THE

GLADES

JOHN NETTI

Black Rose Writing | Texas

The author grants the final approval for this literary material.

Second printing

This is a work of fiction. Names, characters, businesses, places, events, and incidents are either the products of the author's imagination or used in a fictitious manner. Any resemblance to actual persons, living or dead, or actual events is purely coincidental.

ISBN: 978-1-68433-990-7
PUBLISHED BY BLACK ROSE WRITING
www.blackrosewriting.com

Printed in the United States of America
Suggested Retail Price (SRP) $20.95

The Glades is printed in EB Garamond

*As a planet-friendly publisher, Black Rose Writing does its best to eliminate unnecessary waste to reduce paper usage and energy costs, while never compromising the reading experience. As a result, the final word count vs. page count may not meet common expectations.

The Glades is dedicated to victims of sexual exploitation.

THE GLADES

"Hell is empty, and all the devils are here."
–William Shakespeare, *The Tempest*

CHAPTER 1

Utica, New York,
Thursday, November 10, 1983
Maddy Reynolds

"How long do we have to wait?"

"As long as it takes, Johnny."

"What if they're not in there?"

"They're in there, alright." Maddy didn't have patience with the kid. He wasn't a bad kid, but he was green, and everything was a big adventure. She'd seen junior detectives like him before, excited to jump into the action, but when the guns started flashing, they pissed their pants. Johnny was eager to learn alright, which was good, but it made him restless, which was not.

Maddy remembered what it was like when she first started, always wanting to dive into a difficult situation and use her analytic skills to solve a big case. Yet, when it finally happened, it came too soon; she wasn't ready. Sure, she adapted. Sure, she figured it out, but at what cost? Almost her life and she lived in pain nearly every day because of it. It wasn't just physical pain, either. No, Maddy wasn't eager for action anymore; Maddy wanted out.

"Calm down, Johnny. Let things unfold. Situations have a life of their own. If we're patient, maybe nobody gets hurt." That's all she wanted, for nobody to get hurt, neither the good guys nor the bad guys. She'd seen enough of blood-smeared floors, heads dangling from rubbery necks, and eyes glazed over. Waiting for an exit ticket was the name of the game now. Until it came, she'd have to wait for crazy bastards to come out of houses with guns blazing and looking to go out with a headline. She wasn't about to fuck it all up now just because some kid couldn't control his testosterone.

"How about a cup of coffee? It's nice and hot." It was a chilly, damp, and gray Upstate New York morning, the kind that made your bones ache. She reached for the thermos in the back seat.

Wet pavements reflected the gray light of early morning, and the streets shimmered. The neighborhood was still asleep, and the coffee smelled good. Maddy loved hot coffee in the morning and even enjoyed the ritual of making it just the way she liked it before leaving for work; it made a gloomy day better.

"No, thank you, Detective," Johnny said, looking straight ahead, eyes fixed on a green door between the two storefront windows of a dilapidated building.

"You can call me Maddy, you know." Johnny flushed pink around the neck.

Maddy giggled and thought maybe fifteen years ago, she might have found him attractive. But then again, maybe not. He was too much of a Boy Scout for her.

He curled his lips as though he knew she was just playing with him. She poured the coffee into its screw-on plastic cap and the steam condensed on the windshield as she took a sip. Zep's voice came over the radio. "What ya got, Maddy?"

"Just sitting tight."

"Maybe they're not in there."

"Oh, they're in there."

"I'm sending backup, then. I just got a fax from Boston. Jake Donnelly is probably the guy in the building, and he's a real badass. He works with his brother and sister, and sometimes a guy named Rico, so hang tight and wait for Al and Bud."

"Got it," Maddy said. She turned to the kid. "Have you checked your weapon?"

Johnny looked at her, eyes wide, as though caught cheating on a test. She knew he didn't do it. "Why don't you do it now?"

He pulled out his revolver, checked it, and said, "Do you think we'll need these?" He didn't sound as excited as he did an hour earlier.

"Always assume so," Maddy said, with her eyes focused ahead.

The green door cracked open. She poured the coffee back into the thermos. "Here we go. They're checking the street, so don't move. When I say so, roll down your window, open the door and crouch down. Place your weapon through the window opening. Whatever you do, don't stand up."

Three people stepped out into the street. "See those coats they're carrying?"

"Yeah."

"They're hiding guns."

She waited until the three started crossing the street, then shouted over to Johnny, "Okay, now." She opened her door with the window rolled down, kneeled behind it, and pointed her weapon. "Police. Freeze!" Like synchronized swimmers, they dropped their coats simultaneously and started shooting.

She ducked behind the door as windshield glass pattered the car's seats and bullets banged against metal. She felt a kick in the ribs; *I'm shot!* A fiery pain ran up her side. The shooting stopped, she looked, and the Donnelly gang was bolting toward a parked car. Maddy popped up and shot four times through the open window. Two dropped to the pavement with the slapping sound that flesh makes when it hits something immoveable. Another fell, screaming in pain. The guy struggled to his feet and started limping to the car.

Where the hell's the kid? She dared not take her eyes off the guy in the street. Moving around the car door into firing position, she shouted, "Stop, motherfucker!" The man stopped. "On the ground." He remained standing but had no gun. She realized he must have dropped it when he fell but probably had another in the car. "I swear, I'll blow out your knee if you don't hit the pavement." The guy looked at his partners in the street. They weren't moving; they looked dead. He turned, glared at Maddy, and dropped to the pavement. The backup unit pulled up. Two detectives jumped out and ran over to secure him.

A searing pain ate at Maddy's ribcage, and her knees buckled. Blood soaked through her shirt and puddled on the pavement. She pushed herself to her feet and gimped to the patrol car but didn't see Johnny. She hobbled around the cruiser and stopped. The kid lay in the street with his eyes open, staring at the sky, blood oozing from a hole in his chest; he was dead. "Johnny, I told you not to stand up!" *Why is this happening again?* Her arms dropped, and Maddy sobbed as she leaned her head on the open car door.

Twenty Minutes Later

Al and Bud carried Maddy to the back seat of the cruiser. It felt like a chain saw opened up her rib cage when they let her down. She screamed, "It hurts like a son of a bitch." The ceiling spun, and her stomach slid around like eggs in a greasy frying pan. She reached out to Al, and the warmth of his hand calmed her. In a weak, old woman's voice, she said, "Can you contact my ex and tell him what happened? I don't want my daughter to find out on the news."

"Sure, but right now, don't talk; save your strength," Al said.

An unfamiliar voice outside the car said, "Where is she hit?"

"On the right side, near her ribs," Al said.

"I'm Mike, a paramedic," the guy said to Maddy. "I'm going to give you something for the pain. You're losing a lot of blood, and we have to move fast. When we jostle you out of here, it's going to hurt."

She closed her eyes. Firm hands gripped her body and lifted her out of the car. Hot molten steel ran into her back. She shrieked. Resting on the soft surface of the gurney, warmth moved through her. "The worst is over," Mike said. "You should start feeling the medication soon."

She heard a familiar voice outside the ambulance. "Is she okay?"

"Who are you?" Mike responded.

"Captain Frank Zepatello, Oneida County Sheriffs. Is she fucking going to be okay?"

"She's lost blood, but I don't think the bullet struck any vitals."

"Where are you taking her?"

"St. Elizabeth's."

Zep yelled so Maddy could hear, "We'll meet you at the hospital, Maddy!"

The siren blared. The ambulance swayed as it sped through the Utica streets. She lost track of time. Conscious but dreamy, she floated like in a hot-air balloon. Then, rolling through a hallway filled with people, a voice said, "We're bringing her right up to surgery." Her head spun out of control. "Hold that elevator." She smelled the stale air of a confined space; the hot-air balloon lifted off the ground.

A deep male voice spoke, and through her blurred vision, Maddy saw a sunburned face, gray eyebrows, and a blue mask. "I'm Dr. Burke, Maddy." His voice was soothing and confident. "We're preparing you for surgery. The next sound you'll hear will be a nurse in the recovery room, telling you it's over." Although she only saw his brown eyes above the mask, Maddy could tell he was smiling at her.

Tuesday, November 15, 1983

When Maddy opened her eyes, she was in a dimly lit room. They had attached wires and tubes to her body. Instruments beeped, and she heard air entering and leaving her lungs. *Where am I?* She tried to lift herself, but they tied her down. *This isn't the recovery room.* She panicked, her heart raced, the beeping became rapid, and she started looking around for help. She tried to cry out, but the tube stopped her. Her face grew warm, sweat dripped from her forehead into her eyes, and they burned; everything was fuzzy.

The machine beeped faster. A nurse shouted, "It's Reynolds; she's coming out of it!" A figure in white stood before her, wiped the sweat from her forehead, and spoke comforting words. "You're back, dear, and you're going to be alright." The nurse injected medication into the IV, and Maddy heard as she floated into a dream, "Paging Dr. Burke to the ICU."

Friday, November 18, 1983.

"Are you awake, Mom?"

Maddy's eyes opened; her daughter was smiling. The room was bright, and the window blinds were open. Outside, snow fell. "Where am I?"

"You've been in Intensive Care, but now you're in a regular room," Amber said.

"How long was I out?"

"Five days." Jack, her ex-husband, sat in the back of the room. "You've been out for five days." He stepped forward where Maddy could see him. In his typical sad-sack tone he used ever since the divorce, he added, "Welcome back."

"Hi, Jack," she mumbled, trying to smile. Struggling to speak, she asked, "What happened? I didn't think I got hit that badly."

"Dr. Burke said a bone fragment nicked an artery and caused internal bleeding," Jack said. "The blood loss put you into a coma."

Maddy turned to Amber and asked her if she was doing okay.

"I'm much better now," she said. "I was so worried that you'd never come out of it."

"I feel like I've been on a long trip."

"You have, Mom. You really have."

The nurse came in and said Maddy needed to rest. Amber kissed her mother and said goodbye; Jack waited near the door and waved before leaving. Alone, Maddy lay looking at the ceiling, thinking, *I can't believe this is happening.*

Monday, November 21, 1983

Maddy returned from physical therapy. Zep and Al were waiting in the room, reading newspapers. "Aren't you two supposed to be catching bad guys?" she asked with a smile.

Al dropped the paper onto his lap and quipped, "You caught them all; now we have nothing to do."

She sat in a chair and shifted her body to find a comfortable position; her thoughts went to a more serious matter. "The kid who got shot, Johnny, did he have children?"

"Twin six-month-old girls," Zep said.

She shook her head, and a pang of sadness tugged at her insides. Her mind flashed back to Johnny before the shoot-out. *Instead of being so annoyed, I wish I'd asked him about his kids.*

"The department will get involved and help the family, the way we always do," Zep said.

"How about the people I shot? What happened to them?"

"You killed Rico Parma and Lizzy Donnelly. The wounded guy was Jake Donnelly, Lizzy's brother. Teddy Donnelly, Jake's younger brother, was detained on a DUI in Albany."

"What's going to happen to Jake?" she asked.

"He's charged with three counts of murder in Westchester," Zep said.

"He's one crazy bastard, Maddy," Al added. "It's good you got him off the street."

Maddy said Jake might want vengeance for killing his sister. Al and Zep glanced at one another. "What's that all about?" she asked.

"Jake swore he'd kill you when he gets out," Al said.

"That's just great," she blurted. "And when will that be?"

"It won't be for a long time," Zep said. "And where he's going, they don't let people out for bullshit reasons."

"Enlighten me. Where is he going?"

"Dannemora. It's a prison for the criminally insane up near the Canadian border."

Maddy's stomach was in knots, and her wound ached from physical therapy. She looked at Zep and shook her head. "I can't take this. I mean, I'm thirty-five, and not only is this my second time wounded, but Donnelly is the second pathological killer who wants me dead."

"Maddy, no one has done more than you. No matter what you decide to do, I'll support your decision."

"Me too," Al added.

"Look," she said. "I'm tired, and I'm in pain. Please take nothing I've said as gospel." She knew she might think differently in a few days. *I can't afford to not work, yet something in me is changing.*

Zep and Al left, and Maddy spent the morning watching snowflakes dancing around a lamppost outside her window, thinking of her future. *I'm sick of doing battle with ruthless people. Why is this happening to me?*

CHAPTER 2

New Orleans, Louisiana, Thursday, September 19, 1974
Avery Jordan

I hate him, Avery said to himself when his father left the room. He took the gun out of the drawer and laid it on the bed. It was the same one his father gave him for Christmas two years earlier. He thought it was strange because his father knew he wasn't into weapons. He ran his finger along the barrel, felt its cold smoothness, and marveled. *How can something so small change everything?* It dawned on him maybe his father wanted him dead.

All night, his father's voice was in his head. It told him he was worthless. "But he gave me this voice silencer," he said, holding the gun, laughing as tears ran down his face. Avery disregarded the meeting his old man set up. *It's probably another attempt to save me from myself.*

He lifted the revolver to his face and looked into the barrel. *This tiny hole makes things permanent. Do I have the balls to do it? Damn right, I do.*

He raised it near his face and put his lips around the barrel. His heart pounded as his thumb touched the trigger. He applied the slightest pressure, then relaxed. Again, pressure, and relax. Everything in his conscious mind teetered on the brink between flesh and steel, thumb and trigger. Everything—his next breath, the cool air blowing through the open window, even the creaking sounds of the old hotel—it all hinged on pressure.

Bang! His eyes opened. *Am I dead?* Confused, he pulled the gun out and ran to the window. A man lay in the street, and blood oozed from his head. Shaking, Avery set the gun on the table, turned the barrel away from himself, and thought, *I can't even do this right.* He buried his face in his hands. His stomach churned, he was about to vomit, and he ran to the window for air. Outside, people gathered around a body. Sirens screamed as rain mixed with blood and streamed into a sewer.

The nameless, faceless dead man was like him, insignificant and alone. It was as if someone used a spoon to carve out his insides, leaving a hollow space. He wrapped his arms around his emptiness and dropped to the bed, crying. *I'm a pathetic heap of human debris.* He lay for a long time as air blew in, and he shivered. He sat up, reached for the slip of paper his father left with directions to the meeting and walked out.

The stairway of the decrepit hotel reeked of urine. The cold numbed Avery's brain when he stepped outside; it was a gray and misty New Orleans morning. He didn't think the meeting would make a difference, and if he was right, he'd go back and try again.

Chilled and shaking, he walked through the French Quarter, turning up his collar against the raw dampness. When he got to the bar, it was a shithole; dingy, smoke-filled, and smelled of stale beer. He checked the paper; it was the right place. He waited for his eyes to adjust to the dim light, then looked for the guy as he walked through the bar. Unshaven, with messy hair; no one looked at him or cared. He sat at an empty table, and when a waitress came by, he asked for a shot of Jack. His eyes stayed glued to the front door.

According to the note, the guy should have a brimmed hat with a single red feather and a black trench coat; that was all he knew. His father's words from the visit that morning kept repeating in his brain. The old man had acted disgusted and stood as Avery lay in bed.

"You shame your mother and me before our friends. You hurt us. What I'm doing is for her—not you." His father pulled out the paper. "This might be your last chance to become something, Avery. Don't fuck it up as you've done with everything else."

Holding the paper as though it was priceless, his father added, "I'm handing your fate over to people who don't care about you. If you treat them the way you've treated us, they will kill you. I believe it's your last chance, and from now on, you will answer to them; I don't want to see you again until you've fulfilled their conditions." His father looked at him like it might be for the last time. "Goodby, Avery," He put the paper on the bed, turned, and walked out.

He gulped the last of the Jack, slammed the glass on the table, and shouted, "Fuck him!" He lifted his eyes, and a man stood at the front door. Avery raised his hand, and the man walked to the table.

"Avery Jordan?" His voice was deep; it sounded like his throat was full of gravel. Avery nodded. The man sat. He pulled out an envelope, placed it on the table, and with a strong Italian accent, said, "We've known your father for years. He's done favors for us; now he asks we do one for him." The guy's bulging neck, deep black eyes, and the realization he was mafioso sent a shudder through Avery. He looked away, trying to compose himself.

"We made a deal with your father. He put up the money, and when we get it back, it becomes ours." The guy looked at the envelope. "We made the check inside out for you. If you accept our terms, you can use the funds for ten years; then you will pay back every penny to us, capisce?"

"Yes, I understand."

"Remember, ten years from today!" Avery reached for the envelope, and the guy slammed his hand on top. "Not so fast. You play by our rules. Your father cannot protect you. Do you know what that means?"

"Yes."

"Say it," the guy shouted, adding something in Italian Avery didn't understand.

"If I don't pay back every penny by September Nineteenth, Nineteen-eighty-four, I'll be..." His voice trailed off.

"Dead!" the guy said as he stared into Avery's eyes. "Do you accept this condition?"

"Yes. Yes, I do." The guy pushed the envelope across the table, stood up, and left the bar.

Avery stared at the envelope, afraid to move, wondering if it contained only enough for him to leave the country and stay out of his father's sight or enough to build his dream business. He pulled it close and looked around, then yanked out the check. Avery counted the zeros twice to be sure he understood the amount correctly. His heart raced; he leaned back in his chair and thought, *My luck has changed.*

Morning light shimmered in the rain; the bells of St. Louis Cathedral rang before mass, and Avery laughed to himself as he walked back to the hotel in the drizzle. In his room, he unloaded the revolver, showered, searched for his cleanest dirty clothes, and headed to Naomi's, the finest brothel in New Orleans, to spend the last of the cash in his pocket.

8:38 *That Evening*

A large man with curly hair and massive arms stood in a restored French colonial vestibule. "Can I help you?"

Avery stammered, "I think so."

The guy barked, "Do you have an appointment?" Avery said no. "Wait here," the guy said.

Avery watched women walk by in loose-fitting gowns, strolling arm-in-arm with gentlemen in tuxedos. *What an operation,* he thought to himself, enthralled with the ambiance and sophistication of Naomi's. Music played, the scent of jasmine filled the air, and people moved as though attending the Queen's Ball, sporting elegant gestures and smiles. *I want to be in this business.* Every venture he had tried failed, but the sex trade, he believed, could make him rich.

The big man returned, a woman accompanied him; Avery froze. *She's a goddess.* His eyes roved over her extraordinary white skin, hair the color of snow, gray eyes, and lips with a hint of pink. When she asked what he wanted, he struggled to answer. "Well... ah... um... I want to be with someone."

She said her name was Naomi, and they service by appointment. "It's a slow evening. I'll see if someone is available."

Unable to control himself, words spilled out of Avery's mouth. "Are you available?" he asked.

Naomi looked at the big man. She smirked, then turned back to him. "Hang on, big fella. We'll find someone to take care of you tonight."

Shit! Embarrassed, Avery watched Naomi walk away. Her glittering silver gown clung to her perfect body and drew out the animal in him. He waited, counting the dollars rolling into Naomi's coffers as couple after couple walked across the room and up the stairs. *This is a gold mine.*

The guy returned with a brunette. "I'm Tara; come with me, honey." The girl wore a sleek blue gown and looked in her teens. She took his hand, and as he followed, Avery watched her wavy, lush hair bounce while her body remained firm, clinging to the dress. She led him to a bedroom carpeted with Oriental rugs, its walls covered with burgundy patterned drapes. In the middle stood a large canopy bed.

Tara moved close, and Avery said it had been a while.

"That's okay, honey." Tara unbuttoned his shirt and nuzzled him toward the bed. He buried his face in the softness of her sweet-smelling hair, and as they made love, images of Naomi intruded on his thoughts. Soon it was the luscious albino squirming beneath him and not Tara. They finished, and as the girl lay with her head on his chest, Avery's thoughts remained with the alluring Naomi.

CHAPTER 3

New Orleans, Louisiana, Wednesday, October 23, 1974

"I'm here to see Naomi."

"You again?" the big man with the massive arms said.

Avery held out a fifty-dollar bill. "I'm here on business. She'll want to hear what I have to say." The man grabbed the fifty, shoved it in his pocket, and told him to hang tight.

Avery waited, thinking how his plan needed Naomi's talents. Every time he'd asked someone who the most knowledgeable person in sex trafficking was, they pointed to Naomi White. *I want the best!*

"You don't give up, do you?" Naomi said when she came out.

"Someone sent me," Avery said.

Naomi asked who. He leaned over and whispered a name. Without expression, she said she'd meet with him. He followed her to a lush room, and Naomi sat behind a big black desk gesturing to a chair in front; Avery sat. "Tell me what you want, Mr. Jordan, but make it brief; I'm swamped." She pulled out a cigarette and lit up.

"You," Avery said. "I want you."

Naomi exhaled and threw her head back, laughing. "You and many others. Why are you bothering me?"

Avery pulled a cigar from his sports coat. After lighting up, he calmly said, "Ms. White, I'm thinking of a business arrangement."

Naomi looked at him with a cat-like stare as though sizing him up. "I'm listening."

"I have a big idea and the money to make it happen. I need someone who knows the sex business. I heard you are the best, so I want you."

"What makes you think you can afford me?"

Avery took control. He stood up and strolled around Naomi's office. He walked to a painting of a naked woman lying on a sofa. "I see you appreciate art."

"Yes, I do," she said in a quizzical tone.

"I bet you wish you owned the original," he said, still looking at the wall hanging. The woman said nothing. Avery turned to her. "If you join me, you won't be hanging knockoffs on your walls; they'll be the real thing."

Naomi stood and walked around the desk. She leaned back and let the length of her milky white leg show through the split in her skirt. Avery knew he was being manipulated but let it happen. "Tell me of your idea," she said.

"You do a good business here in New Orleans, right?" Naomi gave a slight nod. "Of course, the geography limits your opportunity. What I mean is, limited to this city." Naomi said nothing, but her look conveyed she understood.

"You are under the scrutiny of the law, and it cramps your operations. Agree?" Again, she concurred with her eyes.

"Imagine not being limited to this city, or any city, or any country. Imagine hiding your business in a wilderness, where no one would know what you're doing." Naomi's eyes opened wide. "My plan gives us access to anywhere."

Naomi pushed herself away from the desk, walked a few steps closer, smiled, and gestured to the sofa. "Come, let's sit and talk business."

Berry Lake, New York, Adirondack Mountains
Thursday, January 30, 1975

"How long before we land?"

"It's a short flight. We should arrive in Syracuse in forty-five minutes," Naomi said.

Completing his arrangement with the sophisticated madame, Avery's confidence in her grew each day. Although her mind for business was not a problem, his sexual attraction to the alluring vixen was. Avery tried to keep a safe distance with so much at stake and the shameful thought of his father finding out he'd messed up another business arrangement.

Naomi planned every detail of each step along the path to the new business. Her knowledge of sex trafficking far exceeded anyone Avery knew. With his resources and Naomi's knowledge, the plan extended a potential business beyond the United States' borders. The next step—not a small one—was finding a discreet location to operate undetected and large enough to handle an airfield.

"How did you find this property?" Avery asked.

"One of my past clients is an executive at the Adirondack Park Agency, and he owes me a favor." Naomi smiled as she spoke, and Avery wondered what favor she did for the man, noticing a pang of jealousy in his gut. "The place overlooks Berry Lake, an enormous expanse of water. It's one of the Great Camps of the Adirondack Mountains formed in the eighteen hundreds. It's called The Glades, and for historical reasons, we cannot change the name."

"Can it fit an airfield?"

"I guess we'll find out when we see it."

A limousine at the Syracuse Airport waited to drive them to Berry Lake. Avery was exhausted from the air travel and drifted between sleep and semiconscious slumber for the entire three-hour drive. Naomi read documents from her briefcase. She'd say, "Hmm," and "I see," and "no way." When she wasn't taunting him by rubbing her breasts up against him or bending over while wearing a low-cut blouse, Naomi was all business.

As his mind drifted off, Avery recalled the first time he learned of Naomi White, the person. Everyone in New Orleans heard of her brothel, but she was a mystery. The day he had lunch with his friend Carmine Augustino, a young rising mafioso figure in town, Avery told him he was looking for someone with experience in the sex trade.

"I need someone with a vision bigger than New Orleans. I want to go big, real big."

"Naomi White. That's who you want," Carmine said.

"She runs a great brothel; I'll give you that, and she's hot as hell," Avery said, "but what makes you think she has what it takes to set up a national enterprise?"

"Naomi is smart, and she is as cunning as a snake. She took down Vito Campese. That whorehouse she runs used to belong to him; he's now doing thirty for tax evasion, and she owns the place. If you do business with her, don't let her in your head, or you'll end up like Campese."

Recalling Carmine's words sent a shudder through Avery that snapped him wide awake. His eyes opened, and he was struck by sunlight reflecting off vast mounds of snow. "Where the hell are we, Alaska?"

"You want remote? This is remote," Naomi said. "We are here." Tall evergreens with boughs hanging low from the weight of snow reminded him of the Alps when he was a boy. "Driver, we've planned for the road up the mountain to be cleared of snow. Please go right to the top," Naomi instructed.

The pristine natural wonder impressed Avery, and he let his imagination run wild. They drove past gigantic white pines on their way to the mountain retreat. At the top, the terrain leveled off, and an ancient log camp stood in a snow-covered field. Though in obvious disrepair, its charm was inescapable. The driver stopped, and Avery got out. He considered the cost of rebuilding the log building, then gazed at the massive body of water, its many islands, and surrounding mountains.

"What do you think?" Naomi asked.

"I must have this!"

Naomi laughed. "Is there enough room for an airfield?" He knew she was kidding because the mountaintop's immensity could fit five airfields.

Together, they walked to the faltering building, and Avery thought how magnificent it must have been in its heyday. "According to the historical society, if we rebuild, it must keep its original charm," Naomi said.

"That's not a problem; it will be magnificent." Avery's body was cold and stiff, but his elation warmed his insides. As he took in the grand vista, he felt Naomi's body snuggling up next to his and her arm around his waist. Her steamy breath rose to his face, and she closed her eyes and kissed him.

He knew Naomi intended to take him to an erotic place when her hand moved up his thigh.

"We have hours in that limo together," she said. "I think the back seat turns into a bed."

Naomi looked into Avery's eyes. He wanted her and thought to himself, *Maybe just this once.*

CHAPTER 4

New Orleans, Marti Gras, Tuesday, February 11, 1975

"The man is a stone-cold killer," Naomi said as she and Avery walked through the French Quarter. They bumped and shoved amid a throng of inebriated revelers as girls flashed their breasts and poured champagne on the crowd below from upper hotel porches. They neared a bar several blocks beyond the madness. "Sedgwick Neri is a very unusual person. He's known by few and liked by no one. Only the people who need his services tolerate his presence."

"I don't get it. Why?" Avery asked.

"What he enjoys is cutting people's throats."

Naomi convinced Avery people might need to disappear occasionally. She said few individuals have such skills, and Sedgwick Neri was one.

"I'm not looking forward to meeting this guy."

"You're not going to marry him, Avery; you're just going to hire him. And you'll be damn glad you did when the time comes he's needed." They walked into Niko's. The place was grungy and dark. "That's him," Naomi said. "At the far end of the bar, the tall one."

"He's a monster," Avery said.

"Six foot five," Naomi said as she led the way. Neri leaned over the bar, clutching a beer, and his eyes locked on them as they approached. He appeared prepared for trouble. Avery whispered, "He doesn't seem the trusting type."

"You don't want the trusting type for that job," Naomi whispered back as she kept smiling at Neri. "Hello, Sedgwick. This is Avery Jordan."

"Hello," the big man said. Naomi gestured to a lone table, and they sat. Avery looked at Neri's curly black hair, smooth skin, and handsome features; they were inconsistent with the coldness radiating from his presence. Neri's hands were enormous, and Avery imagined him holding someone's head with one while cutting his throat with the other.

He put out his hand, and Neri shook it. Avery never shook a hand larger than his own; his hand disappeared in Neri's. The big man's vice-like grip and icy stare made him question the decision, but a telepathic look from Naomi said, *He's our man*, and Avery capitulated. He consummated an arrangement with the killer at the bar.

Avery saw himself as a big picture person. He brought vision and strategy to the new venture. Naomi opened his mind to the dirty underside of sex trafficking, and though Sedgwick Neri frightened him, he accepted such unpleasantries were part of the business.

Berry Lake, New York, Sunday, August 26, 1979

Avery and Naomi stood out on the great lawn behind The Glades. They watched the third and last airplane disappear into a cloud. "I think this will work." Pleased with the successful weekend, Avery said, "Think of it—The Glades's first multi-guest sales event. We've come a long way by doing three in a single night; let's continue this."

Naomi pulled away, turned with her arms folded, and grinned. "Why not twelve? Our airfield can handle the traffic with no trouble."

Embarrassed by his lack of vision, Avery looked out, squinting into the afternoon sun. He realized that, once again, she was right. He had lost sight of his original idea, became small-minded and complacent. *Well, at least it was my idea to hire Naomi*, he thought to himself. It was no accident she operated the most successful whorehouse in New Orleans. Her sexual games aside, Avery was glad she was his partner. "You're right, and that's what we will do."

They strolled together across the lawn back to his suite, and he realized he might love the woman who he toyed with since New Orleans. *She has everything I want: good looks, intelligence, and money. We even share the same values in business. How many women are interested in sex trafficking?*

Avery never gave himself to just one woman. He suspected Naomi was the same way. He believed when she wasn't in his bed at night; she was in Neri's.

After changing into leisure clothes, Avery dropped into an oversized leather chair to relax while Naomi went behind the desk and pulled out a notebook. "If we're going to increase our numbers," she said, "we need to develop our messaging, then push it out to a network of clients." As if she was a parent telling her child to do his homework, she added, "You need to work the phones more, Avery." He marveled at the woman's ambition. He knew no one who loved money as much as him until Naomi, and he realized romance, beyond pure sex, might jeopardize The Glades's business. The thought brought him to his senses, and he nixed any inclination to reset the nature of their relationship.

Over the next several months, with Naomi's constant prodding and support, Avery began devoting himself to developing his and Naomi's New Orleans contacts. Discreetness and anonymity were the primary elements of his pitch. He watched as The Glades network grew beyond New Orleans contacts to the entire United States and other countries. As the business became global, Naomi came to him with additional concerns.

"We need to talk," she said, barging into his office on a Monday after their most successful weekend ever.

"Why are you upset?"

"If anything ruins this operation," she bemoaned, "it won't be the FBI; it'll be that half-assed town down there and its Barney Fife police department." Naomi was fuming because one of the town's deputies drove to The Glades in the middle of an auction Saturday night. "That redneck deputy Mosher wanted to know if everything was okay up here. He's just nosy is what he is," she ranted. "Get these people on the payroll, Avery!"

Avery decided Naomi was right again. The issue was a long time coming, but he'd been avoiding it. Insulated from society at large, The Glades still dwelled in a township with villagers and law enforcement, and it needed to contend with both.

Avery asked Darius Girard, his assistant, to arrange a meeting with Jed Smith, the town's police chief. "See if he'll meet at my office." To his surprise, Smith agreed to meet at The Glades.

Girard buzzed Avery at ten thirty the morning of the meeting. "Sir, Chief Smith is here."

"Isn't the meeting at eleven o'clock?"

"Yes, he's early."

Hmm, what gives with this guy? "Send him in."

A tall man with an enormous beer belly hanging over his belt entered. He was holding his hat in front of him with both hands. *What a pathetic-looking person*, Avery thought. He shook Smith's clammy hand and told him to have a seat. "Thank you for meeting with me today."

"Sure, no problem," Smith said.

"The reason I've asked you here is to discuss our special needs for police protection." The Chief gazed at him as he spoke, as though he didn't want to miss a word. "We'll need more attention than others in town. Perhaps we can compensate you and your team for the extra work."

Smith sat rigid, biting his lip. His knee started bouncing. *Is he about to arrest me?* Avery wondered. *Maybe he wants to know how much?* He made a calculated move and said, "I'm willing to pay you five hundred dollars a week for the extra service."

Chief Smith cleared his throat and said, "Sure, that would be great."

Avery continued. "I will pay each of your deputies two hundred a week, and for each one who signs up, I'll add another fifty dollars a week for you."

Smith looked ready to jump off the chair. "Sure, Mr. Jordan. I'm sure my four guys will want to help."

Avery reached into his coat pocket, pulled out an envelope stuffed with cash, and handed it to Smith. "Here's a good faith starting bonus. Darius Girard will be your contact unless I want to meet with you. Questions?"

Smith said, "No, no questions," clutching the envelope with one hand and holding his hat with the other. He smiled and started leaving, and Avery thought, *How pitiful.*

As The Glades became more renowned, so did its visibility, and it didn't take long for Naomi to bring other matters to Avery's attention. They lay in bed one night after making love, and she said, "We need a legitimate front business to cover up what we're doing up here."

He believed Naomi knew what she was talking about and paid attention to what she said. "I'm listening, dear."

"To be sure we keep the shiny veneer on our clandestine business, we should position The Glades as a five-star mountain resort and cater to well-known public figures, politicians, and aristocrats. We can showcase charities and worthy causes at our own expense. This will endear us to powerful politicians and give us a layer of legitimacy."

Brilliant! He didn't want to give Naomi too much credit, so he said, "That sounds good; I'll give it thought." Avery researched the idea, and like every brainstorm Naomi came up with, things fell into place.

The hardest part of setting up the new initiative was hiring specialized staff, cooks, purchasers, and waiters and keeping them separate from the dark side of The Glades. They added another wing, and Neri's job was to keep the catering staff and the traffickers from knowing what each was doing.

After reviewing the books at the end of its second year, Avery realized the legitimate aspect was so successful it operated as a profitable stand-alone business. Its margins paled compared to sex trafficking but proved to be just the image The Glades needed.

Its location and airfield were keys to The Glades' success. Avery's marketing pitch to the downstate crowd for catering services was, "With New York City an hour's flight away, you can escape to a wilderness setting with the ambiance of the best Manhattan resorts. The wonders of untouched mountains, forests, and sprawling lakes will surround you." When he calmed the fears of his sex auction clients, he added, "It's so remote, no one will ever know why you were here."

Filled with confidence by the time 1979 drew to a close, Avery envisioned the day The Glades paid off his debt. *I'll make my father's holdings pale in comparison. I can't wait to make that phone call.*

CHAPTER 5

Utica, New York, Monday, December 19, 1983
Maddy Reynolds

Time dragged to a halt when Maddy returned home from the hospital. Each day ran into the next. Tired of daytime soaps, she grabbed the remote and turned off the television. She had good days when she did housework and bad days when she did nothing. That afternoon was a bad day. Her ribs hurt, and every movement sent high voltage electricity through her side. She tried putting a few ornaments on the Christmas tree that Amber started, but in pain, she stopped.

It was nearing four o'clock, and Maddy expected Amber soon. She folded the blanket. She didn't want her daughter to think she was lying around all day. She started a pot of coffee and felt as gray inside as the dark sky outside her window. *I can't bear a green Christmas this year*, she thought to herself, looking at the brown lawn.

She poured the coffee, turned, and snow was falling. A smile broke across her face. *It feels like Christmas.* With her spirits lifted, she started making dinner. She heard the school bus stop outside and the front door open. "Mom, I'm home," Amber called out.

"I'm in the kitchen," Maddy chirped.

"What are you making? It smells so good."

"Chocolate chip pancakes, hash brown potatoes, and bacon."

Amber snuck up and stole a piece of bacon. "Go up and get comfortable; food will be ready soon." As they ate, Maddy asked Amber how her day went.

"I met with my English Lit teacher, Mrs. Jamison, to discuss the short story I'm writing for the Wilson Grant. She thinks it's great but gave me suggestions."

"Such as?" Maddy prodded.

"She thinks I'm holding back on the darker parts of the story. If something's disturbing, don't sugarcoat it."

"You like her, don't you?"

Amber smiled and said Mrs. Jamison was the main reason she wanted to pursue literature the following year in college. She explained how her teacher encouraged her to apply for the esteemed Wilson Grant. "It would mean a lot of money toward tuition, but kids from all over are entering the competition; I don't think I have much of a chance."

Maddy placed her hand on her daughter's and told her how proud she was. They finished with dinner, and she suggested leaving the dishes in the sink. "I'll do them tomorrow; let's relax in the living room." One of the few things Maddy enjoyed during her recovery was talking with her daughter.

"Okay, but I'll clean the kitchen and do the dishes first. I can tell you're in pain. I don't want you to have to do them tomorrow."

Grateful that Amber volunteered, Maddy found a comfortable position in a living room chair. Amber came out to join her, pulled a box filled with glass ornaments from the hall closet, and started placing white snowflakes on the tree. "You just sit, Mom. Say if an ornament is out of place." *I feel so helpless.*

Midway, Amber stopped. She went to a chair across from her mother. "I have something on my mind. Let's talk." *Oh, boy. I wonder what this is about.*

Amber moved to the floor and folded her hands, resting her elbows on her knees as if trying to command her mother's full attention. "I know it's important to you I go to a good college. You invested all the money Grandma left for my education. But, if I attend a less expensive school, you can use the money to quit your job." Amber's words cut into Maddy. "I'm terrified the next time you're going to get killed." Amber's voice cracked, and her eyes watered. "There's nothing wrong with a community college; at least I'd know you're safe."

Cornell already accepted Amber. The idea of sending her to a lesser school was unthinkable. "Honey, look, I know you're worried about my well-being, but I tie my happiness to you. I want you to go as far as you're capable. Please, just for tonight, let's not worry. Let's finish the tree." Maddy pointed to a space just below the star that needed an ornament.

Utica and Berry Lake, New York, Thursday, March 1, 1984

It was winter, but that day, it felt like spring. Maddy saw her first robin, smiled, slid open the back door, and stepped into the sunlight. Closing her eyes, looking up, she let the sun warm her face. *This feels so good; I've been too long indoors.* It was a long winter cooped up, pampering her wound. She saw yellow crocus breaking through the earth and heard birds singing. It reminded her of the birthday party her grandma gave when she was seven. The phone rang, and when she ran inside, Maddy felt strength returning to her body.

"Hey, it's me; how's your recovery coming?" It was her friend Jodi.

"Oh, Jodi, it's good to hear your voice. Things are progressing slower than I'd like, I'm afraid, but today's a good day."

Jodi was more than just her friend; Jodi saved her life when Maddy killed Cupid, the serial killer. Twenty-two, Jodi was more mature than most adults Maddy knew, and through the horrific experience with Cupid, they formed a lasting bond.

"How are things at Cornell?" Jodi was a natural outdoors person, a trait Maddy thought she developed growing up in Vietnam. She entered the prestigious environmental studies program at the Ivy League school, and since Amber's acceptance at Cornell, Maddy was interested in what Jodi thought of the place.

"Well, that's why I'm calling. I'm thinking of transferring to the ranger school at Berry Lake."

"Is it the school?"

"No, Cornell is great. I realize I'm more of a hands-on person than an academic. The ranger school might fit me better. I'm planning on driving there to check it out and wonder if you want to come."

"I'd love to go. I am so up for doing this." The two friends made plans to leave the following Friday.

The next few days, she ruminated over the trip. As a city girl, it amazed her how visiting the mountains captured her imagination the way it did. She'd heard of the Adirondack Park but never been. She researched maps and articles. Captivated by the natural wonder on her doorstep, Maddy realized a world of possibilities awaited only hours away.

The night before they left, Maddy couldn't sleep. *I can't believe myself,* she thought, as she lay awake. *It's like being a kid on the night before going to summer camp.* Knowing she needed to return to work soon, she hoped the trip might revive her. Yet, the thought of work was troubling, and she tried to push it from her mind.

Jodi arrived the following day, and Maddy was excited to get out of town. They loaded Jodi's Volvo, stopped for gas, burgers, and fries, then hit Route 28 North. Fresh air blew in from the passenger side window as Maddy nibbled at her fries. She laughed to herself, thinking, *I feel like I'm on spring break driving to Fort Lauderdale.*

"Why do you want to visit the ranger school?" she asked Jodi.

"I want to make sure it's everything I want," Jodi said. "I have a list of questions for my meeting tomorrow." She glanced at Maddy. "If you're up for it, we can go for a short hike."

"Absolutely," Maddy said. Inside, she wondered how much her body could handle.

An hour into the drive, Jodi brought up a guy who'd dumped her. "He gave no explanation; he just stopped calling." With a pained look on her face, she added, "I haven't heard a word from him, and he won't answer my calls. I even wrote him a letter but got nothing in return."

"Not a word?" Maddy asked in disbelief.

"I saw him in the grocery store one day, and I smiled. He saw me and turned his cart up another aisle to avoid me." Tears filled Jodi's eyes. Maddy listened in silence to the cruel treatment her friend endured.

Jodi was beautiful, inside and out, Maddy thought. With her jet black hair, silky smooth complexion (inherited from her Vietnamese mother), and deep blue eyes (inherited from her American soldier father), Jodi always turned heads whenever Maddy was with her in public. Maddy thought the girl's physical attributes, along with the calm and secure way she carried herself, made her a gem for any guy.

How can someone do that? she wondered as she reached over and rubbed her friend's arm. "Want me to drive awhile?"

"Nah, if I was to kill myself, I'd wait until I was alone." Jodi turned to Maddy, smiling through her tears; they both laughed.

They caught their breath, and Maddy confessed things weren't great with her either. Jodi glanced over, and Maddy unloaded. "I've lost my desire for detective work. I never thought it could happen to me. I've seen it with others, but law enforcement runs in my family." Maddy was quiet for a while, looked out the window, and added, "It's just that I didn't realize how afraid I am of getting killed."

"Geez, Maddy. Think of what you've been through. You were in three gun battles; each might have cost your life."

Maddy sat back. *She's right!* Reflecting on what had happened to her— the Donnelly incident, Cupid, Benny Bowls—they were near-death experiences. *It's no wonder Amber wants me to retire.* She recalled the night Cupid murdered her father. Maddy was twelve and severely traumatized, fearing the man would come to kill her too. She coaxed her grandmother into joining a gun club. Maddy learned how to shoot and eventually became a High Master Shooter. Her anxiety subsided; shooting was the only way she knew to fight off her fears. But Maddy's talent with a weapon brought her into battles with wicked men; she was running on emotional empty.

"I've lost my confidence," she said to her friend.

Jodi reached over and put her hand on Maddy's. "Be patient. You've been through difficulties before. Things will work out." Maddy smiled and thought if anyone knew of hard times, it was Jodi. She grew up in the middle of a war. Abandoned by her mother, she barely escaped Saigon when the Americans pulled out. *What an amazing person,* Maddy thought.

"We're getting close," Jodi said. "Look for the White Inn. It's on the right. It's not in the village of Berry Lake; it's near Wanakena, where the ranger school is located."

"I see it," Maddy said. It was a white building with pillars and a porch out front. Empty rocking chairs looked like they waited for guests.

After they checked in, they found Josie's diner. The restaurant was a small house gutted and converted for dining. It had a limited menu, but the aroma made Maddy think of walking into her grandmother's kitchen on Thanksgiving. They feasted on chicken and biscuits with mashed potatoes, cranberry relish, a pickle tray, and homemade bread. The waitress cleared the table; Jodi sat back and sighed. "I can't move."

"Are you interested in dessert?" the woman asked. They shared glances and burst into laughter. "Let's do it," Maddy said. The delicacies looked outrageous, and they split an order of strawberry shortcake with lots of whipped cream.

Back at the inn, exhausted and with full stomachs, Jodi sat, reviewing papers for her meeting while Maddy lay reading. She looked at the pages, but her mind wandered. Miles away from home, her situation seemed more clear. It was harder to pretend everything was going to be okay. *I'm an animal in a cage. My life is not my own.* She'd been running from her unhappiness for years, but it grew more intense after the shootout. *I'm tired, and thinking this way only makes things worse.* She pushed the uncomfortable thoughts from her mind and went back to reading.

The following morning Jodi showered and was out the door; Maddy stayed in bed. It was eleven o'clock when Jodi returned. Maddy sat outside, basking in the sun with her book.

Jodi walked out, and Maddy said, "I haven't been this relaxed since"— Maddy stopped, thought, and said — "since I can't remember when." It bothered her that her life had become a grind, and she couldn't remember the last time she'd enjoyed sitting in the sun.

"Up for a hike?" Jodi asked. "The professor I met with gave me directions to a trail. He said it was nearly clear of snow. If you get tired, we can turn back."

"I'll try it." They dressed in warm clothes and drove a few miles east. A half-mile onto a muddy road, tall white pines with branches heavy with snow blocked the sun.

"Wow, so cool," Maddy said.

Jodi smiled as she navigated the bumpy road. *She's like a kid on her way to the county fair;* Maddy laughed to herself, appreciating her friend's childlike enthusiasm for nature. The car stopped at a sign. "Ruttenberg Peak Trail, 3.6 miles." *That's 7.2 miles. I hope I can do this.*

They got out, and Jodi packed a map, compass, canteen, and a camera inside a small duffel bag. "If you get tired, just tell me."

Maddy wanted to carry something but didn't risk it. *I hate being so helpless.* Snow-filled ravines and windfalls blocked the way in places; Maddy's confidence grew as they traversed the first few miles. At the second mile, the trail vanished. "Let's hold up a minute," Jodi said. Maddy thought Jodi might suggest turning back, but she pulled out a map and spread it on a rock.

"Do you know where we are?" Maddy asked.

Jodi laughed. "Look at this topographical map; it marks the trails. See that ridge? Look at the map. Here's the stream. The lines are close together, where the land is elevated, representing that ridge. We're right where we should be."

"Cool," Maddy said with a smile. *It's a good thing I'm not navigating.* They soon found the trail and started up again toward the summit. Maddy saw a small mountain across the valley with a clearing on its flat top that captured her imagination. *What a spot for a house.* They stopped, and Jodi rechecked the map as Maddy gazed at the sprawling lake below and its swaying waters in a rhythmic motion. "I'd love to build a house on that mountain," she said.

"I thought you were a city girl," Jodi said when she looked up at the flat top mountain.

"Me too."

Jodi folded up the map, and the two continued upward, soon entering a place where the trail ascended sharply, making it necessary to grab tree roots to pull themselves upward. Concerned about the hike's stress on Maddy's body, Jodi suggested they rest. As they leaned against a tree, sharing a canteen of water, Jodi froze. "Shush." She looked off to one side. "Move your head to the left, slow," she whispered.

Maddy turned her head, and her eyes locked on a creature of magnificence and power. It was a beaming free spirit. "It's a wolf," Jodi whispered. "Don't move." The imposing figure stood with its eyes fixed on Maddy; it looked into her soul. Mesmerized, she stood frozen. Out of the corner of her eye, she noticed Jodi lift a camera from her coat. With the click of a shutter, the wolf disappeared.

Maddy leaned against the tree as though spellbound. A bolt of lightning activated something within her she didn't understand. *What just happened?* She felt strange and somehow changed.

"I think I got it," Jodi said, looking at her camera.

Maddy pushed away from the tree and broke into a sweat. Her heart pounded; she took deep breaths as if she'd just run a sprint. Lightheaded, she didn't speak. "Are you okay?" Jodi asked. Maddy gave a slight nod. Jodi added, "I heard there've been a few sightings. They're native to these mountains but are scarce now." Again, she looked at Maddy. "You don't look well. Why don't we head back?"

"Okay," Maddy said, her mind trying to understand the experience.

As they hiked back, the wolf's penetrating stare reverberated in Maddy's mind; stirrings bubbled up uncomfortable emotions from deep inside that made her stomach tingle. At the car, Jodi asked again if she was alright.

"Yes. It's just that, well, something happened when I saw it. It drew something out of me I've been fighting. It's something I don't want to acknowledge." Maddy took off her jacket and placed it in the back seat. "I want to understand this." Maddy couldn't put her finger on what changed when she saw the wolf.

As civilization approached and home neared, a gnawing in Maddy's stomach grew. She realized how unhappy she was with her life. Out of nowhere, distracting her from her thoughts, Jodi said, "I just realized something."

Maddy looked at her. "George cut me off after a weekend we spent together at his apartment. It started out fantastic. On Friday, he made me dinner, and we watched old movies. It was very romantic. On Saturday, I got sick. By evening, I was vomiting with diarrhea and fever. I felt awful and looked worse. He drove me home Sunday morning and didn't walk me to the door; he didn't kiss me or even throw me a kiss goodbye. Since that day, I haven't heard from him."

"Are you saying he liked you because of your looks?"

Jodi took a breath. "I think so."

"It's a blessing he's out of your life." Jodi nodded as if she was processing the new revelation. Silence returned to the car. They continued the long drive, but Jodi noticed Maddy's silence and asked if she was okay.

"Yeah, I'm okay. Just thinking of work. I'm trapped." The two friends remained quiet, but Maddy's mind was on her job. *Be honest with yourself, Maddy. You don't want to do detective work anymore. You have bills to pay and have no choice, but don't lie to yourself. It's better to live unhappy than in self-deceit.*

CHAPTER 6

Utica, New York, Friday, March 9, 1984

Maddy folded clothes upstairs when she heard Amber open the front door and scream, "Mom, come quick!" Panicked, she ran to see what the matter was. "It's the Wilson Grant."

Amber jumped around, reminding Maddy of when she got her first two-wheeler.

"They say if it's a big envelope, you got the scholarship. You open it— I'm too afraid."

Maddy took the parcel. Amber covered her mouth as if was in the House of Horrors at the county fair, anticipating Dracula might jump out of a closet. Her mother ripped it open and slipped out a packet of papers.

"Read it, Mom, read it."

"'Dear Ms. Reynolds, for your wonderful short story, *The Upside of Down,* the Eva Wilson Grant Committee has conveyed to you its highest award, first prize. This scholarship entitles you to tuition, room, board, and academic accessories for four years at the university of your choice. Congratulations, Rosland M. Krug.'"

"I won, I won, I won!" Amber bounced to the kitchen. "I have to call Dad and Abby. I've got to call everybody."

Maddy sat, gazing at the papers, trying to grasp their ramifications. It meant the money saved for tuition, room, and board was available. It was too good to be true. Not wanting to be disappointed, she remained cautious.

They ordered Chinese for delivery. Amber went to her room to peruse the grant paperwork, and Maddy poured a glass of wine. She tried to sort out what had just happened and needed to talk with someone. She called Jodi.

"You will not believe this."

"Try me."

"Something just happened that might change everything. Amber won a scholarship that pays all expenses for four years at Cornell."

"What does that change?" Jodi asked. Maddy hesitated, remained quiet, and wasn't sure if she should share her crazy idea with her friend. "Don't tell me," Jodi said. "You're thinking of quitting your job."

"How did you know?"

"You've been dreading going back. Don't you remember the ride back from Berry Lake after we saw the wolf?"

"I didn't think I was so obvious to everyone."

"I'm not everyone," Jodi said.

"I know that; you're a great friend." She added, "Do you think I'm crazy doing this?"

"No, I don't. I'm happy for you; you've suffered through a lot these past several years. The question I have is, do you have the money?"

"Well, there's more." Maddy paused. "I want to build a house on that mountain in Berry Lake."

"And live there?" Jodi asked.

"Yes." After an even longer silence, Maddy said, "Are you there, Jodi?"

"Wow, that's a big move. Are you sure?"

"It's been on my mind ever since you dropped me off that day. I couldn't afford it, but I believe I can do it with the money I've invested in Amber's college fund and the proceeds from selling this place. I need to meet with my accountant to be sure." She hesitated and said, "It's just that—" then stopped herself.

"What, Maddy. What is it?"

"I don't know. It's just that—" Maddy stopped again. She waited, then blurted out, "It's just that it's not me. I mean, I don't do these types of things."

"Maybe it's time you do," Jodi reacted. "Maybe you're discovering an unknown part of yourself. Face it, being a detective doesn't make you happy anymore."

Maddy knew it was true, but just hearing Jodi's reaffirming words was like a cool breeze blowing in an open window on a hot day. "Leaving a job at my age is alien to me. I don't believe I deserve it. Isn't that strange?"

"If anyone deserves it, it's you."

Maddy realized that although she conquered the fear of monsters in childhood and overcame evil men who tried to kill her, she was about to face her greatest obstacle—herself. Becoming a detective was a promise made to her father at his graveside when she was twelve. As she sat in her living room, alone, after hanging up with Jodi, she heard her dad saying, "It's okay, Maddy, you've done enough." She realized her father never held her to that promise; it was her all along. *I'm the only one who can set me free.*

She spent the following week mulling over her decision. After reviewing the finances with her accountant and coming to terms with making a move from Utica to Berry Lake, she was ready to discuss her thoughts with Amber, expecting her to be nothing less than ecstatic.

It was a typical Sunday morning at the kitchen table; Maddy read the paper, nursing a cup of coffee, and Amber ate Cheerios, skimming through a magazine. "Honey, I have something to discuss with you." Amber lay the magazine on the table. "Do you remember how you wanted me to quit detective work?" Amber gave a quizzical look that signaled she remembered. "Well, I have decided you're right; I told Zep I'm resigning."

Amber's eyes opened wide. "Oh, Mom, you do not know how happy this makes me."

Maddy still needed to explain the rest of her decision. "Wait, there's more." She folded her hands and placed them on the table. "I want to move to the Adirondacks." Maddy watched Amber's balloon deflate. She looked like she'd just lost her puppy.

"This is our home. It's the only place I've ever lived." Amber covered her face and wept; Maddy didn't know what to say.

Oh my God, what am I doing? Confused, she didn't expect Amber's reaction. A pang of guilt rocked her. She looked at her daughter, holding her head, sobbing, and thought, *I should have gotten her involved in my decision sooner.*

Maddy sighed and paused. *Wait a minute. Amber doesn't realize it yet, but she's starting on a road to her future. She has her whole life ahead of her. I have a right to happiness, too.*

She reached deep inside for courage and said, "Honey, both of our lives are going to change. We'll be changing together, but in different places."

Amber looked at her mother, wiped her face with a napkin, and said, "I know."

Berry Lake, New York, Wednesday, March 21, 1984

"I think I see it," Amber said, looking for the red mailbox. Maddy slowed the car and turned onto a narrow, unkempt road.

"I hope this car will make it," Maddy said. Rocks and ruts jostled her and Amber as they climbed the steep hill. Tall trees cast shadows part of the way, then there was a sudden burst of light, and they shielded their eyes from the point where the trees ended. Fifty yards ahead, the ground leveled; they stopped and got out.

Amber stretched and then, as if just realizing her surroundings, said, "Oh, my God, it's incredible." The hill's flat top was at least a hundred yards in diameter and covered with wild, knee-high grass. Amber turned to the lake. "Look at that!"

It's breathtaking, Maddy thought, as she looked out at the ten miles of blue water with islands scattered throughout. A few low-hanging clouds covered mountain tops and a scent of evergreens mixed with the smell of earth in spring. *It's heaven.*

"Are you sure this is for sale?"

"I'm sure." Maddy's eyes focused on the other end of the lake.

"Buy it, Mom. You must buy it."

Maddy stopped in the center, turned in a circle with arms spread out, imagining her future home. "Here's where I'll put the house. The morning sunlight will strike those mountains. I want the kitchen right there so I can see the first light of day when I drink my coffee."

She struggled to believe it was true. A few months earlier, she was indoors, watching soap operas. The weather was raw, and her future seemed as bleak. *I thought nothing would change. It's incredible how life can turn on a dime.* She folded her arms, thought of her dad, and said to herself, *I'm hooked on a dream, and I'm not going back.*

CHAPTER 7

Utica and Berry Lake, New York, Thursday, June 7, 1984

"Does anyone want another beer?" Maddy asked as the hamburgers sizzled and the hot dogs popped. Al worked tongs with one hand, holding a beer in the other. Zep and Bud talked baseball at the picnic table, arguing over who'd take the World Series, still four months away. "My Girl" by the Temptations played on the radio. Everything was perfect.

Bud raised his hand. "I'll take one. Is there pizza left?"

"I believe so; I'll be right back." Bud gave an affirmative wink. Bud was her nemesis when she first started at the department. He hated the idea of female detectives. That changed the night Maddy killed Benny Bowls in a shoot-out.

She returned to the table, and a sudden thought hit her; *I wonder how Amber's doing.* Her daughter left for Cornell's summer program. Maddy avoided thinking of it, but the sadness in her gut told her she missed her more than she realized.

The doorbell rang. *Hmm, who can that be?* She handed Bud the beer and pizza and went to answer. A black woman, tall and dressed in a pantsuit, stood erect. *She's a cop.*

"Can I help you?" Maddy asked.

"I'm Hannah Bates with the New York State Police." The woman flashed a gold shield.

"Come on in. Are you here on police business?"

"Yes, I am."

"I'm here with friends, detectives. Why don't you join us." After the Cupid case, law enforcement often asked Maddy for help with serial killer investigations. She introduced Hannah to her friends and asked her to sit. "Something to eat or drink?"

"I'm on duty; no thanks."

Maddy explained to the men that Hannah was there on police business. "Frank Zepatello, here, is captain of detectives with the Oneida County Sheriffs; I'm sure he'll be interested in what you have to say."

"Detective Reynolds, what I have to say is for you." Hannah's solemn tone got Maddy's attention.

"Okay." Maddy's stomach tensed. It reminded her of when she learned the man who killed her father wanted to kill her. It was a sensation she'd never forget.

Hannah said, "This afternoon, at 1:38 PM, Jake Donnelly, with the help of his brother Teddy, broke out of Dannemora State Prison." Maddy's eyes fixed on Hannah. She turned to Zep; his look confirmed Hannah's words were as ominous as they sounded. "There's more," Hannah said. "We believe they're coming to kill you."

Maddy looked away. *So much for living in peace and harmony with nature.* She turned to The investigator and asked why she thought that?"

"Several inmates at the prison said Jake talked of revenge for his sister's death. We found this article in his cell." Hannah handed Maddy an Adirondack magazine with her photo on the cover. She was standing in front of a house under construction. The story explained how the famous detective was retiring to live a more serene life at Berry Lake. Someone circled the image of Maddy over and over in black ink.

Hannah pulled out a map, opened it, and laid it on the table. "We found this in Teddy's apartment." Highlighted were several routes from Dannemora to Berry Lake, through the wilderness of the Adirondack Park. She pulled papers from her purse. "These receipts for hiking equipment were in Teddy's apartment." Remaining stoic, Hannah said, "We think they intend to stay in the wild. The Donnellys are experienced outdoorsmen."

Maddy slid the map and receipts to herself and examined them. *They planned this well*, she realized.

"It's a hundred miles as the crow flies to Berry Lake from Dannemora," Hannah continued. "It's forests, mountains, lakes, and streams. We estimate it will take between twelve and fifteen days to get to your place in Berry Lake." Hannah sighed. "We don't think you should be there when they arrive."

Maddy snapped at her, "What do you want me to do, run?"

An uncomfortable silence fell over the backyard. Minutes earlier, laughter, music, and talk of the World Series filled the air.

Zep piped in, "What are you thinking, Maddy?" Maddy knew the men at the table wouldn't try to convince her to change her plans. It wasn't just because she was stubborn. They knew that. It was because they had faced danger, too. Each decided whether fear was going to drive the truck or themselves.

"I'm sorry, Detective Bates," Maddy said as she stood up. "In three days, the Vigalotti and Sons moving truck will be here. By five o'clock, this house will be empty. On Saturday, I will meet them at my new home on Flat Top Mountain in Berry Lake. I plan on sleeping there for the rest of my life. If the Donnelly brothers want me, they know where to find me. I'm afraid that's all there is to it."

There wasn't a decision to be made. Maddy made it when she was fourteen after her father's murder. Faced with cowering under the covers of her bed for the rest of her life or saying, fuck it, if I'm going down, I'm going down swinging, Maddy opted for fuck it. For her, being dead was better than living in fear.

"They told me you'd respond this way," Hannah said as she got up. "We'll do our best to protect you. I can find my way out." Hannah stuck out her hand with a half-smile. Maddy shook it, and Hannah said she'd be in touch. She watched the investigator disappear into the house, and her thoughts turned inward. The three men at the table sat in silence, each withdrawn into themselves.

Bud stared at his beer bottle, rolling it back and forth with his hand as though inspecting it for a flaw in the glass. Al placed a consoling hand on

Maddy's shoulder and shook his head, looking at the beer stains on the tablecloth.

Zep's eyes, bloodshot from a few too many beers, stared at Maddy. "Let's go kill those fuckers!" The backyard erupted with laughter like a crowd cheering a winning last-second field goal.

"I'm for that," Bud concurred, lifting his beer in the air.

Spirits raised as Maddy sat among her battle-hardened friends. But she knew in a week, she would be alone.

It was too good to be true. I was given a get-out-of-jail-free card, and just like that, it was taken away. But I'm not rolling over. If I have to fight it out with those assholes, I'll take at least one with me.

Friday, June 8, 1984

Maddy spent her last night in the old Victorian house alone with the lights turned low. She'd poured a glass of wine, sat in the living room, and let memories flow into her head. She listened to the walls replay the voices of the past. "Maddy, get up for school; you're gonna be late," and she heard, "I'll be making your favorite cake for your birthday; you can have friends over." It was her grandma's voice.

The day Maddy said she wanted to marry Jack, her grandma pulled out a handkerchief, buried her face, and wept. "He isn't right for you," she remembered her say. "Just because you're pregnant, you still have a right to happiness; he will not give that to you."

She sipped her wine, looked over at the reclining chair where her grandmother sat one afternoon with her head tilted to the side, as though she were sleeping, but she was dead. "Oh, Grandma, I miss you so much," she whispered from her depth, remembering the woman who gave her a second life after her father died.

Her grandma's fateful words came roaring back a few years later when Maddy found out about Jack's affair. She remembered screaming at him, "You were not at work; I called, they told me you left at five o'clock. It's after one in the morning, Jack. I found out her name. It's Sheila; deny it."

She took off her wedding ring, threw it, and whimpered the words, "I want a divorce."

There were beautiful memories, too—Amber's first steps and helping her get dressed for the junior prom. The time her daughter cried, with her head in Maddy's lap, after her first broken heart, and Maddy ended up crying with her.

The Cupid experience was near as well. He stalked the house, left a dead kitten on the front porch, and hid a valentine in Amber's backpack. The way Maddy saw it, everything was for a reason; the good and the not-so-good brought her to where she was.

Jackson Brown's words played on the stereo. *All good times, all good friends, all good things, got to come to an end.* Tears welled up in Maddy's eyes. She looked around, held up her glass of wine, and toasted the years. "Goodbye, old house." She swallowed a final swig and got up to go to bed but stopped on the landing, looked around, and heard the house whisper back, "Farewell."

CHAPTER 8

Utica and Berry Lake, New York, Saturday, June 9, 1984

Maddy left for Berry Lake on a bright, chilly morning. A golden hue hung over the Utica neighborhood. She cracked the window of her new Chevy truck to let fresh air in while the heater warmed her feet. She hit the highway, and a chain broke. A lifetime of serving other people was over. She was free to do as she pleased.

I act like I know what I'm doing, she thought, laughing at herself as she drove the truck. The pickup was Amber's idea. "Mom, women who drive pickups are cool." Maddy bought it to please her daughter. She agreed it was damn practical. Amber suggested the cowboy boots, but they were a bridge too far. Maddy settled for a good pair of leather hiking boots. The vehicle still smelled new. *New, Maddy thought. Everything in my life is new—a new home, new people, new surroundings.* As an afterthought, *New danger.* Jake Donnelly popped into her head.

She approached the forever wild region, and the sky was as blue as her grandma's sapphire ring. The road curved like a river, and the hills grew higher the further she went. She was moving into an unfamiliar world. *There it is.* A wooden sign that proclaimed, "You Are Entering the Adirondack Park." Excitement, like droplets of ice, ran down her back.

It was six million acres of hills and mountains, ten thousand lakes, and thirty thousand miles of rivers—bigger than Yosemite, Yellowstone, Glacier, Grand Canyon, and the Great Smokies National Park together.

The idea was daunting to a city girl. Maddy was born in Chicago and raised in Utica, New York, but determined to live among nature's wonder.

Off to her right, a massive expanse of water glittered. She shouted, "I'm home!" It was Berry Lake. She slowed the truck and scrutinized the tree line on her left, looking for the red mailbox that marked the entry to her road. She found it, turned, and climbed the hill; at the top stood her new house.

It's just the way I imagined. It was the first time she'd seen it finished. She was moving in before it was ready. There were still odds and ends the builder needed to complete. But for Maddy, it was good enough. The basement was above ground. The living space was on the second floor, and a deck surrounded it on four sides. White lattice covered beneath the deck, and wide stairs descended to a fieldstone walkway.

Maddy stepped up to the deck, stopped, and looked out at ten miles of crystal blue water. A mountain on the opposite side of the lake she hadn't noticed before caught her attention. It was higher than the rest, and a sprawling log building was on top. *I wonder what that is?*

She carried in a few things from the truck. She stepped inside, took in the bright open space, the smell of fresh paint, and the newness of everything. Walking from room to room, she absorbed the colors of the varnished hardwood floors and the gray fieldstone ceiling-high fireplace.

As she marveled at it all, her footsteps echoed through the living room. Vaulted oak ceilings amplified them. It was the rustic look she wanted. She put her hand on the granite mantle and thought of her dad. *Look at this place. Can you believe it? I wish you were here with me.*

Thinking of how she might place her father's detective badge on the mantle, she took it from her pocket and set it on top. In times of peril, she'd held it and asked him for help. *I'll put his green metal box next to the badge.* The metal box became a keepsake because it contained the clue that broke the Cupid case wide open. *I'll want my wolf photo and my puzzles right there.*

Maddy loved complex puzzles. She looked at every criminal case as a giant puzzle with missing pieces. Each clue in an investigation became a puzzle piece that made the mystery clearer when put in place.

The sound of tires crunching gravel distracted her; she looked, and a jeep with the top down raced up her road. Its long-haired driver wearing sunglasses, Bermuda shorts, and a gold shield stood up in the jeep. He seemed more of a Boy Scout than law enforcement.

"Are you Maddy Reynolds?"

"That's me," she said, looking down from her deck.

"I'm Danny Mosher, Chief Smith's deputy. The troopers contacted us about those Donnellys. The Chief wants you to know that we're keeping a close eye out for them, and if they come around here, we'll get them."

"Thank you, that's reassuring," Maddy said, thinking to herself that Jake Donnelly would eat the kid for lunch. Danny sat, started the jeep, gave Maddy a toothy smile, and barreled away. *Hmm, that's interesting.*

It was pushing two o'clock in the afternoon, and Maddy was famished. Nothing in the ice chest she'd brought was appealing, so she headed into the village to scope out a diner or general store for food. Driving through Main Street, she saw hardware, grocery, and sporting goods stores; a laundromat; and an antique shop. At the far end of the strip was Lena's. The sign read, "No One Walks Away Hungry." *We'll find out because I'm starving.*

Inside looked like something from the 1950s. Fifteen stools with red seats and silver bases bolted to a black-and-white checkered linoleum floor ran along a white counter. A group of men occupied one of the ten booths, drinking coffee and smoking cigarettes. They seemed to laugh at each other's jokes. As she walked through the entranceway, Maddy glimpsed a newspaper dispenser. The headline read, "Camp Ransacked Near Ausable Forks Believed Work of Escaped Cons." She gave her head a shake and sat at the counter.

A heavyset waitress walked over. "What will you have?"

"A great big cheeseburger, fries, and a Coke?"

The woman winked. "Joe, did you get that?"

"I heard it," a deep voice in the kitchen said.

"You're not from around here, are you?"

"I wasn't, but I am now."

"Oh, you built the place up on Flat Top Rock, didn't you?"

"I haven't heard it called that."

"It's called lots of things, but we've always called it Flat Top Rock. My name is Rose." The woman stuck out her hand; Maddy shook it and introduced herself.

"Aren't you the famous detective?"

"I used to be a detective, but not anymore. I retired."

"Well, good for you, honey; I hope to be joining you in thirty years." Rose gave a hearty laugh that made her chubby cheeks jiggle and turn red. *The woman makes a perfect Mrs. Claus.*

Rose brought back a monster burger and a plateful of French fries. "My God, it's huge," Maddy said.

"You said you wanted a great big burger, didn't ya? This is Lena's Ass-Kickin' Burger, and they don't get any bigger or better." After devouring the burger, Maddy paid the bill and asked where to buy seasoned firewood. "Try Lester's. He'll take care of ya."

"Oh," Maddy said, "What's that place on the mountain overlooking the village?" The jolliness drained from Rose's plump face.

"That's The Glades, honey." She took the dirty plates and walked away.

A bell chimed when she opened the door to Lester's Hardware Store. A voice called out, "What can I do ya for?" Maddy couldn't see anyone. She walked past shelves filled with everything from nails and screws to chainsaws and sledgehammers. A sixty-ish man behind the counter looked over his spectacles. "How can I help ya?"

"I'm looking for ten cords of seasoned firewood."

"Sure, I can get you your ten cords. I suppose you're gonna want it delivered too."

"And stacked," Maddy added.

"Oh, and stacked. Of course, you do," Lester lamented, made a disgruntled face, and rolled his eyes. He finished expressing his disapproval at the stacking of the wood and added, "It's twenty-five dollars a cord, plus five for delivery. Where do you live?"

"Flat Top Rock."

"Shit, Flat Top Rock! Make it seven dollars for delivery. I don't know if my tractor can even make it up that hill. I gotta have cash now, and I'll have Hector bring it Friday morning."

"And stacking?"

"You talk to Hector about that. If you're nice to him, he'll do it." *If I'm nice to him. What the hell does that mean?*

Maddy placed the money on the counter. Lester took it with a growl, then disappeared. *He's a happy fella,* she thought to herself.

It was a lovely afternoon, and when Maddy returned to her place, she walked through the field behind her house, toward the woods. The grass grew taller since her and Amber's visit in the spring, but the exhilaration she felt was the same. At the tree line, bushes thick with blackberries, fat, round, and dark, lined the edge of the field. Delighted, she picked a few and tasted. Juicy sweetness melted on her tongue, and she thought that if it weren't for the Donnellys, she'd be in heaven.

As she feasted, she glimpsed something fifty yards into the trees that looked unnatural to a forest. Intrigued, she moved closer, stepping over branches and rocks to get a look. She drew nearer to the object and saw a white wooden cross. It reminded her of a cross she'd seen near a fatal car accident on the highway. It stood four feet high, and withered wildflowers, still green, lay before it. *Did someone die here?* She moved closer when a sudden breeze blew through the treetops, rustling the leaves, and she stopped. The draft ceased and left an eerie stillness. Maddy was not superstitious but had developed a healthy respect for things beyond understanding. She slowly backed away from the cross and walked out of the woods.

She poured a glass of wine when she returned to the house and waited on the deck for sunset. Next to her, on an ice chest, lay a Glock, a bottle of Cabernet, and the leftover French fries from Lena's.

Clouds moved across the fading blue sky, and Maddy's mind drifted. The air was crisp, and the wine went down smooth. The strangeness of the cross bothered her, but she convinced herself it was probably a pet some child buried. *But why here, so far away from other houses?* She was less concerned after the second glass of wine. The sun began descending the mountains when the Donnelly's popped into her head. Unable to enjoy the moment, Maddy went inside and locked the windows and doors. She lay on a sleeping bag and rested her head on bunched-up clothes. Numb from fatigue, she fell off to sleep.

The next day, the movers arrived before one-thirty. It was nearly six-thirty when the truck was empty and the furniture in place. Tony Vigalotti and his two sons helped Maddy unpack kitchen supplies and put beds together. It was time to leave, and Tony, the fatherly type, said he didn't like leaving her alone.

"You guys should be going. My God, you won't get back to Utica until midnight." She watched the big truck kick up dust, rumbling away on her road, and her stomach dropped. *Now, I am alone.*

Katydids and field crickets filled the air with familiar summer night sounds. Maddy walked up the steps to the house, her legs as heavy as tree trunks. She stopped and marveled at the ancient mountains surrounding her. A dark thought disturbed her reverie. The humped edifices of silhouetted hills reminded her of ghouls shrouded in black cloaks.

She thought of the Donnellys coming to kill her and stared at the frightening figures until she found the courage to set herself free from fear.

CHAPTER 9

Berry Lake, New York, Monday, September 6, 1979
Hector Lemont

It was the first school day, and Hector Lemont led the charge to bust open the brass schoolhouse doors when the afternoon bell rang. He had one thing on his mind: the enormous brown trout in Eddy's Pond. The previous day, he and Stick Larson fished until dark, and as Hector reeled the monster to shore, it spat out the hook. Stick wasn't in school, and Hector worried his friend went back to the pond to nail the trophy for himself.

As he ran to Eddy's, plenty of daylight remained to grapple with the trout. He'd left his fishing pole behind a bush near the water's edge and knew where the behemoth rested in the afternoon shadows. *It will surprise Ma when I show my catch.*

"Stick!" he shouted as he rounded a bend. His friend strolled with a poll in hand and the honker over his shoulder.

"You son of a bitch, you stole my fish."

"I'm sorry, Hector. I just couldn't help myself."

"You knew I was in school and went behind my back. Why weren't you in school?"

"My dad says that school's a waste of time, so I just don't go. Don't be mad, Hector. Here, you can have the brown." Stick held the fish in his outstretched hand. Hector was eleven, and Stick fourteen, yet he intimidated Stick. Hector figured it was because everybody rattled Stick.

"Ahh, you keep the damn thing," Hector said. "It's probably old and tough. Come on—walk with me to get my pole." The two boys walked back to the pond, Hector grabbed his pole, and they headed for the village on their way home. The sun was low near the mountain overlooking Main Street, casting a long shadow over the stores and houses, extending several hundred yards into Berry Lake.

"Hey, look," Stick said. "There's Luellen Hicks."

"So?"

"I'm in love with her."

"In love with her?" Hector exclaimed, stopping to stare at his friend. "What's there to love? She's a girl!"

"Just wait a few years, Hector, and you won't be saying that." Stick kept his eyes glued across the street on the cute blond with the tight blue jeans and the sweatshirt that said Thriller. "Hey Hector, you won't be mad if I go over and talk with her, will ya?"

"Go ahead, but you better hope she likes the smell of dead fish because that brown is rank."

"Oh. Will you take it and my pole?"

Hector shook his head, smirking. "Love," he said, taking the fish and the pole. He didn't understand the hubbub over falling in love. His older sister, Anna Jean, was making a fool of herself over a boy, and seeing Stick do the same thing, affirmed that he'd never stoop so low.

Hector's mother sat, holding her head as dinner cooked on the stove when he reached his house.

"Are you okay, Ma?"

"Yeah, just tired."

His mother looked run down for weeks, but Hector figured it was because Pa was into the sauce since he lost his job. It took little to drive his father to binge, so Hector paid it no mind. He laid the trout on the table. "What do you think?"

His mother's expressionless glance said that it was one more thing that had to be done. "You better clean it and put it in the ice chest before it goes bad." As an afterthought, she added, "Then go find your sister and tell her it's time to eat."

After finishing the fish, Hector went out back where Anna Jean took clothes off the line. "A.J., Ma wants us to come in for dinner."

"In a minute," she said, her morose tone catching her brother's attention.

"What's wrong with you?"

"Oh, Hector, don't you know nothing? Don't you see how Ma's acting? She's sick."

"What do you mean, she's sick? Does she got a cold?"

"No, she ain't got no cold! Doc Abrams told her she's got the cancer."

"What's the cancer?"

"The cancer is something people die from, and it makes you sick first. That's the reason she's been acting so tired."

"I didn't know," Hector said.

"I know you didn't," A.J. said. "Help me get these clothes down before Ma gets upset."

Hector helped, wondering if his mother was really going to die. As they sat at the dinner table, he kept looking over at her. "Pass the potatoes, Ma?" She handed him the bowl, and he tried to imagine her not sitting at her spot anymore. It was hard to do, but powerful loneliness ran through him when he saw the empty chair.

"What's the matter, Hector? You didn't put any potatoes in your dish," his mother said.

"I guess my eyes are bigger than my stomach," he said, but he'd lost his appetite.

Wednesday, June 22, 1980

Anna Jean held the screen door in place while Hector screwed on the hinges. "I wish Pa would quit kicking out this door when he gets drunk," Hector said. "With these days getting hotter, the fresh air should help Ma feel better, don't you think?"

"I hope so," A.J. said. The stuffy air inside has made her awful ornery."

They finished, and A.J. opened the solid door, letting in the fresh air. "How's that, Ma?" Hector asked.

"Oh, so much better." She took a deep breath, and color returned to her face. "I have something special to ask of you," she said. They looked at each other.

"Sure, Ma. What is it?" Hector asked.

"Up on Flat Top Rock, the blackberries must be as big as plums. I want you to go pick me a basketful."

"Ma, you ain't thinking of baking a pie, are ya?" A.J. asked.

"Why yes, I am. I can still do some things. Making my mother's blackberry pie is one of them. I'm gonna do it while I can. Please, run up there and get me real ripe ones. Oh, on the way home, stop by Doc's and get my medicine; I'm out."

Hector and Anna Jean headed to Flat Top Rock through the woods, with Hector grumbling, "Ma shouldn't be trying to do no baking, as sick as she is."

"Hector, you don't understand. Ma's just got a little time left, and Grandma's blackberry pie brings her good thoughts." In her playful way, A.J. shoved her brother to the ground, saying, "I'll beat you to the foot of the hill," and took off running. Hector ran after her, laughing as he went. Out of breath, A.J. stopped, and Hector passed her. With her hands on her knees, she huffed, "I almost had you this time."

Hector came back and put his hand on her shoulders. "You know what the problem is? You run like a girl." His older sister, still larger than Hector, pushed him down, took off, and made it to the Flat Top Rock trailhead first. Hector walked the rest of the way, holding his stomach, laughing. He reached her, and they lay on the tall grass at the foot of the hill, looking up into the summer sky. "That was too much," he said.

He started thinking of his mother, and when A.J. began talking about Everett Turley, a boy who took an interest in her, he was half-listening. He finally said, "I don't like him."

"Why, Hector? He's real nice."

Hector was twelve, but he knew what Turley was after. His friends kept telling him how pretty his sister was, and Turley—a rich, stuck-up kid—wasn't someone with honorable intentions. "I just don't like him. That's all there is to it." Out of nowhere, as he often did, he changed the subject. "What's gonna happen to us when Ma dies? Pa ain't gonna take care of us."

A.J. sat up, looked at her brother, and yelped, "Stop, Hector. You gotta have faith that God is good, and Jesus is watching over us."

Hector sat and gave her a half-smile. *A.J. believes Jesus will take care of everything. I'm not so sure.* There were an awful lot of problems that didn't get fixed, including his father's drunkenness and his mother's cancer. Lost in their thoughts, they started up the hill to where the blackberries caught the sunlight all day.

"Oh my God! What's that awful smell?" A.J. screeched.

"Smells like a dead animal," Hector said. "It must be a big one."

Pointing to a heap covered with flies, A.J. shouted, "Look!" Hector moved toward it; A.J. followed.

"It looks human." Hector saw a black shoe with a foot inside, several feet from the rest. "An animal must have chewed off its leg." His sister screamed, turned, and ran. Hector covered his nose, moved closer, and shooed away flies. "I think it's a girl!" The corpse lay on its stomach with its head turned away from him. He grabbed a broken tree limb and began prying the body over until it flipped; he jumped back.

One eye opened, and the socket filled with squirming maggots repulsed Hector. A smile-shaped hole across the girl's neck was like a carved Halloween pumpkin. Blood caked on the shirt reminded Hector of his own when he ate watermelon. He forced himself to inspect further and saw a rusted object lodged in the hand. *It's a knife. She cut her own throat?*

"Hector, come on. Let's get out of here!" He walked back to A.J., trying to imagine someone cutting their own throat. The two went home through town while the gaping hole in the girl's neck remained stuck in Hector's head. They reached Main Street, and like homing pigeons, they went to the person in town they trusted most, Doc Peters.

Doc was a black man and was Berry Lake's only physician. Beloved by all, he had a soft spot for people with troubles, and no family had more than the Lemonts. He lived behind his office, and that's where Hector and A.J. ran. They knocked hard, and Doc opened. "What in tarnation is wrong?" he asked.

"We found a dead body, Doc," A.J. said.

"What? Come on in here, you two. Sit, take deep breaths, and try to calm yourselves." Doc sat and said, "Okay, now. Slowly tell me what happened."

Hector did the talking. "We were heading up to Flat Top Rock to pick blackberries for Ma, and as we climbed the hill, we saw a dead body. It was a girl, and she cut her own throat."

"What color hair did the girl have?" Hector said it was blonde.

"It might be Luellen Hicks," Doc said.

"Luellen. Why Luellen?" Hector asked.

"She went missing a week ago. Her mother told me Luellen's been acting strange ever since she got a job up at The Glades."

"What should we do?" A.J. asked.

"Just tell me where the body is, and I'll let Chief Smith know. Then, you two get on home." Hector drew a map on a napkin, and before they left, Doc handed A.J. a small package. "Give this to your mother; it's her medication."

As they walked home, Hector ruminated how beautiful Luellen Hicks looked decrepit. She was rotting in the dirt. He couldn't get the smiling hole and the maggots out of his head.

CHAPTER 10

Berry Lake, New York, Saturday, June 9, 1984

Hector fed sticks into a campfire, wrapped up in a sleeping blanket. He sat on a fallen tree and watched the smoke rise through the pines. It was June in the mountains, and it was cold. He was waiting for daylight while thinking of how unfair life had become since his mother died.

A twig snapped, he looked up, and a figure emerged from the darkness; it was his sister.

"What are you doing here?"

"I brought biscuits and pork." A.J. sat next to him, holding a basket.

"Was Pa drunk last night?"

"He sure was. It was a doozy, too. You should have seen him singing and trying to get me to dance. I got right out of there as soon as I finished cooking."

"Did he give you any money for food from the welfare check?"

"You know he never does."

"Well, how the hell does he expect us to eat when he drinks the money away?" Hector chomped into a biscuit, shaking his head with disgust.

"You had me worried," A.J. said.

"You know I always come back. I knew Pa was drunk and didn't want to see him."

"I know, but I still worry,"

Ignoring A.J.'s concerns, Hector stood up and started rolling up the sleeping bag. "Come on, help me pack my stuff back into the cave, and I'll walk you home."

Hector found the cave when he was eight, after one of his father's beatings. He would go there to calm himself at first, but, in time, he stayed the night. He fixed it up with a tree limb to sit on and a fire pit. The cave was just 15 feet deep but had a ledge in the back where he stored sleeping bags, cooking utensils, and a few supplies. It became Hector's home away from home most of the year, but it was his home in summer.

They finished putting things away and pulled tree branches over to cover the entrance. Unless someone knew where it was, they'd walk right past it. As they started hiking the trail home, the eastern sky turned red, making silhouettes of the rounded peaks. The mountains in the morning always made Hector's troubles smaller.

"I've got to tell you something, and I don't want you to get mad," A.J. said as she walked behind her brother.

"What is it, now? You got another boyfriend?" Ever since Everett Turley broke A.J.'s heart, Hector tried to protect her from guys he thought were just using her. She was eighteen, and several older men were interested in her. Hector knew it wasn't because his sister was smart or sophisticated; it was that she was downright beautiful. He was only fifteen but wasn't afraid to fight guys who might hurt her.

"No, it's not a boyfriend. It's about getting a job and making money." Hector stopped and looked at her. He wasn't pleased but realized they needed money.

"Where?" he asked.

"The Glades," she said. "I have an interview next week." Her brother said nothing; instead, he mulled the matter over in his head. When they reached the village, people were milling around Main Street. "I don't think you should go home until Pa's off his bender," A.J. said.

Hector said that maybe he'd stop by the hardware store to see if Lester had any work. When he walked in, and he saw Hector, Lester smiled. "I was just thinking of you."

"Hey Lester, any work for me?"

"Not today, but soon. I'll have cordwood deliveries if you want to make a little money?"

"Not too little, I hope." Hector smiled.

"Stop back. I'm sure I'll have something soon."

Hector had time to kill, so he walked over to Doc's next. The old physician was a good listener, and in Hector's eyes, Doc was like a dad. He knocked on the side door. When no one answered, he walked in, grabbed an apple, and sat at the table.

When he finished with his patients, Doc came into the kitchen. "Hector, I haven't seen you in a week; where have you been?"

"Hey, Doc. I've been out at the cave."

"Has your pa been drinking again?"

"Yep, the welfare check came the other day, and he won't stop until it's gone."

"You're nothing like him," the old man said. "You're a good boy."

Hector smiled. He wasn't used to such talk, but he trusted Doc and wished he could believe him. Deep inside, he didn't. Doc tried to make him feel good. His words were comforting, and even though Hector seldom used the word love, he believed he loved Doc.

"What's new in your world, Hector."

"A.J. has an interview at The Glades."

The look on Doc's face said he disapproved. "I wish she'd work at the grocery store or ice cream stand instead." Doc opened the refrigerator, pulled out a bowl of leftover stew, and asked Hector if he wanted lunch.

Doc's reaction bothered Hector.

"Why is everybody so scared of The Glades?" he asked.

"It's not that people are afraid; it's they don't understand it. It's another world up there."

Hector nodded, but it seemed Doc was holding something back. He worried the rest of the day about his sister being with people no one knew. *How will I protect her? The Glades is different from the village. At least here, I know everyone.*

CHAPTER 11

Sunday, June 10, 1984
Maddy Reynolds

Maddy didn't sleep well her first night in the new house. She gave up on trying after 7:30 and went to the kitchen to find the coffee among a few unpacked moving boxes. She walked to the deck with a cup and her Glock. The sun was warm; the sky was blue, and it looked to be a glorious day. Several loud pops rang out; she went for her weapon and realized a tractor bouncing up to her house made the sound.

The driver turned, looking at a wagon piled high with firewood, and Maddy couldn't see his face. She tucked the gun under her shirt and watched as the guy drove up close. A boy, around fifteen, jumped off. He walked up over with a sideways saunter, pulled out a red handkerchief to wipe the sweat from his forehead, squinted with the sun in his eyes, and said, "You Maddy Reynolds?"

The kid was tall, thin, fair-complexioned, with sunburned skin and long, messy blond hair. His body was approaching manhood, but his voice belonged to a boy. Something about him touched her.

"That's me," she said.

"Where do you want it?"

She worked at not laughing out loud. "Behind the house."

The kid turned his head, spat, and looked at her, squinting. "Is that a basement beneath your house?"

"Why, yes."

"Does that basement have doors on the side?"

"It does indeed," she said, smiling, holding in a guffaw.

"Then why put the wood in the back? Do you know the snow we get up here, lady? Christ, it'll take till spring to dig your body out after you freeze to death trying to haul that wood." He spat again.

Faced with insurmountable odds and inevitable defeat, retreat and try another approach, she thought. "You know my name, but I'm not sure I know yours." She put out her hand.

The boy hesitated. "I'm Hector Lemont." He looked unsure of what to do. Scratching his neck, he stared at the outstretched hand, and, with little enthusiasm, he shook it.

"How do you do?" he said in a softer tone. Maddy noticed a tenderness in his penetrating blue eyes that he tried to hide.

"Let's start over, okay?"

"Okay," Hector said.

"I think you're suggesting that I should place the wood near the double basement doors so that it will be easier for me to bring inside during the winter months, correct?"

"That's right."

"I think that's a good idea. Can I pay you to stack it for me?"

"Stack it!" he said with a harsh sigh. He shook his head, smacked his lips, and said, "How much?"

"Well, what's it worth to you?"

"Ten dollars, and I stand firm."

"I'll pay you fifteen and throw in some lemonade?"

"Deal," Hector said. He turned to the tractor with Maddy close behind.

"Oh, Hector, do you know about the cross in the woods behind my house?"

"Sure," he said. "That's where Luellen Hicks's body was found."

"What happened?"

"They said she went off the deep end. You know... she killed herself." Hector ran his index finger across his throat.

"You mean she cut her own throat?"

"Yep. My sister and me came blackberry pickin' and found her. She damn near cut her head off."

Hector started the tractor engine and pulled around to unload the wood, and Maddy went inside. She'd never heard of a woman cutting her own throat. She started making the lemonade when a loud scream came from the back of the house. She dropped what she was doing and ran to the deck. The boy was smacking his leg, shouting, "He's getting me good." He pulled up his pant leg. A large bumblebee fell out, and half a dozen red welts ran up his calf.

"Are you alright, Hector?"

"I'm allergic to bee stings. You gotta get me to Doc Abrams."

By the time Maddy got to him, Hector had fallen to the ground, his lips had swelled, and he was gasping for air. Maddy's heart pounded. "Where is Doc Abrams' office?"

Hector wheezed out the words, "Red house... west end of Main Street." Maddy drove the truck around, lifted him inside, and took off. Hector's head lay on her lap, and she placed her hand on his chest to comfort him. Air flowed unevenly into his chest as he struggled to breathe, and Maddy worried he might suffocate.

Hector's lips were blue when she reached Main Street. His eyes were wide open and reminded Maddy of dead people she'd seen over the years. Beyond the diner and hardware store, a red house stood by itself. A woman walking out said Doc was at lunch. "He just locked up. He opens again at one o'clock."

Maddy ran into the vestibule, but the door to the office was locked. When she came back out, a black Subaru in the driveway waited for traffic. "Hold on!" she shouted. An older black man turned and rolled down the window. "I need help. Hector Lemont is in my truck; a bee stung him." Before she said another word, the guy left the car and ran to Hector.

"Help me get him out," he yelled.

Maddy and Doctor Abrams slid the boy out, and Abrams grunted as he picked him up. He handed Maddy a set of keys. "The one with blue tape opens the office door." Hector's eyes were closed as Abrams carried him. He lay him on a table and went to a medicine cabinet where keys hung from its lock. Doc grabbed a bottle and prepared a syringe. Maddy noticed Demerol set off to the side. *If this were Utica, that bottle would be stolen and on the street,* she thought.

"This is epinephrine; it should bring him out of it." Maddy watched as the boy on the table struggled for his life. She thought back to how it happened. It wasn't the first time she'd seen tragedy come from nowhere, but usually, it came from a knife or a gun—not a bee stinger.

As Abrams held Hector's wrist and waited, Maddy noticed how Doc's expression changed; the corners of his mouth started turning upward. "His pulse is stabilizing; I think he's going to be alright."

Throwing herself back in her chair, Maddy exhaled a sigh of relief. Hector stopped struggling, and Abrams asked for help to get him to the sofa. "We'll let him sleep for a while." Maddy and Abrams sat where they could see Hector and one another. He looked at Maddy, smiled, and put out his hand. "I'm Doc Abrams; everyone just calls me Doc."

"I'm Maddy Reynolds."

Doc pulled out a pipe and said, "How long have you known Hector, Maddy?"

"I just met him this morning. He was delivering firewood when this happened."

"This boy's quite a character," Doc said. "He carries a lot of weight on his shoulders for someone his age. He can be a sassy one, but he's just a boy longing for his mother." Doc looked at Hector with a tender smile. Maddy heard both love and pity in his voice.

"So, you're the detective that built a house up at Flat Top Rock."

"Everyone seems to know that."

"The magazine with your article went through town like a brushfire. Every coffee table in Berry Lake has one. I've got a couple in my waiting room." He took a couple of puffs off his pipe.

"Are you the only physician in town?" she asked.

"Yep, grew up in Philadelphia, got a scholarship to the University of Pittsburgh, and, when I finished my residency, believe it or not, I couldn't find a job. I heard rural communities were desperate, so Jenny and I moved here. She's my wife, or was my wife; she's gone now. I guess when people are sick, the color of one's skin doesn't mean much." Doc bellowed out an old man's laugh, deep and heartfelt. "Why did you decide to retire to Berry Lake?" he asked.

"I had my fill of crazy. You know, life on the streets."

Doc looked at her. She could see the glow leave his face. "You thought you were going to escape crazy here?" He wasn't joking.

"Hector looks like a typical country boy," she said.

Doc pulled the pipe from his mouth. "Hector is anything but typical. He lives outside of town with his father and sister in what you might call less than optimal conditions. The father, Bart, is unpredictable. Sober, he's as lucid as you or me, but if he falls into a bottle, he becomes the meanest drunk you'll ever see. Hector there, he takes the brunt of it. If it wasn't for Anna Jean—that's his sister—he'd have run away after his mother passed."

Maddy understood what it was in Hector's voice that drew her sympathy. It's the sadness people who have known more than their fair share of heartache carry with them and can't hide. She thought that a listener familiar with such sorrow can always detect it in someone's voice.

Groaning from the sofa turned both their heads. "He's waking up." Doc went to him. "How are you doing, Hector?" He held the boy's wrist, checking his pulse while trying to converse.

"Oh, I'm okay. Where's the lady detective?"

"I'm right here."

"I didn't finish stacking your wood," Hector said, rubbing his eyes.

"Don't worry about that."

"Oh, I'll finish it. I will."

"Let me take you home, and we'll deal with the wood another day."

Maddy and Doc helped Hector to his feet and then to Maddy's truck. Maddy offered to pay Doc, but he refused the money.

She got in the truck and drove out of town to a long dirt road, following Hector's directions. Hector leaned against the driver's side door with his eyes closed. When Maddy thought she was near, she slowed the truck. Hector sat up. "Up there, passed the big oak," he said. "Just pull over."

Washing machines, refrigerators, and unrecognizable objects surrounded a small shack, set fifty yards into the trees, and Maddy's heart sank. Hector got out. He spoke through the open window. "I'll be back to finish the wood and to get Lester's tractor." He looked over his shoulder at his house, then back at Maddy, grimacing as though he was ashamed. As Maddy turned the truck around in the road, Hector waited and watched. In the rearview mirror, as she drove off, Maddy saw the boy disappear into the trees across from his house. *Why did he do that?*

CHAPTER 12

Wednesday, June 13, 1984

My God, it's ten-thirty, Maddy thought when she rolled over in bed the following day. She planned to putter around the house and bemoaned that the morning was half shot. She dragged herself out of bed, threw on sweats, and didn't bother taking a shower. She kept the Glock close even though the Donnellys were a week away, and as she filled the coffeepot, she looked out the window and shook her head. *What is this?*

A black limousine glistened in the sunlight behind her house. She walked outside, the limo's rear door opened, and a tall, dark-skinned man in a black suit got out. "Hello, Ms. Reynolds. I am Darius Girard." He smiled and put out his hand. As Maddy shook, she noticed Girard's smooth hand was softer than her sandpaper skin, roughed up from pulling weeds.

"I work for Avery Jordan," Girard said, dignified. "He owns The Glades and wants to meet you."

"I don't think I know of Mr. Jordan," she said.

Girard chuckled, turned, and pointed to the mountain across the lake. "That's The Glades, and Avery Jordan is its founder. I'm sorry to show up unannounced; I hope I'm not inconveniencing you."

"Oh, no. It's just that, well, as you can see, I'm not presentable," Maddy said, running her fingers through her hair, trying to make it obey.

"We can return in an hour if that's alright with you." She smiled and said she'd be ready. The limo left, and as she returned to the house, she thought, *What's next, Elvis?*

Maddy showered, got dressed, and walked to the kitchen in a bathrobe. The limousine was back. *Shit, he's twenty-five minutes early; these people are awful pushy.* She rushed to finish.

"You look lovely, Ms. Reynolds," Girard said when she came out of the house.

"Why, thank you." She didn't think she was wearing fancy clothes. Girard opened the limousine door, and Maddy slid onto a leather seat that was more comfortable than any furniture in her house.

They drove nearly ten minutes before turning up a paved road. The limo ascended a hill that was much steeper than Flat Top Rock's and was covered with a tall pine tree forest. They reached the top, where a massive log building stood. *Wow, look at that!*

The vehicle pulled under an overhang, and a man wearing a black bowtie came out to open her door. *This isn't the Berry Lake of Lester's Hardware Store or Lena's Diner,* she mused to herself as the gentleman escorted her into Castile Room. They stepped into a massive open hall. A janitor polished a wall-to-wall marble floor with a machine. *My God, what is this place?*

As she looked at the golden oak-stained log walls, forty-foot-high ceilings, and three chandeliers, loaded with lights hanging from beams, she remembered gawking at tall buildings the first time she was in New York City.

"Come," Girard said. "Mr. Jordan will meet us in the garden." Their footsteps echoed in the open space as they crossed the hall. They walked toward a wall made of hundreds of small-pane glass windows. The wall reached the ceiling, and in its center, three sets of large French doors let in pillars of light that opened to a colorful garden.

"Out here is the Nadia Arboretum." Girard held the door, and Maddy stepped outside. She walked into an exotic paradise that reminded her of Kew Gardens in London. *This is marvelous,* she thought. It was like entering another world.

"Come. This way," Girard said. They walked across a stone terrace lined with hedges to a long pathway around a circular pool. A fountain flowed in its center, and entrances to other walkways with plaques identified its type. "Mr. Jordan loves hydrangeas. That's where he'll be."

They entered a place about the size of a tennis court. It was filled with purple, blue, burgundy, and white flowers. In its center, covered with large-leafed Dutchman's pipe vines, a wrought iron gazebo stood, and inside, waiting, with his hands in his pockets, smiling at her, was a tall, handsome man. In his mid-forties, with blonde and white hair and a tightly groomed beard, the man looked like a movie star.

As Maddy approached, his face lit up. "It's a pleasure to meet you, Ms. Reynolds." Maddy smiled. A strange attraction drew her to him, yet she also felt repelled. Unsure of what to make of him, she remained guarded. "Please, let's sit," he said, gesturing to cushioned iron chairs. Girard brought a pitcher of sangria and two glasses half-filled with ice. He poured the red concoction into the glasses and left them alone.

Avery settled into his chair and introduced himself. "I've wanted to meet you for the longest time. I thought you were a model when I saw your photo on that magazine cover. But with your long hair and smooth dark skin, you are even more attractive in person. I found your work intriguing, and oh, what you did in that horrible serial killer case." Avery's voice was a babbling brook, melodic, soothing, seductive. He was masculine yet gentle, and Maddy was attracted to him.

"Thank you, Mr. Jordan, you're very kind." His knowledge of her past disquieted Maddy.

"Is it alright for me to call you Maddy?" he asked. She nodded. "Maddy, I keep close track of notable people. I said I must know this woman." Avery drew Maddy in with his charm.

"That's most flattering," she said as she tried to move the discussion away from herself. "The Glades is magnificent."

Avery's face beamed. "Thank you. It means everything to me."

"I feel foolish that I didn't know of you before today," she said.

"You're not foolish at all. I try very hard to stay off the radar. That you didn't know of me is testimony to my success."

Avery's force field kept pulling at her. He spoke deliberately, contrived, and with purpose, and Maddy wondered what his purpose might be. Her uneasiness kept her on guard; she felt a powerful strangeness. *I stepped through a time warp into the kingdom of Avalon. I wish I stayed home to yank weeds out of the garden or spray-paint that old chair I bought at the barn sale.*

"Come with me," he said. "I'd want to show you something." Maddy placed the sangria down and followed him to a path. Along the way, short flowering pink trees gave off an exotic fragrance. She asked what they were.

"These are myrtles. Wonderful, aren't they?"

"They're perfect," she replied, but in her mind, she thought, *Perfect makes me uneasy because it's never what it seems.*

They went further and reached an opening, and Avery spread his arms. "See." A magnificent vista opened up before them. Berry Lake's deep blue water contrasted with dark green, tree-covered mountains and islands. It was similar to Maddy's home view, but she saw further from where she stood; it was much higher.

Shocking, she thought as she gazed at the wonder. The rounded peaks of ancient mountains, covered with thick, lush green trees, stood in silence beneath the afternoon sun, lazy and unbothered by time. Maddy whispered to herself, "Yes."

Avery turned to her, smiling. "I fell in love with it, too. I said I must make it mine." Maddy gazed at him, thinking, *I've known no one with such a need to own what he sees.* She found the quality disturbing.

He pointed across the lake. "See, there's your place." Maddy saw her house sitting atop Flat Top Rock, and she felt exposed. "And there," he said, pointing. "There's the village of Berry Lake." Tiny houses glimmered in the sunlight, and cars scurried.

"Do you go there much?" she asked.

Avery looked away. "No, never been." *How unfortunate,* Maddy thought. *Great people live there.* Avery gave off an air of self-importance and superiority. Maddy stared at him as he looked at his cherished view, then he said, "I'm peckish. Lunch?"

They walked along a path to a veranda where Girard waited, and a woman dressed in a housemaid uniform rolled a cart with thick sandwiches, cut in quarters and filled with different meats, cheeses, and vegetables. She placed bowls of soup, salad dishes, and fruit cups before Avery and Maddy.

Girard and the woman left them. Avery arranged his plate and said, "I've admired your work. I remember when you killed Benny Bowls. That must have been some shoot-out."

How does he know of Bowls? That was five years ago.

"I have an aversion to violence," he added, "but sometimes it's necessary." Changing subjects, he said, "So what made you retire to this remote part of New York?" Maddy said she fell in love with its natural wonders.

"You have law enforcement blood in you. Your father and grandfather were detectives. You don't mean to say your inquisitive, analytic mind has retired too, do you?" Maddy realized Avery did extensive research on her history. He was fishing for something.

"I guess time will tell," she responded. Avery's expression, which changed from a smile to a grimace, startled her. *I hit a nerve.* She wanted to ask why he'd moved to Berry Lake but refrained. "The food is wonderful," she said.

Finished with lunch, Avery looked at his watch and said, "Oh, it's nearly two o'clock. It's my favorite time to be at the summit. Come, let's hurry before we miss it." Avery choreographed the afternoon to a T. Maddy sensed an unknown reason he invited her, but he couldn't seem to get at what he was after.

"I should go," she said.

"Oh, no. You don't have to go. Come, the sun hits the mountains at a unique angle for ten minutes." He leaned his body toward a path to the summit. He stretched out his hand. "Come on."

"If you insist." *This guy won't take no for an answer.*

The view from the summit was indeed spectacular. Mountains to the west cast shadows that made silhouettes on the waters below, and the sun colored the village in amber. "Isn't it magnificent?" he said as he gazed at the marvel.

"It is indeed," she said.

She caught a whiff of Avery's cologne in a warm, intoxicating breeze. She noticed how well kept he was. Something was unique yet odd about him.

The sun moved from its position, and he turned to her. "It was a delightful afternoon. Thank you, Maddy."

"Thank you for inviting me," she said.

As Darius Girard escorted her through the complex to the limousine, Maddy saw a young woman running from a building screaming. A man chased her and forced her back inside. Alarmed, Maddy turned to Girard. "What's that about?"

"Oh, it's a domestic thing. Those two are always at it."

"Even domestic things have limits, Mr. Girard." Maddy was concerned for the woman.

In the evening, she sat with the Magical Forrest, a 9,000-piece puzzle spread out before her, and could not concentrate. Avery Jordan and The Glades haunted her thoughts. Her eyes rested on the puzzle's surreal figures as she sorted the pieces. A warped grandfather clock stood in a forest with a pair of eyes. A tree had arms and hands, and moonlight shrouded everything in a foggy haze. *My God, that's where I was today. Being at The Glades is like being in the Twilight Zone.* She pushed away from the table and brought her wine outside to gaze at the mountains.

She heard an airplane, located its red light in the dark sky, and watched as it moved among the stars. When it landed at The Glades, she shook her head and, unable to absorb any more weirdness, went to bed.

CHAPTER 13

Wednesday, June 16, 1984

It was late afternoon. Maddy hung up from talking with Amber when she heard a car racing up her road. An unmarked police vehicle slid along the gravel and stopped. Hannah Bates got out, and as Maddy walked to her; she knew something was wrong.

"I have news, but it's not good," Hanna said. Maddy's stomach did a backflip. "The Donnellys stole a car near Lake Placid and ditched it twenty miles from here. We found it this afternoon. They're continuing on foot, and unless we stop them, they could be at your place tonight."

Maddy looked out at the surrounding hills, wondering why this was happening to her. *I only wanted to retire.*

"Let me find you a safe place to stay for a few nights," Bates said.

"Not happening, Hannah." Maddy remembered what her old friend Mary told her about herself. Unlike most people who avoid fear, she said Maddy always lived with it. She told Maddy that she would drown if she ran, and as strange as it sounded, her fear made her strong.

"I'm not running, I can't," she reiterated to Hannah.

Hannah sighed. "Okay. Then, let me put two units here."

"No units at my house," Maddy said.

"Ms. Reynolds, you're putting yourself at grave risk."

"My choice, Hannah." She thought of Johnny lying in the street with his face blank and eyes wide open. "Don't you think those troopers you send here will be at risk? No units!"

"We'll do our best to protect you, but you are damn stubborn." Hannah got in her car, slammed the door, and sped off.

Maddy retreated to the house and watched the afternoon drift by in her living room. She kept two guns at her side and a fresh pot of coffee going to help her stay alert. The overcast sky dimmed, and a sense of foreboding grew. Darkness fell, night sounds came to life, and Maddy moved to a corner of the room, with one thought in her head: *They will not make me run!*

She sat in the dark, listening for any noise that might be the Donnellys. As the hours passed, her mind wandered. *Why is this happening? Am I cursed? No matter where I go, killers follow me.* Her thoughts raced as the night grew long. *Will it ever end? The hatred, violence, killings, vendettas—does it end?*

She remained agitated until the sun chased the shadows away. She opened the windows and breathed fresh air, then went outside with a cup of high test, her weapon, and a cordless phone. The lake below came to life as fishing boats set out from shore. Halfway through her first cup, the phone rang. It was Hannah.

"You won't believe this."

"What?"

"We found Teddy Donnelly with his throat cut."

As if hit with a baseball bat, Maddy was speechless.

"One of our helicopters was scanning a creek-bed four miles southeast of you. They spotted something at the foot of the ravine. We checked it out, and it was him, deader than dead."

"Talk to me, Bates. This isn't making any sense. Do you think Jake killed his brother?"

"No, I do not. Something else is going on in Berry Lake that we don't understand. But there's one thing for damn sure: Jake wasn't with him. That means he's getting closer to you. Maddy, you must leave"

"Investigator Bates, let's not go through this shit again."

"You are goddamn bullheaded; you know that?"

Bates hung up the phone. Maddy sat, trying to grasp what had just happened. *Teddy Donnelly is dead, with his throat cut. How can this be?* She forced Teddy out of her head, retreated to the house, and focused on Jake. Running on pure adrenaline, Maddy returned to being on the defensive. Inside, she moved from room to room, keeping a close eye on the tree line around her place. Several hours passed, she got tired, made more coffee, and counted on the caffeine to keep her awake.

Hours dragged. Maddy moved to the sofa and used it for cover, keeping an eye on the three entrances to her house. She knew it would be hard to stay alert—her nourishment was a large bottle of water and a box of Cheerios. After several hours of fighting boredom, she struggled to keep from nodding. She recalled frightening experiences from her past to pump adrenaline into her bloodstream. The day Cupid left a dead kitten inside her door. He blasted her friend Allison's face with a shotgun when he thought she was Maddy. After a while, her tricks stopped working.

Daylight faded, and the clock on the mantel read nine forty-five. It was dark. The wind picked up and made it hard to detect sounds that might be Jake Donnelly. She snapped out of a sound sleep. *Shit! That was reckless.* She sat up, eyes wide, listening to the wind rattling the windows.

She looked into the darkness of the house, trying to detect movement. She wondered if someone might have entered while she snoozed. A tiny red light on the message machine glowed in the dark. Time passed, and again, her mind faded. Her eyes closed for a minute, five minutes, maybe fifteen; she wasn't sure. When they opened, she saw the red light suddenly disappeared. A shot of adrenaline shocked her mind awake. She waited. Nothing. *He has to be right there.* The red light appeared. That's him! Maddy lifted the Glock. *If I can't see him, he can't see me.*

A switch clicked on and light-filled the room. Jake Donnelly stood with a gun in hand. His black eyes glared at Maddy, and he wheeled his weapon. Two shots rang out, shattering the silence. A loud poof and sofa stuffing splattered into her eyes. She wiped them clear. Jake lay on the floor, with a hole in his throat, gurgling blood. He lifted his arm to shoot, and Maddy shot first; Jake's hair, scalp, and brains covered the stone fireplace.

She flopped onto the sofa; a locomotive chugged through her chest. She tried to catch her breath. Sweat dripped from her face, her stomach curled into a knot, and the smell of Jake's blood and brains made her want to vomit. She ran outside for fresh air and saw headlight beams bouncing around on trees. Tires crunched gravel on her road as five state police vehicles skidded to a stop. Hannah Bates got out and came running. "Are you hit?"

"No, I'm okay." Huffing and exhausted, Maddy said, "Jake's inside. He's dead."

"We set up at the end of your road and heard the shots." Hannah gestured to the other detectives to go inside. "Treat this as a crime scene. And make sure he's dead." Hannah put her hand on Maddy's shoulder. "Come, let's sit." They moved to the picnic table; Maddy felt weak. "We're going to have to run this through forensics—just procedure. You understand, right?"

Maddy nodded. "There's a mess in there," Maddy said. Hannah said they'd take care of it.

"Are you sure you're okay?"

"Yeah, I'll be alright; I just need to calm myself." Familiar disturbing memories returned whenever Maddy took life as she thought of the people she'd killed.

They stayed outside in the cool air while a special team took care of the scene in the house. Hannah stayed close and brought a blanket to cover Maddy's shoulders. She went to her car and returned with a thermos of hot coffee, poured a cup for each of them, and they drank it without talking. The eastern sky turned pink over the mountains as the troopers finished. It was time to leave.

"This was a very traumatic experience for you, Maddy. Are you sure you don't want to stay at a hotel?"

Maddy had been in similar situations before and knew she'd get through it. "I'm more comfortable staying here, close to the things I'm familiar with, but thanks."

The other troopers left Flat Top Rock, and the two women walked together to Hannah's car. The sun peeked over the hill, birds sang, and things felt normal. Maddy just killed a man who wanted to kill her, and that, too, was becoming normal.

Hannah turned to her before getting into her vehicle. "I owe you an apology."

"I don't understand."

"I underestimated you; I thought you were signing your death warrant."

"One of these days, I might be; I was lucky to get through the night alive." Hannah gave her an appreciative look, climbed inside, and drove off.

As Maddy lay in bed thinking that night, one thought haunted her: *Who killed Teddy Donnelly?*

CHAPTER 14

Wednesday, June 20th,1984
Avery Jordan

Avery was on the phone when Darius Girard knocked and stuck his head inside without his boss saying it was okay. Avery scowled and put his hand over the speaker. "What is it?"

"Sir, The Guy is holding on line one."

"Are you sure it's The Guy?"

"It's him, Mr. Jordan, I'm sure." Avery switched calls.

"Do you know what the date is?" the man said with a gruff, unflinching voice.

"June twentieth," Avery replied.

"Do you know how many days until September nineteenth?"

"No."

"Ninety-one!" The phone slammed, a dial tone rang out, and Avery sat, unable to move.

"Have Naomi come to my office," he barked to Girard over the intercom.

The albino entered while he was at the window. "I just got a call to remind me that September nineteenth is getting close." He faced her and added, "Everything rides on the masquerade party. I hope you have left no stone unturned."

"You worry too much," she said, walking to him and putting her arms around his waist.

He loosened her grip and snapped, "That's because I'm the one who'll be dead if we don't deliver." Avery went to the wall safe to get the ledger. Next to the vital journal lay the revolver his father gave him years earlier. His mind flashed back to the day he'd wrapped his lips around its barrel, and he forced the thought from his mind.

He scrolled down the attendee list. "I think we have enough people, but a few more won't hurt. I'll have to make more calls." Naomi sat, watching Avery fret. She lit a cigarette and exhaled a cloud of smoke. "And the gala. Are we set? We must satisfy that congresswoman. If we blow that, we blow our front. Both events need to go without a hitch."

"Everything controllable is being controlled," Naomi said. "I can't do anything about the weather."

Avery looked over his calendar and saw an interview scheduled for one o'clock. "Who is Anna Jean Lemont?"

"She's a local girl who's interested in a customer service position."

"I don't have time for this; I'm supposed to meet Chief Smith any minute," he said, tapping his fingers on the table.

"It's your policy to interview every new hire, Avery."

He sighed. "Let's do the interview in my quarters when I'm done with Smith." As Naomi started for the door, the phone rang. He answered, and Girard said Congresswoman Fieldstone was on the line. Avery waved Naomi out of his office and took the call.

"Oh yes, Congresswoman, I'm delighted to host your gala." Avery thought the only delight was that it distracted the law from September's masquerade party.

"Our women's group is very grateful," Fieldstone said. "This is our fifth Single but Not Alone Gala, and we are so pleased you offered to host it at The Glades."

"It's a very worthy cause assisting these unwed mothers, and it's a pleasure to help. You will not find a finer venue than The Glades, I assure you."

"I hope the weather will hold out up there," the congresswoman lamented.

"September nights are enchanting in the mountains," Avery assured her.

"Are you sure you can accommodate five hundred guests, Mr. Jordan?"

"We have the capacity for eight hundred, Congresswoman."

"I am so looking forward to it."

When Fieldstone said goodbye, Avery buzzed Girard. "Has the Chief arrived?"

"He's been waiting, sir." Jed Smith walked in with his hat in his hand. *He looks like a suck-up,* Avery said to himself.

"Chief, I called you here because we are putting on a few important events these next few weeks, and we can't afford to have any disruptions by the locals. I want you to be extra vigilant."

"I will, Mr. Jordan, I will."

"This detective from Utica."

"Maddy Reynolds?"

"Yes, Maddy Reynolds. What do you know of her?"

"Well, she's retiring to Berry Lake."

"That's what everyone knows, Chief. I had her here for lunch last week. She told me she moved here to be near nature. That's odd, isn't it? Why is a single woman with her credential coming to Berry Lake?" Smith's face was blank. "There has to be more to it. Find out what you can." The chief crept out of the room, looking like a puppy scolded for peeing on the carpet.

Free to do the interview, Avery went to his quarters. A girl about eighteen sat waiting with crossed legs, smiling and playing with her hair. She flipped it over her shoulder when she saw Avery. *Cheap dress, scuffed up white shoes,* Avery thought as he inspected her. *Wow! She's gorgeous,* he realized when he looked closer. Her unconquered innocence sent a shot of testosterone through his body.

Naomi entered, smiled at the girl, and gave Avery a look that telegraphed an earlier warning. She told him the girl was a local, and he needed to keep the conversation to business.

Avery locked on Anna Jean, imagining her naked in his bed. He introduced himself and Naomi. "I understand you're interested in the Customer Specialist position." He sat on the sofa across from her, reached into his coat pocket, and pulled out a cigar.

"Yes, I'm very interested," she said. Avery lit up and looked at her between puffs of smoke, knowing it was causing her to be anxious by the way she shifted around on the sofa.

"What do you bring to this position?" Avery knew that the country bumpkin brought nothing, but demeaning his prey was a favorite tactic for women with low esteem.

"Ah, I'm not sure; um, what do you mean?"

"A person must bring something to a job—a talent, experience, an attribute, something. There's no reason to hire them otherwise." A.J. looked to the side, uncrossed her legs, and appeared stumped.

"I can cook," she blurted out. Avery laughed loud, shook his head, and gazed at Naomi, smiling. Naomi looked away, obviously embarrassed at the girl's lack of sophistication.

"You can cook!" he roared. "Oh, dear."

Anna Jean's face flushed, and Avery saw her eyes watering. In that instant, something went wrong inside of him. A pang of sympathy bubbled up. He pushed it back down. "Our cooks are among the finest; we don't need you to cook," he mocked.

"What do you need?" she asked.

He sat back, rubbing his fingers over his chin. "I want you to be available whenever I need you. To do what I ask without question. Occasionally, you'll take on a special assignment. If you do an outstanding job, we'll pay you special rates—say, a hundred dollars each time."

"A hundred dollars!" A.J. thundered with her eyes opening wide.

Naomi shook her head when Avery guffawed.

"Is it a deal?" he asked.

"Damn right," A.J. said, stood up, and stuck out her hand. Avery caressed it, moving his thumb up and down on her wrist. Her soft, creamy skin felt delightful. He glimpsed at Naomi, saw her glaring, and he let Anna Jean's hand drop.

He stood and looked down at the girl. "You'll begin training tomorrow, Miss. Lemont. You'll learn how to do the important things that we expect of our specialists."

As he left the room, Naomi brushed against him and whispered, "Keep it in your pants, Avery." He smiled. Making Naomi jealous was fun; it made her crazy in bed.

CHAPTER 15

Friday, July 6, 1984

Avery's favorite ritual was ending a workday with a stroll in a garden. He was about to leave his office when Girard appeared at the door. "We have an issue, Mr. Jordan." Irritated and eager to get outside, Avery asked if it could wait. "It's serious," Girard said.

"What is it?"

Girard opened a large envelope and pulled out several glossy photos. He lay them on the desk. "This is the problem." He spread out the glossies.

Avery dropped himself into the chair and picked up the photos. His face grew hot. "Who did this?"

"The guy's name is Silas Glumper. He tends one of our safe houses near the Canadian border."

"Where's the girl?"

"She arrived on last night's flight very upset. She's in the infirmary." Avery said he wanted to see her, and together they walked through Castile Room to C-wing.

C-wing was three floors of housing, and on the ground level were grooming facilities, saunas, whirlpools, tailors, hairdressers, and an infirmary. Everyone stood when Avery entered. He went to the exam room where a girl, around seventeen, sat. A nurse consoled her. The room emptied, and Avery pulled a chair near the girl and asked her name.

She said it was Nikita. "Did a man hurt you, dear?" She nodded, trembling. "We'll take good care of you. Are you in pain?" She nodded again. "Where did he hurt you?" She pointed to her right breast. "Let me see what he did."

"No!" she said, pulling her shirt tight.

"I can't help you if you don't show me what happened." He stroked her hair. "Come, come, it will be alright."

Nikita dropped her hands, rested them on the table, and Avery unbuttoned her blouse. The red, bloody bite marks surrounding her nipple ignited a firestorm inside of him. He stood, told the girl to button her blouse, and walked outside the room where Girard waited. "In my office, Mr. Girard."

Avery Jordan seldom showed anger to others. It was a trait he'd learned from watching his father conduct business. His father considered displays of anger, fear, or love signs of weakness. When Avery reached his office, he smashed his fist on his desk like a hammer. His eyes locked on Girard. "Mr. Girard, I have stressed to you the absolute importance of hiring people who are responsible, discreet, and can exercise self-restraint." He walked to the window. "Is Mr. Neri on the premises?"

"I believe he's out for a flight in one of our planes."

Avery turned to Girard. "Flight? Is he a licensed pilot?"

"Yes, sir, he has considerable experience."

"Find me when he returns. I'll be in my quarters."

It was mid-afternoon, and Avery took a nap as he often did. Unlike most people who might lie on a sofa or bed for a short snooze, he changed into his pajamas, slid between silk sheets, covered his eyes with a mask, and fell fast asleep. When he awoke, Girard told him Neri had returned. "Send him to my office."

Avery was uneasy around Sedgwick Neri. He seemed to look right through him. When he walked in the room, the big man put out his hand, and Avery shook. Neri's eyes riveted on him as though he were analyzing Avery's motivation for the meeting.

"Please have a seat." Avery walked around his desk and sat across from the throat cutter. "First, Mr. Neri, thank you for taking care of one of those

Donnelly thugs. I was hoping you'd get them both before they reached Maddy Reynolds. Thank goodness she took care of the other one; if anyone is going to take that woman, it's going to be me."

"Why is she so important to you?" Neri asked.

"There are things I prefer to keep to myself, and my little fetishes are among them." He offered Neri a cigar, but the big man declined. Avery lit up, thinking to himself how he didn't want to share his need to claim ownership over everything he fancied. It irked him when someone he desired wasn't under his power, and he was becoming inclined to have Maddy Reynolds within his control. Her youth, beauty, intelligence, and proven analytic skills made him think of her as erotic. But she was also a threat.

"I have another situation for you to take care of," he said, exhaling smoke away from his guest. "One of our own has overstepped his boundaries and must go."

"And the evidence?"

"The location is far enough away. No one will associate it with The Glades; do what you will with the body. The person is Silas Glumper. Mr. Girard will give you the details. Please handle it as soon as possible."

Neri's forte of cutting throats was repulsive to Avery, but he believed it was one of the dirty little necessities that went along with the business. Expert in hand-to-hand combat and a superior marksman, it bewildered him that a man with such talents enjoyed getting close enough to his prey to hear it gasp its last breath.

Neri left, and Avery's stomach was as tight as a violin string. *The man unnerves me,* he thought. *Maybe it's that he enjoys his work a smidge too much.*

Wednesday, July 18, 1984

Avery went to the staff training room more often since Anna Jean had come on board. "You again?" Naomi asked when he walked in, interrupting a training session. He ignored her and walked over to the tender young girl.

"How are you today, Anna Jean?"

She appeared sheepish, and she blushed. "There's an awful lot to know about sitting," she said. Avery laughed as Naomi watched with an eagle's eye.

"You're doing just fine," he said. "Why don't you stop by my office when you finish the class." As he walked out, Naomi turned her back. Avery thought their relationship could tolerate his messing around.

A long-standing private client, Ronald Aster, was waiting on hold when Avery returned to his office. Wealthy and a frequent guest at The Glades, Aster called to arrange a night of relaxation. "The eighteenth works for us," Avery said, finalizing Aster's visit. He hung up and thought he heard a faint knock at the door.

"Come in!" he shouted, and Anna Jean walked into the room. It was like the sun coming out from behind a cloud when he saw her shy innocence radiating. It triggered his primal, animalistic drive for conquest. Anna Jean stood with her hands clasped in front. She reminded him of a school girl asking her daddy for candy. "Please have a seat," he said, surprised at his boyish excitement. He watched her long legs breaking through the blue silk dress that was split in the front. Her skin was sleek and glowing from expensive imported retinol oils; her flowing blond hair bounced as she walked, and Avery's exhilaration grew with each move.

Anna Jean sat, crossed her legs, and folded her hands in her lap, just like the other girls at The Glades learned to do. "I've been told you go by another name with your friends," Avery said.

"A.J.," she said.

"Oh, of course—A.J., short for Anna Jean. Is it okay if I call you A.J.?"
She giggled and said that she'd like that.

"So, tell me, A.J., do you have folks here in Berry Lake?"

She explained she lived with her brother and father and that her mother passed on a few years back. Briefed by Chief Smith ahead of time, he already knew all that. "Are you close with your father?" The girl's honesty surprised him. "My pa, well, he's got a drinking problem. He doesn't treat my brother and me too good." A.J. look down and to the side. A pang of sadness ran through Avery as he thought of his pain from years of his father's rejection.

"My brother Hector is almost fifteen. He tries to act like he's thirty and looks out for me, but he's pretty wild, too."

"I'm sorry to hear that," Avery said, dropping his come-on facade and talking in an authentic tone to the girl. "My father hasn't treated me very well, either." He glanced over at A.J., saw her sympathetic expression, and, for an instant, was disarmed. Uncomfortable with his tender feelings, he got up. "If you ever need anything, ask me." He walked over with his hand out. A.J. got up and stood close to him. He smelled the sweet fragrance of her hair, and when she looked at him with her brown eyes wide open, he could not stop himself from kissing her.

It wasn't what he planned. Avery didn't allow tenderness for a woman. Sex was all he cared about. Right then, he felt at one with A.J. Her warmth, apparent innocence, and sheer gentle beauty were almost more than he could bear. His face grew warm, and he trembled in his vulnerability. He looked down, their eyes met, and A.J. caressed him. She leaned her head on his chest, and Avery put his arms around her; neither spoke for several minutes. "Come, A.J., let's get comfortable on the sofa."

"I'm a virgin." She pulled away with fear in her voice. The phone rang and broke the awkward moment. He answered, and it was Naomi.

"What's going on, Mr. Jordan?"

Avery put a hand over the receiver. "You can leave, A.J., and don't forget, come see me if you need anything." She closed the door. "Naomi, you are a real pain. I was chatting with one of our new employees."

"Mr. Neri has asked me to go for an airplane ride, and we'll be leaving soon." She hung up. Avery sat and held his head in his hands, trying to unscramble all that just happened. He remembered catching Neri staring at Naomi from afar in Castile Room and suspected they were sneaking around, but that was the nature of his relationship with Naomi; what Naomi and he didn't tell each other didn't exist.

How did I let myself get here? He tried to understand why he was so attracted to young Anna Jean. Becoming obsessed with a person or an object he desired was nothing new, and when he wanted something, Avery remained single-minded until he got it.

It was like when, as a teenager, he had a crush on Clair James, Luke James's wife. Luke was one of his father's employees, and Clair was twice Avery's age. One afternoon when her husband came by to visit Avery's father on business, and she was with him, Avery was sure the woman's gaze signaled she wanted him to pursue her.

He convinced his father that Luke should go on an overnight trip to New York City to buy a unique mink coat for his mother's upcoming birthday. When the man was away, Avery made his move. With a bottle of wine in hand, he visited Claire and made small talk. The alcohol gave him the courage he needed to make his move, and he quenched his thirst for the married woman.

It was the beginning of a scorching affair. Luke eventually found out and came within inches of crushing Avery's head with a baseball bat. His father was forced to sever ties with his dedicated employee. The incident was one of many humiliations that broke off relations with his son.

She's a virgin; she's innocent and afraid, he pondered, thinking of Anna Jean. *And I want her.*

The next day, Avery summons Chief Smith to his office. "The Chief has arrived," Darius said when he called on the intercom.

Avery folded the ledger, walked it to the wall safe, and placed it inside. Smith entered, and Avery greeted him differently from usual. "Thank you for coming, Jed. How are you?"

"I'm fine," Smith said, taken aback by Avery's sudden kind demeanor.

"Would you like a cigar?"

"No, thanks, I smoke Camels."

Camels, Avery chuckled to himself. "Have a seat, please." Smith sat, and his eyes narrowed with suspicion. "I understand that this boy, Hector Lemont, is rather wild. Am I right?"

"I'll say," Smith said. "He has a truancy problem, and he thinks he can live on state land. He's a pain in my butt just like his drunkard old man."

"Jed, if you do me a small favor, I'll show my gratitude." The chief's face lost all expression. "Do you see that rather thick envelope sitting on my desk?" Smith looked over at the desktop. "That envelope expresses my gratitude." The chief's eyes locked on the bulging envelope.

"What kind of favor are you talking about?"

"The kind that would get Hector Lemont arrested."

Smith leaned forward in his chair, and his leg started bobbing up and down. "I'm not sure I can do that, Mr. Jordan; he has done nothing that bad."

"Do you remember the deputy who didn't do what I asked?" Avery snapped.

Smith's leg stopped bobbing. He seemed frozen to the chair. "When do you want this to happen?"

"Soon!" Avery went to the desk and opened the envelope. He took out about half of the money, all twenty-dollar bills. "Here is a down payment." The chief took the cash, and Avery said to let him know when it was done.

CHAPTER 16

Saturday, August 4, 1984
Maddy Reynold

It was Saturday morning, and Maddy had her first good night's sleep since moving to Flat Top Rock. She felt energetic, walked out to the yard, and inspected the weed-infested flower bed. *Maybe I'll attack this today*, she thought. She kicked over a rock, looked around, realized the job was more than she wanted to tackle, and started inside. A voice called her name, and it was Hector.

"You scared the devil out of me, Hector."

He hopped off the stacked woodpile, toothpick protruding from his mouth, smiling. He handed over a stack of envelopes. "I got your mail. Thought I'd save you a trip."

"Thanks," Maddy said. "And thanks for stacking the wood."

"I told you I'd finish the job, didn't I?"

Maddy asked how he was feeling since the bee sting. "Bees are the least of my problems," he said as Maddy thumbed through the mail.

"Want to join me for breakfast at Lena's? My treat," she said.

"Aww, Lena's. Nothing like a gut full of grease to get my day started right." Hector laughed. "Sure, I'll go."

"This is interesting." Maddy held up a small textured envelope from the stack of mail. "It's an invitation to a gala at The Glades."

"Looks like you'll be hobnobbing with the bigwigs," Hector said with a sarcastic chuckle.

Avery Jordan popped into Maddy's head. She remembered his haughty swagger and the way he looked down on the townspeople; she wasn't inclined to go back to The Glades anytime soon. After she changed and they were driving into town, Hector said, "The whole town is buzzing about those two dead guys. You know, the ones who came to kill you."

Maddy didn't want to talk about the Donnellys. Hector continued. "One guy's throat was cut. You know, a lot of people get their throats cut on Flat Top Rock," he said, smirking, obviously making a connection to Luellen Hicks.

Maddy looked at him. "I was thinking the same thing. How well did you know the Hicks girl?"

"Not too well. My buddy, Stick Larson, was goo-goo for her. She dumped him when she started at The Glades."

Maddy decided it was time to make mental notes about what was going on around Berry Lake, the way she used to do when she was a detective. She filed away that Luellen Hicks worked at The Glades. "What do you know about The Glades?" she asked.

Hector squinched his lips together. "I don't know what to think about it. All I know is my sister just got a job up there." Maddy thought she'd hit a nerve and dropped the subject.

They walked into Lena's, and Rose pointed them to an empty booth and came over. "Hello, Maddy. Hey, Hector, what ya have?"

"Oatmeal, an order of toast, and coffee," Maddy said.

"Huh!" Hector grunted as he looked at Maddy. "Give me the flapjack special with eggs over easy, a glass of milk, and a double order of bacon." Maddy looked at the kid. He was as skinny as the toothpick sticking out of his mouth. *I'd weigh two hundred pounds if I ate like that.*

The retired detective's mind churned as they waited for the food. "The day I dropped you off at your house, you didn't go inside. You took off across the road. Why did you do that?"

"My pa was drunk, and I don't enjoy being around him when he's like that."

Rose brought the food, and Hector smothered his pancakes with syrup. "There's a cave in the woods where I go to be alone," he continued. "The trees don't talk back, and it's really peaceful."

A fat uniformed man walked up to the table and stopped. He glared at Hector, looked at Maddy, smirked, and continued out the door.

"Who is that?" Maddy asked.

"That's Jed Smith, the police chief," Hector said with a mouthful. "He ain't a very nice guy."

That's the police chief? Maddy asked herself. She was trying to gauge the sort of town she had made her home in when she glimpsed a woman a few booths ahead who looked like Hannah Bates. She looked closer, and it was her. "Hector, I'll be right back."

Hannah looked up when Maddy walked over. "Oh, hi, have a seat," Bates said.

"What are you doing up here?" Maddy asked as she sat down.

"Investigating a homicide, execution might be a better word for it."

"Really? I have heard nothing on the news; it must be recent."

"They found the body up near the Canadian border yesterday. That's where I'm headed from here."

"You said execution-style?"

"The guy's throat was cut."

Throat cut? Are you kidding me? "An awful lot of throats getting cut around here."

"Tell me about it," Hannah said. "We still don't have any leads on who took out Teddy Donnelly."

"What was the guy up north into?" Maddy asked.

"We think he was running something from Canada. Maybe drugs, guns ... we're not sure. We found what looks to be a safe house nearby."

Something started moving inside of Maddy. There were too many coincidences. "Two similar-style executions in unrelated murders," she said. "It sounds like there's a connection." She didn't even mention Luellen Hicks.

"I know," Hannah said, looking worried as she placed her coffee cup down.

"Missing pieces," Maddy whispered under her breath, shaking her head. "What was that?"

"Missing pieces," she said louder. "There are always missing pieces." Maddy returned to the booth, and it was empty. "Aww, damn it, Hector."

"It looks like your guest took off," Rose said when she brought the check.

"He's a hard boy to figure out," Maddy said.

"He's a lost boy, a very lost boy," Rose said.

Maddy walked out into the sunshine, and before she reached her truck, she noticed people gathering on Main Street looking in the same direction. Three police cars with flashing lights blocked the street. The chaos drew her in like a magnet. She moved toward the cops and saw Danny Mosher shove Hector into a police cruiser. Hector's face was red, his nose bloodied, and he screamed something through the closed window. She didn't hear what the boy said but was enraged as she walked to Chief Smith with her fists clenched. Maddy asked what the boy did. "He's been trespassing on state land."

"He's a minor, for God's sake. Why are you roughing him up like that?"

"He resisted arrest—hit one of my deputies. We're taking him in. If you know what's good for you, Miss Big Shot Detective, you'll turn around and leave before we take you in for obstruction."

About to lose her temper, Maddy backed off. As she started for her car, she saw Hector looking out the closed cruiser window with his eyes wide and face wet with tears. Her stomach sank. She wanted to go to him but knew it was a bad idea.

Maddy trembled with indignation as she neared her truck. Rose stood with her arms crossed, watching the drama and shaking her head. "Hector will never survive this town," Rose said as she turned and walked back inside.

Too agitated to hang around her house, Maddy stopped by Doc's. "Why what a surprise!" he said when he opened up.

"Do you have a few minutes?"

"Sure. Come in." Doc led her to the living room. "What's wrong, Maddy?"

"The police just arrested Hector on a trespassing charge." She tapped her fingers.

Doc shifted position and looked away. Maddy cringed. "Talk to me, Doc. What's going on here?"

He hesitated. "I'm not sure." She suspected he knew more than he shared. "I mean, there must be a reason we don't know about. Where could Hector be trespassing around here?"

He's leaving something out. Maddy stood up and walked across the room with her arms folded.

"You're not telling me something," she said.

After a long silence, Doc said, "Look, anything I say right now will be pure speculation."

Maddy sighed, frustrated, and thought, *He's not going to tell me anything.* "Okay," she said. "But bizarre things are going on in Berry Lake. If I'm going to live here, I have a right to know what they are." She started for the door, and Doc got up.

"Maddy!" She turned. "I'm not keeping anything from you. It's just that, well, I've been uneasy about Chief Smith's involvement with The Glades. It's possible what happened to Hector might involve the place. I'm not sure my concerns are real, or it's my imagination. I don't like saying things I'm not sure about, that's all."

Maddy gave him a half-smile as she was leaving. "We're going to have to find a way to help him out of this jam. I'll be in touch." When she walked outside, her head was swimming, and she drove to Flat Top Rock, with a powerful longing for the people she'd left behind in Utica. I need to hear a familiar voice, she thought, and when she walked into her place, she called Jodi.

"Hello."

"Oh, my God, Jodi, I'm so glad you're there."

"Are you okay?"

"I'm in la-la land; everything here is strange." Maddy explained all that happened in the short time she'd been in Berry Lake: Teddy Donnelly found with his throat cut, her shoot-out with Jake, the cross behind her house where the Hicks girl cut her own throat, and the guy up in the North Country who succumbed the same way. She told Jodi about Hector's near-death experience with a bee sting, how the kid just got beaten up by the police and arrested on a trumped-up charge. "And there's this place called The Glades," she said. "It's a retreat that sits high on top of a mountain. The guy who owns it, Avery Jordan, sent a limousine to my house. We had lunch, and it was one of the weirdest experiences of my life. He has charisma and acts like some kind of prince."

"What made you feel uncomfortable about Avery Jordan?" Jodi asked.

"It was like he had an ulterior motive, and it involved me," Maddy said, continuing to unload on her friend. She realized what she was doing and stopped. "I'm sorry; I'm just frustrated. Tell me what's been going on with you."

After a deep breath, Jodi said, "I've been a little depressed."

"George, right?"

"How did you know?"

"When you love someone, even if they're an asshole, you can't just flip a switch and shut off your feelings. You have to grieve your losses; that takes time.

"I haven't talked to anyone about how I'm feeling in a while. My friends think I should be over him by now, and my roommate stopped listening to me a month ago. I feel so alone."

"That's because they've never been through it. Or maybe haven't loved as deeply as you. I have an idea," Maddy said. "Why don't you come and visit me for a few days? Hang on, let me check something."

Maddy grabbed the invitation. "There's an event at The Glades, and I'm invited. If you come with me, you'll see what I'm talking about."

"What kind of event?"

"Well, it's a fancy ordeal, which is why I'm not cool about going, but if you're with me, we can make it fun. How about it?"

"Okay, but what do I wear?"

"Do you have a formal dress?"

"I have the one I wore to my prom."

They made their plans, and Maddy's gloom lifted. Jodi was the solid point of reference she needed. She looked outside toward The Glades as it shined in the afternoon sun. The uncomfortable thought of Avery Jordan's perfect world came back. She learned long ago, people obsessed with perfection were hiding something. *What are you hiding up there, Mr. Jordan?*

CHAPTER 17

Friday, August 10, 1984
Avery Jordan

A mourning dove cooed somewhere outside Avery's window, keeping him awake. It was nearly light when he got out of bed. He slipped on a silk bathrobe and called for Robert. "I'm ready."

Robert knocked and came in. He was the only person allowed to bring Avery his meals. He placed a tray on the small table near the window. Avery inspected the food, nodded, and Robert poured the coffee. Although he typically didn't work while he ate, Girard sent in a call from Chief Smith.

"Yes, Chief."

"We have Hector Lemont at the juvenile detention center, but we can't hold him for long."

"Good," Avery said. "And Chief, remember I want you to find the real reason Reynolds is in our backyard." Avery anguished over anything that might screw up the masquerade party. He wanted to turn up the heat on Smith to be more aggressive. He tried to go back to his breakfast, but his stomach was too tense. Girard stuck his head in. Avery screeched, "What now?"

"Sir, Mr. Neri said he has one trapped, and you should come with your rifle."

Avery was on a quest to surpass his father's hunting accomplishments. He got dressed, grabbed his new rifle, and followed Girard to a jeep. They drove down a rutted trail until it disappeared in the thickness of trees. "This way, sir," Girard said when they got out. He led Avery to where Neri stood with a rifle in hand; yelping and squealing echoed throughout the forest.

"I have the female in a trap," Neri said. "Keep an eye out for the male; he's been circling, wanting to rescue her." Avery walked about ten yards and saw the wolf gnawing at a steel trap, trying to free itself. "Aim for the heart," Neri said. "If you hit it above the neck, you won't be able to hang the head on your wall."

With his heart thumping against his chest, Avery aimed, but his arms trembled, and he let the gun down. He took another breath, exhaled, then raised it again, steadied himself, and fired. The wolf screeched, fell, kicked its hind leg for several seconds, then went limp. There was a howl on the ridge. Neri reeled and fired, but the round hit a tree, and the male disappeared. "We'll get him another time," Neri said.

Avery ran to the animal, relishing having its head on his wall. More importantly, he just outdid his father. *I can't wait to let him know.*

That night, he sipped brandy at an open window. The scent of hemlocks entered, and he thought of all he'd accomplish. *In a month, this will be all mine.*

He heard an eerie howl somewhere in the night, realizing it was the male wolf. He pulled the window closed and started for his desk when he heard someone at the door. "It's me, Anna Jean. Can I come in?"

"Certainly, dear. Come in and have a seat." Avery gestured to the couch, and he sat across from her. "So, what brings you to visit me tonight?"

She looked down into her lap, holding a crinkled tissue in her hands. "I need your help."

"What is it, A.J.?" Avery asked, sounding very concerned about the girl.

"My brother Hector has gotten himself in trouble and is in a detention center. My pa is a terrible drunk, and I'm afraid to be home alone with him. I noticed that most of the staff live here at The Glades. I wonder if I can move in too."

She wept, and Avery got up, sat next to her, put his arm around her, and stroked her hair. "Everything will be fine, dear," he said. "Sure, you can move in here."

It must be my lucky day. First the wolf, now A.J. Let nature take its course, and she'll be in my bed. "Tell me what happened to your brother."

"Hector got arrested for trespassing, and when the police tried to take him in, he punched a deputy and broke his nose. He's in a world of trouble."

Avery took a tissue and dabbed tears from her face. He put his hands on her arms and looked into her eyes. "Would you like me to see if I can get him released?"

The girl lit up. "Do you think you can do that?"

Avery touched his lips to hers. "Yes, I think I can," he whispered, pulling her close and then laying her down on the sofa.

A.J. said, "But Avery, I told you, I'm a virgin."

"I'll be very gentle, dear."

The following day, as he sipped a mimosa in the garden, his spectacles on the tip of his nose, and reading the New York Times society pages, Avery marveled when he saw an article about The Glades. "Hmm, what do we have here?" he said out loud to himself when he saw the headline: "Extravagance in the Adirondacks: The Glades to Host the Single but Not Alone Gala." It was about his mountain creation and how Avery was a champion for women. *The press,* he thought to himself. *It's where perception changes into illusion and illusion into reality.* He heard footsteps, looked up, and saw Naomi drawing near.

She stopped, looked at him, stuck out her hip, and tilted her head. "Did you have sweet dreams last night?" *How the hell did she find out?*

"Yes. How about you?"

"You might say mine was jam-packed."

Avery knew it meant she was with another man. *She is such a vindictive bitch.*

"Remember, Ron Aster is visiting this weekend," she said. "We need to find a partner or two for him."

"I'll leave that to you," Avery said.

"Very well." She smiled in a way that meant she was scheming. When Avery was alone again, thoughts of Anna Jean's body lying next to his flowed back into his head. *Sweet dreams, indeed.*

CHAPTER 18

Wednesday, August 15, 1984
Maddy Reynolds

It was approaching late afternoon, and the sky grew overcast. Maddy dragged herself around the house, thinking her move to Flat Top Rock was a mistake. Ever since she'd seen Hector abused by the police, she longed for her old life of chasing street criminals.

Nature opened up a new world of beauty for Maddy since she'd come to the mountains, yet gnawing loneliness lingered as well. She breathed in the refreshing fragrance of pines, and they seemed to whisper, "We do not belong to you, and you do not belong to us." Her uneasiness drove her to the bedroom closet. She pulled out a Glock, lay on the bed, and fell asleep with the weapon at her side. When she awoke, it was near dark.

She grabbed a leftover pizza slice, uncorked a bottle of cabernet, and sat before the Magical Forest puzzle pieces with a glass of wine. She began the ritual of searching and matching and turned on the radio, hoping to listen to oldies. The only station without static was WADK out of Saranac Lake. A talk show was about to start.

"This is Randy the Man. You're listening to Late Night with Randy. Hello, insomniacs, unemployed, and the graveyard shift. Our first caller tonight is from Old Forge; go ahead, you're on the air."

Maddy half-listened while she sorted puzzle pieces, sipped her wine, and replayed the events of the past twenty-four hours in her head.

"I'm Sally," and then a bleep.

"No last names, please," Randy said.

"Oh, sorry. Anyway, I'm calling because I want my dog back."

"I don't have your dog," the host quipped.

The woman laughed. "I know you don't have my dog, Randy; Ralph took Firpo when he moved in with Jeannie."

"You named your dog Firpo?"

"Why yes, after my father."

Maddy laughed to herself. This can't be real, she thought as she sorted.

"Ralph has a right to Firpo, too, doesn't he?" the host said.

"Firpo loves me more."

"How do you know that?"

"He told me."

"Firpo told you he loves you more?" Maddy smiled and realized it was the first time she'd done so in days.

"Hold on, Sally. Folks, we'll get to the bottom of this when we return from a break. Don't go anywhere; we're going to hear about Firpo, the talking dog."

"This is silly," Maddy said out loud and lowered the volume. "I wonder where they find these people; it has to be staged. No one can be that dumb."

She turned the volume back up a few minutes later, and she heard Randy say, "Okay, now for the serious part of tonight's program with our special guest, Pasha Lermontov. I hope I got that right," he said.

"Close enough," a female voice with a slight accent responded. The girl sounded young; her voice was soft and humorless.

Randy gave a short preamble before starting the interview. "I know most of you tune in to my show to lighten the load from your busy day, and so I want to forewarn you that tonight's subject is not lighthearted; it is serious. It's 1984, and most of us believe the things we'll talk about are from a different era or another country. But we are not immune. Everything you'll hear about is happening now, here, in the United States." Maddy turned up the volume. Randy continued, "Pasha is from Russia. I'll shut up now and let her talk."

"Thank you, Randy, for letting me come onto your show. I'm nineteen. Three years ago, in my hometown in northwest Russia, I was invited to a party by a girl I had recently met. Before I left the house, my mother said, 'Be home by eleven o'clock, Pasha.' I kissed her goodbye, and the next time I saw her was two years later." Maddy's glass was empty. She got up and brought the bottle to the table.

Pasha said she passed out at the party and woke up in a strange apartment the following day. "I'm sure someone drugged my Coke at the party," she said. "That started a long nightmare. For weeks, I was in apartments with other girls. Men came and went. They brought food and things we needed. With the doors locked, we couldn't escape." The girl's story drew Maddy further in as she imagined it happening to Amber.

"Before we moved to other locations, they put something in our food to make us pass out, and we traveled using small airplanes. Near the end, I knew we were in Montreal, Canada, because I heard it on a radio station in the next room."

Her voice quivered; Randy jumped in. "Let's take a break. We'll be right back."

Something stirred inside Maddy, but she couldn't pinpoint what it was. "We're back with Pasha Lermontov, telling her story of sex slavery."

"One of the last places they took us was a small safe house in the United States where almost a dozen girls stayed. The last airplane ride brought me to a beautiful estate outside of Detroit. I lived with six other girls. We knew two women as Bev and Dot, who took care of us. We'd sit by the pool during the day to get tanned, fed healthy foods, and forced to exercise to keep our bodies trim. We could never use our last names."

"Why do you suppose that was?" Randy asked.

"If anyone heard our last name, it would make it much easier for authorities to trace us back to our hometowns. There are millions of Pashas in my country but not so many Pasha Lermontovs."

The girl's voice trailed off as though she had difficulty continuing, and Randy asked if she'd like to take a break. "No, I want to go on." Maddy thought the girl was courageous. "After about a month, they started forcing us to take drugs."

When Randy asked what kind, she said Heroin and sounded ashamed. "It wasn't long before we needed it, and that's when they forced us into sex acts of every kind." Maddy squirmed in her chair. "They told us if we didn't cooperate, they would withhold the drugs, and our lives would become miserable." Maddy could hear Pasha take a deep breath and exhale. "One girl resisted. She was very young and scared. She didn't appear one day, and they told us we would not be seeing her anymore. From then on, we all did everything they told us, and everything was filmed."

"One day, out of nowhere, men came crashing through the doors, and helicopters landed everywhere. One of the workers was an undercover agent, and if it wasn't for her, God knows where I'd be now."

As the show neared an end, Randy asked a final question. "Do you think this still goes on?"

"Yes, because the people involved are making a lot of money."

"Thank you, Pasha," Randy said. "Folks, you just heard a story that should keep us all awake tonight. Until tomorrow, goodbye."

Safe houses, airplanes, and wealthy men. Can it be? A loud crack in the woods snapped Maddy's head around. She thought she heard a voice and ran for her weapon. She listened to the wind as it blew hard like a storm was coming, and the smell of moisture was in the air. Maddy stood without moving, looked into the darkness, and her heart pounded. *Maybe it's a bear.* She turned off all the house lights and sat outside with the gun on her lap. After a while, she convinced herself it wasn't human.

The night became still, and as she was about to head inside, a painful howl echoed across the lake. It was a wolf. She listened to the mournful requiem with respectful patience, wondering what caused the magnificent animal such heartache. When it ceased, she returned to the house, sure it was her wolf.

Hector was on her mind as she showered the following day, and she thought how the boy needed help. She got dressed and headed into town, hoping to find a way to get him released. The peaceful hills seemed out of place with the beating Hector had endured, and she thought how it's impossible to escape brutality, even among such beauty.

When she reached Doc's house, he greeted her with his usual smile. "Why, hello there, Maddy; I expected to see you here yesterday."

"Sorry, Doc."

"Coffee?" he asked. Doc's warm welcome made her feel she was one of his regulars. She said no and asked about Hector.

"That's what happens when you don't come around," he said. "Hector is free. All charges dropped." Surprised, Maddy asked what had happened. "Some sort of police screw-up." *That's strange*, she thought and asked where he was.

"He stayed here last night. He may be back at his house now."

"You're right," she said. "If you don't come around for a day, everything changes when you return." Maddy was about to leave to run errands when she remembered the gala invitation.

"It looks like I'll be going to a gala at The Glades. Tell me about the place."

"Well, let's see, it's a historical Adirondack Camp, built in the mid-eighteen hundreds by the Seymour family, but it changed hands several times. It was neglected for over twenty years until about 1975 when Avery Jordan purchased it. He keeps the place a world apart from the rest of us, and no one knows much about him. A lot of rich people go up there for fancy events. One thing is for sure, he's sunk millions into its restoration. It even has an airfield, and it is pretty busy too."

Doc described The Glades, but Maddy realized he didn't say what he thought. She drove home frustrated when she left him, thinking that Doc was holding back. *I can't figure out why he's so damn secretive. It's almost like he's scared.* She didn't like secrets, and, more than that, she hated being afraid.

It was late morning when she pulled up to the house. Hector was sitting in his favorite spot, the woodpile.

"You and that woodpile look like you belong together," Maddy said, laughing. "It seems every time I see you, you're sitting on it." She added, "I heard they dropped the charges. Did they give you a reason?"

"Nah, they just said it was because I'm such a nice guy."

They play awful loose with the law around here, she thought. "I have the money I owe you," she said, pulling out cash from her pocket. Hector jumped down and took it.

"I'm glad you brought it up because I didn't want to be rude and ask you for it myself."

As he shoved the bills in his pocket, he said, "You know, you should keep your window blinds shut at night."

She snapped at him, "Are you spying on me?"

"Nope, not me, but someone is."

"You better explain yourself, Hector, because you're not making any sense."

Hector didn't answer right away. He looked at the ground and shook his head, chomping on his toothpick. "For reasons that are none of your business, I'm keeping an eye on a certain place. I followed a couple of fellas here last night. Fortunately, they ain't as good in the forest as they think. They sure made one hell of a racket when they got here. Why do you suppose anyone would want to know what you're doing?"

The sound last night, she thought. She flashed back to when she learned Cupid watched her in her home and asked herself the same question as then: *Why is someone spying on me?*

"Well, I thought I should tell ya," he said and started walking toward the woods.

"Where are you going?"

"I'm headed home."

"Let me give you a ride," Maddy insisted.

"I might just let you do that," he said, smiling.

CHAPTER 19

Wednesday, August 15, 1984
Hector Lemont

When Maddy dropped Hector off at his house, he found A.J. inside, packing a suitcase.

"What's going on?" he asked.

"I'm moving to The Glades; that's what's going on," she said defensively.

Confused, Hector asked why.

"Because I have a future there," she snapped, her eyes glaring as though daring him to stop her. Her brother leaned back, confused. It hurt to see his big sister looking at him with such enmity. She acted the same way when he tried to tell her that Everett Turley was just using her, and he wondered who was making her so crazy now.

"What's happening to you?" he pleaded.

"None of your business." A.J. shoved the rest of her clothes in the bag, and as she tried to force the snaps shut, they jammed. She pushed harder and knocked the suitcase onto the floor. Among the clothes that fell out was a cloth with a hard object wrapped inside, and it hit with a clunk. The bundle unraveled, and a brass ballerina standing on one toe in a tutu rolled out.

"See what you made me do?" she yelled as she gathered up her stuff and shoved it back in the bag. The ballerina was one of their mother's few possessions. She cherished it and gave it to A.J. before she died. The sight of it on the floor cut into Hector.

A.J. picked up the bag and was about to leave but stopped and said to her brother, "Just so you know, Pa's gone. He hasn't been here for three nights, and his friends told me he skipped town. His stuff is gone too. If I were you, I'd find a place to hide because, once Child Protective Services finds out you're alone, they'll try to put you in a foster home." A.J. stormed out the door without saying goodbye.

What just happened? Hector stood in disbelief. It made no sense, and not knowing why made it worse. *Who changed her? She's like a different person.*

He stumbled his way outside and felt like the time he drank a half-pint of cheap whiskey with Stick Larson, only he wasn't drunk. It was approaching dark as he meandered across the road and headed for his secret place. His mind struggled to reconcile the change he'd witnessed in his sister, remembering how, just a few short weeks earlier, she was so excited about the interview at The Glades. She had made him food and explained how she'd bought a new dress. *The Glades has taken control of her mind.*

Hector got to the cave, and it was pitch black. He built a fire and ate a candy bar he had stashed in his stuff. Gazing into the darkness, he covered himself with the sleeping bag, wondering what he would do now. He tried to sleep but couldn't get comfortable.

Lying, listening to night sounds, Hector waited for the glimmer of the morning, then packed up and headed back to town. Numb inside, he walked home, as his world was falling apart. He had promised his mother he'd take care of A.J., now he couldn't even do that.

He arrived at his house, and it looked as empty as he felt inside. The sun rose, and the house's silhouette was dark in the tall woods. He imagined rectangular plywood boards would soon cover the windows, and a Keep Out sign would be nailed to the door. Life seemed cold and cruel. He sat on a log near the old fire pit where he'd spent summer nights watching chunks of wood burn down to embers until the early morning hours with his family. His mother was healthy then, and his father didn't drink as much.

He reached under the log and grabbed the stick he used to stoke fires. Rolling it in his hands, he remembered the sound of his mother's high-pitched cackle and his father's pig-like laughing snort. Their gayety echoed through the hickory trees as they told funny stories of when they first met. *It was the annual Independence Day dance.* He remembered his mother saying that Pa tried to dance and looked like a stiff-necked chicken doing the two-step. *She and Pa laughed real loud until they almost couldn't breathe.*

Tapping the stick on a rock, Hector shook his head and wondered why those days went away. *After Ma passed, and Pa took to drink, it all went wrong,* he thought, *Now everyone's gone.*

A cool breeze stirred the leaves, and his arms chilled. He looked beyond the branches at the rouge-colored sky, remembering a dream he once had of being a pilot. *Hell, they don't let kids who only get to the 8th grade and get arrested become pilots,* he thought, laughing with a cynical barb directed at himself. He broke the stick over his knee, threw it in the empty fire-pit, and started for town. When he got to the hardware store, he found Lester on his knees, counting nuts and bolts. "Doing inventory?" Hector asked.

"Why you're a sight for sore eyes," Lester said. "Wanna do a little work today? I got a lot of nuts and bolts that need counting and sorting."

"I'd like to help ya out, but I got stuff to do. I need two things from you, Lester. The first is my pay. I believe you owe me for a week's work."

"Why, I believe you're right." Lester grabbed a shelf and dragged himself up off the floor with a moaning groan. "I ain't getting any younger, Hector. I sure could use a hand. I know; you're a busy man." Lester took out a small stack of bills from the cash box and counted out two twenties, a ten, and four one-dollar bills. "Here ya go, fifty-four dollars. What was the second thing you wanted?"

"Do you know where Stick's been hanging?"

"Stick Larson?" Lester said indignantly. What do you want with him? He ain't nothin' but trouble."

"He's still doing deliveries up at The Glades, ain't he?"

"Don't go getting involved with The Glades, Hector. You know nothing good happens up there. Stay clear of that place."

"Lester, I realize you're trying to look out for me, but I asked you a simple question: do you know where Stick's been hanging?"

Lester shrugged his shoulders and sighed. "I saw him going into Lenas when I opened up. Knowing him, he'll be there until they throw him out." As Hector started for the door, Lester added, "Now, you be careful, Hector."

When he stepped into Lena's, a pair of long skinny legs stretched out into the aisle. *That's him,* Hector thought . Stick was so tall that he couldn't fit in a chair, a booth, or a car without having to scrunch up his legs. He walked up and heard Stick laughing with Ben Jacobson, the barber, and Johnny Johns.

"Hey, Stick," Hector said when he walked up.

"Why, Hector, I've heard all kinds of things about you. I sure hope half ain't true." The two old men laughed. "Why don't ya have a seat?" he said.

"Well, I'd kind of like a word with ya." Stick seemed to get his drift, and when Hector walked outside, his friend got up and followed. They sat on a bench the town put in along Main Street the previous year.

"What's going on?" Stick asked.

"You're still delivering fresh produce a few times a week for Pendergast Farms, aren't ya?"

"Sure."

"You go to The Glades twice a week, right?"

"Three times," Stick said.

"How about I give you twenty dollars to let me hide in your truck, and when you get there, you can let me out?"

"Are you crazy, Hector? Those people ain't like us. They ain't from around here; they don't talk like us, and there ain't one of them I trust."

"You can make an extra forty or sixty dollars for just giving me a ride."

"How are you gonna get out?"

"I'll find a way. Maybe I'll come back with you. It's getting in; that's the problem."

"They've got a perimeter around the place," Stick said. "It goes well into the woods, and they guard it with dogs. I have even seen guys with guns."

"I know all about the perimeter. Look, I'll make it twenty-five bucks a trip, and that's my last offer. Shake on it." Stick shook Hector's hand. "I'll let you know when," Hector said.

He left Lena's and started for Flat Top Rock with something on his mind. He walked the same way he did when he and A.J. picked blackberries the day they found Luellen's body. His mother was still alive then, and life was brighter. Hector remembered getting a rise out of his sister, running past her before she pushed him down, and how they laughed so hard he couldn't walk. "Stop making me laugh, Hector," Luellen had said. "You're going to make me pee my pants."

When he made it to Flat Top Rock, he was glad Maddy's truck wasn't there. He walked out back and down the hill. Along the tree line past the blackberry bushes, just as Hector remembered from when he and A.J. played there as kids, orange day-lilies basked in the morning sunlight. He picked an armful, brought it to the woodpile where Maddy was sure to see them and spread the lilies on top. "These are for you," he said, pretending she was standing there.

He stood back, gazed at the flowers, and thought, *Why am I doing this?* He wondered if it meant he was in love with Maddy. He shook his head, turned, and walked to the woods.

CHAPTER 20

Friday, August 17, 1984
Avery Jordan

"I'm sure you realize that this weekend's guest is special," Avery said to Naomi. She sat with her legs crossed and hands folded over her knees, acting like it was old information as he continued. "I expect everything to meet or exceed our standards." Anxious that the slightest mishap might destroy The Glades's prominence, he believed his reputation was on the line when he hosted high rollers like Ronald Aster.

"Yes, Avery, I remember what you told me."

"And do you remember his peculiarities?"

Naomi grimaced. "Yes, he likes…"

"Pain, Naomi, pain," Avery interrupted.

"Yes, pain."

"And about the selection?" he asked.

"We have a fine selection for him to choose from."

"Good. Please have Mr. Girard alert me when Astor's flight is about to land. I would like to greet him myself."

Girard was at the door and said Chief Smith had come unannounced. "He would like to see you."

"Send him in," Avery said impatiently. The door opened, and he asked the frumpy man what he wanted.

"I thought you'd want to know that the state police found Silas Glumper's body yesterday."

Avery sat up in his chair. "What do they know?"

"From what I hear, we stumped them."

"I don't need to know that," Avery said. Smith gazed, confused. As he walked out, Avery added, "I hope you're following up on Maddy Reynolds." The Chief nodded and kept on walking. Avery sat, tapping his fingers on the desk, reflecting on his situation. He ruminated that the next several weeks were critical, and he worried about everything that might disrupt his operation. He obsessed about details and buzzed Girard back into his office. "Has Madison Reynolds responded to the gala invitation?"

"Yes, we received her RSVP today. She's bringing a guest, a female."

"A female? I wouldn't have thought that of her." His mind shifted. "We need to know more about her. I told Smith to step up surveillance. I can't afford to have her playing detective at The Glades. I also want her brought to my office for a private chat when she comes to the gala. Make a note of it." He got up, crossed his arms, and snapped, "I'll be resting in my quarters. I don't want to be disturbed until Astor arrives."

Avery Jordan's quarters were not a room or a suite but an entire floor of one of the sprawling structure's wings. A-wing and C-wing flanked Castile Room. Each of the three buildings included a gymnasium, a swimming pool, a kitchen, and various entertainment centers. Avery often boasted his library rivaled some cities'.

He made sure his living quarters were private. Only three people were allowed to communicate with him: Darius Girard, Naomi White, and Robert, who served meals. Everyone knew that any violation of his privacy carried dire consequences.

A voice on the intercom announced Astor's arrival in thirty minutes. "Very well, we'll meet in the drawing-room." He left his room, musing that Ronald Astor, one of Europe's wealthiest men, was visiting again to his remote corner of the Adirondack Mountains.

During World War II, the man's father was a Nazi sympathizer and became wealthy while the war raged. Ronald possessed his father's nose for business and a few quirks his father didn't have. They pertained to women. Few people knew of Astor's peculiarities, and Avery Jordan was one.

"Why hello, Avery," Astor said when he entered the drawing-room.

Avery smiled and shook his hand. "I trust your flight was comfortable."

"I can't say that it was. Those damn small planes cramp my legs."

"Maybe time in a sauna would help that," Avery suggested.

"Yes, perhaps after dinner; I'm famished."

Avery asked Girard to see Astor to his suite. "Make him comfortable and have Naomi come to my office." He asked if the girl was ready when she walked in, and Naomi said she was. "Make sure you keep an eye on him through the cameras. If he gets out of control, we'll have to stop him. We don't need a sticky little mess to clean up."

"By 'sticky little mess,' do you mean a body, Avery? Why don't you just come out and say it?" Naomi's insolence was getting under his skin. He knew it was related to his covert nightly visits to A.J.'s bedroom. No matter how hard he tried to keep secrets, Naomi found out. Her sixth sense was uncanny and frightening.

It was nearing nine o'clock when he retired to his quarters and soon fell asleep. Naomi called at 10:43. "We have a bit of a problem."

"And what is the problem, dear?"

"Mr. Astor is not fond of the lady we presented. He wants someone more innocent and inexperienced. He likes to break them in, he said."

That bitch, Avery thought to himself, knowing where Naomi was going. *She wants me to give Astor Anna Jean.* The thought pained him. A.J. was a woman of virtue in Avery's mind. She was his personal fantasy, she trusted him, and he'd developed a strong urge to take care of her. Naomi was boxing him into a corner.

"I think we should give him Anna Jean," she said.

"No!"

"No? Are you running a business or a daycare? What would your father think?" Her voice trailed off into a snicker. She knew his father's opinion of his incompetence was a deep wound in Avery.

"A.J. isn't used to that sort of thing."

"That is what the man wants. And besides, I already told him we have just the girl for him. I described her, and he is very excited."

Avery's stomach knotted up, and the veins in his neck bulged.

"Well, what will it be? Shall I tell Astor that you've fallen in love with the one woman at The Glades who can give him what he wants, or shall I have A.J. get ready to earn her keep?"

Avery slammed down the phone without answering, and by doing so, he had given her the answer she wanted. He dropped his head into his hands with his gut in turmoil, knowing what was about to happen. I can't believe I'm crying. *I don't understand why A.J. means so much to me?*

Trying to rationalize, he said to himself, *Everything in life is dark and ugly, anyway. She can join the club.* Hardening himself to the idea, he cauterized his sensitive feelings, wiped tears from his face, went back to bed, and tried to sleep. It was 12:24 in the morning when the phone rang, and it was Darius Girard.

"Sir, high-pitched shrieking is coming from Mr. Astor's room." A lightning bolt of pain ran through Avery.

"Have you checked with Naomi?"

"Yes, and she said, you know about it. I peeked at the camera, and it appears excruciating for the girl."

"Let it go, Mr. Girard, and don't disturb me until morning." He opened the bottle of scotch on the bar and poured a large glass, trying to drown his love for the girl. He threw the fiery Chivis into his gullet until the burning in his stomach was greater than the pain in his heart. His father's voice entered his head. *You're not much of a businessman, Avery.*

His father believed that doing hard things made a man good at business. For Avery, letting A.J. be with the sodomizing Ronald Astor was the hardest thing he could ever imagine doing. He walked to the bed, dropped, pulled a pillow over his head, and lay there until his mind went blank.

It was nine o'clock the following day when he awoke and called Girard.

"Mr. Astor is sleeping," Girard said. "It was a very late night for him, and he is quite tired."

"And Anna Jean?"

"She's in the infirmary. She did not enjoy herself."

Avery showered, got dressed, and met Naomi outside the medical offices.

"She will not be nice," Naomi said.

"You wait out here," Avery barked. A nurse greeted him and led him to a room where Anna Jean lay curled up in a fetal position on a bed. She opened her eyes and saw Avery. "Why did you let him do this to me?" she screamed.

A.J. held up her rope-burned wrists toward Avery's face, then stood up, crying, and opened her bathrobe to reveal bite marks around the nipples. She turned around, whimpering, and shifted her robe. Whip marks striped her back; her anus was grotesquely red and bloodied, and she dropped back on the bed, sobbing.

Avery hung his head with his eyes closed. The sting of remorse hurt, and he thought, *Another good thing, ruined. Anna Jean has become tainted like everything else that was pure in my life.* He opened his eyes, and on the floor, a gold chain glittered. It was the crucifix that A.J. always wore around her neck. He picked it up and handed it to her. "This must have fallen off."

She looked at it and struggled to speak. "I can never wear that again."

"Anna Jean—"

She sat up and cut him off. "Stop!" she shouted. She bowed her head and wept; tears, saliva, and mucus dropped onto the floor.

He turned and walked silently from the room to where Naomi waited. "Give her heroin for the pain," he said.

CHAPTER 21

Wednesday, August 22, 1984
Hector Lemont

"Hector, keep your head under them melons," Stick said.

"Jesum, Stick, I'm gonna suffocate," Hector griped from under the tarp. He couldn't help but laugh at the awkward situation he and his friend were in as Stick drove the old truck uphill to The Glades.

"This ain't no joke, Hector. I told you, these people ain't like us. We'll be lucky if we don't get our nuts cut off. Be quiet now; we're coming up to the first gate."

Stick stopped the truck, rolled down the window, and spoke to the attendant. "The guy's walking to the booth," Stick whispered. "He'll be right back." The attendant waved him forward.

The truck tugged up the incline, and gears ground each time he shifted. "Don't you know how to drive?" Hector said.

"I'd like to see you try to drive this piece of shit," Stick said. "Stay low and shut up." The old flatbed struggled up the mountain road with the engine straining. "Okay, Hector, I'm nearing the top now; I can't stop, so you're gonna have to hop out and run into the pines. Be careful because they got guys patrolling everywhere around here with dogs, and those ain't pea shooters they're carrying neither."

"Okay, I'll see ya in a day or two." Hector jumped out. In the cover of the trees, he found a thicket and hid. The location gave him a good view up and down the hill. Stick's warning about armed men patrolling the area with dogs bothered him, and he stayed put until dark. The two peanut butter sandwiches he made at Doc's and a small bottle of water were his dinner. He'd brought along a plastic jar with a screw-on top to pee in. *If those dogs are worth their weight, they'll be able to smell human piss,* he thought. He had also shoved his father's old, eight-inch, wood-handle hunting knife, still in its leather sheath, into his belt.

The afternoon dragged on; he sat, leaning back against a tree, and started to nod. The sound of a branch breaking startled him awake. He got low, peeked up the hill, and didn't see anything, yet knew someone was there. *They must be behind me.*

Remaining still, he wondered if the sound was a deer. He heard footsteps and slid the knife from its cover, clenching it. The sounds of a dog sniffing and rustling branches caused his heart to race.

"Come on, Jake. This way, boy."

Hector looked around the tree. Two men in leather coats carrying rifles walked away behind a German shepherd. He sat and waited for his heart to slow.

Lawnmowers hummed, and laughter from a distance echoed in the woods. As it neared the end of daylight, the low whine of an airplane engine got louder. When the sound stopped, he knew it had landed.

He left his hiding place when it was dark and crawled to the top of the hill. A hundred yards of lawn lay between him and a lit-up log structure. The sprawling campus, with its lights aglow, was like nothing he'd ever seen before, and it made him feel small. *Wow... ain't that something.*

Ducking back into trees, he made his way around to the massive complex. Two three-story wings ran off each side of a larger facility. One wing was dark, the other was lit up like a birthday cake. *A.J. must be in there somewhere.* The ground floor included expansive windows and French doors that opened to patios and gardens. Fancy fountains in the gardens sparkled with glittering colored water. Curtains blew in and out of opened windows; music and voices traveled through the night air. *I ain't never seen anything like this.*

Large hedges scattered across the open lawn provided places to hide. Hector worked his way to the building, scooting from bush to bush. He crawled behind the landscaping that lined the structure and hid.

The windows on the ground floor were dark except for two. One was dim, and a light flickered in the other. He crawled to the one with the faint glow. The curtains were slightly opened. The four inches of separation allowed him to see inside, and he saw a man sitting, gazing at an interior window. He smoked a cigar and sipped from a broad base glass, legs crossed with his eyes fixed on something in the next room. Hector knew the man had to be Avery Jordan. He ducked down and crawled to the next window.

A young woman with long black hair, a slender body, and full breasts stood naked with her hands tied wide over her head, her legs shackled apart. She was positioned in front of the window Jordan looked through. Her head moved from side to side while a white-skinned woman wearing a one-piece black romper suit approached. The woman held a wand with fluffy feathers and ran them up and down the shackled girl's body. When the girl was sexually aroused, the albino turned the wand around in her hand and began probing her with the handle until the girl groaned with either pleasure or pain; Hector couldn't tell which. The girl passed out; her head dangled.

Good Mother of God! Hector screamed to himself. He thought of his sister and shuddered. He was determined to find her and crawled further down the building to a doorway. The sound of airplanes distracted him, and he stopped to look. Two sets of lights floated down from the sky toward the airfield. He maneuvered closer to the doorway, near where the planes would be landing. He holed up behind a small brick building near the runway, waiting for the aircraft to land, all the time thinking of Avery Jordan sitting alone in the dark, drinking brandy, smoking a cigar, and watching as a young girl was being abused against her will.

The first twin-engine plane landed, and the second rolled in behind. Men appeared from nowhere at the aircraft's doors; the doors opened, and stairs dropped to the ground. The men reached up and assisted the women in descending the airplane's stairs.

When the planes turned and took off, about eight women and four men walked toward the brick building Hector hid behind. He felt exposed and slipped into nearby bushes. The group piled into the small building, and Hector wondered where they went. He ran to it, edged his way to the front, and peeked in the door. *It's a tunnel! They even got a damn tunnel from this airfield to that building. If that don't beat all.*

Two men and a dog walking nearby drove him back to the bush. He moved down the hill about 50 yards, found a tree, and rested.

The night air was thin and cold, and Hector's light jacket wasn't much help. He wrapped himself up as best he could and listened to the sounds of radios and televisions. Voices of girls talking captured his attention. The lack of giggling or laughing raised Hector's curiosity. *What the hell are they doing here? Don't tell me...* He thought of the shackled girl. *Naw, it can't be,* he said to himself. The notion that Avery Jordan flew the girls to The Glades for sexual purposes was so alien and repulsive to Hector that he dismissed it. He refocused his thoughts on his sister.

Eventually, the sounds coming from the building quieted down, leaving only crickets and katydids. *It's time to make my move.* He crawled to the building with the tunnel. With his back up against the bricks, he eased his way to the door, then ran down two flights of stairs. At the bottom, he looked down a long, empty hallway, counted to three, ran to the other end, and ducked under a stairwell to catch his breath.

Hector knew A.J. had to be inside somewhere. He went up a flight of stairs, hid, and watched. Young women entered and left a bathroom. He waited, but there was no sign of A.J.

He snuck up to the next floor and waited again. Sitting hunched up behind a door, his mind wandered. Hector heard a familiar rhythm of slippers sliding along the floor, and he realized it was his sister. She looked ragged and tired and somehow different. *It's like she's not the same person.* "A.J.," he whispered.

She looked, squinted her eyes, and seemed semi-aware. "Hector?" she slurred.

"Come here," he said.

She shuffled to him and asked what he was doing there.

"I'm getting you out of here."

"No," she replied in a slow, drawn-out monotone, almost like a pout.

A.J.'s eyes drooped, and she wobbled as though she might fall. "What's wrong with you?" her brother asked.

"Go home, Hector." She turned and walked away.

"A.J., where are you going? Come back here." She stopped but didn't turn around, then disappeared into her room.

A lifelong bond was ripped apart. Hector's mind went numb. Too overwhelmed to comprehend what just happened, he wondered what changed her.

He sat weeping and thought, *Oh, Ma, what's happened to A.J.?* He stayed, looked down the hallway, hoping she'd change her mind. Beaten down inside, he left the building with an avalanche of memories crashing down on him.

He almost forgot the danger when he stepped outside, and the sight of men with dogs brought him to his senses. He slipped back to his spot in the trees, sat, and looked up between two pines. A star-filled sky and the emptiness gnawing at his insides were his entire world. His pain turned to rage, and he focused it on Avery Jordan. *He did this to her. I'm going to expose that son of a bitch.*

The following day, Hector woke to the sound of a diesel engine. He crawled up and looked out. A guy stood at a fuel truck filling an underground tank with airplane fuel. He waited for the man to finish, worried he might miss Stick, then scooted across the open area to the cover of bushes. The guy finally drove off, and he made his way to the road to wait for the produce truck.

Hours passed before the old flatbed struggled up the hill. Stick drove by and yelled he'd catch him on the way down. Within the hour, he returned, and Hector hopped in.

"Was it worth it?" Stick asked.

Hector sat, frozen-faced, staring at the road. He didn't say a word. When they reached the town, Hector got out, and Stick pulled over at Main Street. "See ya, Hector."

CHAPTER 22

Friday, August 24, 1984
Maddy Reynolds

Maddy picked up a few groceries and swung by the post office to buy stamps. A woman in line ahead of her, wearing a dowdy black hat and veil, placed a parcel on the counter. She opened her purse and fished out the four dollars and fifty-six cents fee. With a pen in hand, the clerk asked her name.

"Abigail Hicks."

"Oh, hi, Mrs. Hicks. I didn't recognize you," the clerk said as she handed him the money. The woman walked out, and Maddy stepped to the counter. "Luellen Hicks's mother?" she asked the clerk.

"Yep. Since her daughter's murder, the poor thing never comes out of the house."

"Murder? You mean suicide."

The guy gave Maddy a disbelieving look, handed over the stamps, and glanced away. "Next, please."

Maddy watched Abigail Hicks through the post office window. She wondered how the woman lived after losing her only child. "*Murder.*" The word bounced around in her head like a steel pinball. The possibility the body found behind her house was a murder victim added mystery to the unfolding saga of Berry Lake. Its undercurrent pulled her further into murky waters.

She drove home, preoccupied, and noticed the back door wide-open when she got home. Startled, she hit the brakes. *Did I leave it open? No way!* She grabbed her gun and ran to the stairs, listening for an intruder. There was no sound. She ascended to the deck with her heart pounding and peeked inside a window. *Someone has trashed my place.*

Sweat beaded on her forehead as she leaned back against the house, taking deep breaths. She slid inside with her weapon in a shooting position. Stepping over books and around overturned furniture, she moved to the kitchen; it looked untouched. Her bedroom, however, was ransacked; drawers on the floor, contents scattered everywhere, and her bed was turned over. *I'm sick,* she thought to herself. She looked for the locked metal box that contained her other weapons; it was gone. *Fuck!* She returned to the living room, sat, and stared at the mess.

Wondering if it was a robbery, she thought about her father's gold shield, got up, and ran to the fireplace. The mantel was bare, and she panicked. On her knees, Maddy crawled around, looking for the beloved keepsake.

The badge was more than a memory; it was a part of her soul. She'd held it the night she entered the room where Benny Bowls waited to kill her. It gave her courage as she pursued Cupid through the woods, and she'd used its pin to stick him, freeing her from the maniac's chokehold while they battled to the death.

She saw it. The shiny gold object lay hidden under a sheet of paper in a corner next to her journal. *Thank God!* Holding it near her heart, leaning against the wall, she began to weep.

I can't believe this is happening. Unable to move, staring at her belongings, Maddy felt violated. She wished she had never come to Berry Lake. *Who would do such a thing?*

She placed the badge back where it belonged, looked down, and noticed a book resting on her foot. The author, Dr. Sidney Myers, was a criminal psychologist she had consulted with about Cupid. The guy seemed like a jerk at the time, but his insights proved profound and accurate. Months after she'd recuperated from the ordeal with the maniac, Myers started sending her notes and articles about serial killers, which was his area of expertise.

I forgot about this. The book was entitled, *The Changing Faces of Evil.* She opened the cover, and a note from Myers read: "I hear you are retiring from detective work. Remember who you are, Maddy. See page 171, and be on guard, my friend!—Sidney." She flipped through the pages. Highlighted in yellow on page 171, a sentence read: "The instant you recognize the devil's face, he transforms himself into evil of a different kind."

As she gazed at the surrounding wreckage, the meaning of the message became clear. *Cupid was deranged. The evil in Berry Lake is somehow different, but evil nonetheless.* Maddy's fear gave way to anger. Her steel determination kicked in. She went to the truck and headed for town, and as she drove, the sky grew dark as clouds rolled over the mountains. The wind picked up, and before she reached Main Street, it was pouring buckets.

Nothing seemed the same. The streets had eyes, and Berry Lake was no longer an untouched gem of the Adirondacks. Its depravity seeped through its thin veneer, and something sinister lay beneath. An unknown gravitational force was drawing Maddy into its sticky inner core. What wasn't her business yesterday was her business today.

Myers's book was about how certain people who join forces with good find themselves attacked by the forces of darkness in ways they least expect. Maddy wasn't religious, but somehow, the notion rang true.

The maple trees along Main Street swayed in unison. Day turned to night. People still outside ran for doorways, and one looked like Doc. He carried a laundry bag over his shoulder as he ducked into the Quick and Easy Laundromat. Maddy pulled around to the back and ran inside. She and Doc were alone.

"Doc!"

"Maddy, what are you doing here?"

"We need to talk. Someone ransacked my place." Doc said nothing, but Maddy detected fear in his eyes. "What's going on in this town?" she asked insistently.

Doc checked the window as though looking for people watching. "We can't talk here."

"Why not? We have to talk," she insisted.

Doc pulled a pen from his shirt pocket wrote on the back of a hardware store receipt. He drew a map from her house to a location. "Meet me here at ten o'clock tonight." A woman walked in as Maddy took the map, looked at Doc, nodded, and walked out.

When she got home, she was soaked. The first thing she did was look for a bug, and it wasn't hard to find. It was the type that law enforcement used. *Cops did this,* she realized.

She locked the windows and doors, changed clothes, and began the heart-wrenching task of reassembling her home. She went slowly, doing her best to place each item exactly where it belonged. Someone took something from her—not physical, but spiritual. The sanctity of her home was desecrated, and she had a powerful desire to wash off the filth.

With several hours to kill before meeting Doc, she started a bath, hoping it would drive the chill from her bones. She relaxed in hot water but couldn't stop her thoughts from rambling. The Donnellys popped in her head.

They killed Teddy execution-style by cutting his throat, Hannah said. Who in this half-ass town is capable of taking out a hardened criminal like him? There has to be a connection to the murder up north. Safe houses. Why would there be safe houses in that remote region? She remembered Pasha's story of how sex traffickers use safe houses. No one she'd met in Berry Lake seemed sophisticated enough to run such an operation—not even Avery Jordan. Maddy dismissed the notion. Something extraordinary was going on, however; she felt it. It was dragging her in. She needed to know more and hoped Doc would provide the missing pieces.

***

The rain pounded the windows when Maddy left her house to meet Doc, and her truck slid partway down her road. It was a dark, dreary, and treacherous night. The directions had her turning right at the bottom of her road instead of left toward town. With Doc's map on the seat, illuminated by the truck's overhead light, she navigated to a road that forked off to the right. The truck bounced along the bumpy lane; headlights glowed about fifty yards in. Doc sat in his Subaru in a clearing with the engine running and windshield wipers moving fast. She pulled up, Doc got out, and he slid onto her front seat.

"Hell, of a night?" he said as he wiped the water off his face. "What do you need to know?"

"Everything! Start by telling me why you were so paranoid when I saw you at the laundromat."

As if finishing a sprint, he huffed and turned his head away. He looked into the darkness and spoke slowly. "I've lived in Berry Lake for thirty years. It's always been a fine little town, and for a black man living among uneducated white people, it's been good to me. It used to be a wholesome community. In hard times, people helped out." He turned to Maddy. "Somehow, all that changed; fear crept in, folks started looking over their shoulders, suspicious. You don't recognize it when you first come here because it's so pretty, but it's here, and now you've experienced it."

"I want to know about the death of Luellen Hicks." Doc's body stiffened, and he pushed his hands down on his knees like he was bracing for a fall. He looked out again. Maddy asked what he was so afraid of.

"An accident," he said, looking back, staring straight into her eyes. Maddy shook her head like she didn't understand. "Accidents happen when people ask too many questions."

"You mean like Luellen?"

"Why don't you first tell me what you know about her," Doc said.

"I know young girls don't kill themselves by cutting their goddamn throats! Enough bullshit and double talk; I want answers."

Doc looked into his lap. "No, they don't." He looked out the window as if talking to himself. "Luellen was a very nice young lady. She was her mother's pride and joy. I remember the day she was born; Abigail and Henry were the happiest people you'd ever want to see. Henry died in a logging accident when Luellen was three, and Abigail raised her daughter alone with little means. She did a fine job, mind you, a very fine job, and Luellen grew into an exemplary young lady—intelligent, good manners, and beautiful."

Doc sighed and continued. "Abigail told me her daughter changed after she started working at The Glades. She became irritable and rebellious after she moved there. Luellen's death sent her mother into near hibernation. The last thing she said to me was, 'Someone changed my baby.'"

Rain pounded the metal roof. Doc stopped a moment, waiting for it to let up. Maddy flipped on the heater and defrosted the fogged-up windows. Several moments later, he started again.

"Whenever one of my patients dies in a car accident, hunting mishap, or suicide, the family will ask me to view the body, and it's never a problem with authorities. The medical examiner would not let me get near Luellen. That was the first red flag."

Maddy listened. She could tell Doc was struggling. "It came out she cut her throat, and I could not believe it. Everyone in town knew the unlikelihood of it being true. No one said a word except one person: Reverend Ethan Gillis, the Lutheran minister. Gillis gave a sermon a few weeks after the suicide, admonishing his parishioners about being cowards in the sight of the Lord. 'We should stand up to those who intimidate us against righteousness. Never turn our backs on the truth.' Three days later, the reverend and his wife burned to death in a house fire."

The whole town is drowning in fear, Maddy thought to herself. *This kind of fear will bring a community to its knees.* "Did Luellen tell her mother what was happening at The Glades?"

"I don't know. Abigail stopped talking to people."

"Can we get a copy of the autopsy report?"

Doc laughed a cynical laugh. "Certain people are in other people's back pockets. The medical examiner is one of them."

"And the police chief?"

"Especially him," Doc said.

"And whose back pocket is everyone in?"

Doc clammed up and folded his arms across his chest.

"Is it Avery Jordan?" Doc looked down and nodded.

Maddy thought about the gentle, sophisticated man who entertained her for lunch. "I met him," she said. "He was decent. Yet, there was a strangeness about him. I sensed he was after something. Like I told you, I even got an invitation to a charity at The Glades." Doc looked at her with concern in his eyes and frowned.

"What are you thinking, Doc?"

"I'm thinking you better be damn careful. Maybe you should go back to Utica. Visit friends until things settle down."

"I can't do that," she said sternly.

"Well, do you still keep a gun from your detective days?"

"I do," she said.

"Are you good with it?"

"Damn good."

"If you're going to stay around here, I'd have it close at all times."

She reached into the door and pulled out the Glock. "You mean like this?"

"Yes, just like that." Doc got out of the truck. "Stay safe," he said, then closed the door.

The weather remained brutal; the rain was so thick Maddy couldn't see the road as she went down the path. Doc scooted ahead, and by the time Maddy reached Route 3, he was long gone. *The Glades,* she thought as she drove. *It's all about The Glades. I need to find out more about Jordan and that place.*

As she reviewed the conversation in her head, headlights in the rearview mirror approached at an alarming speed. Maddy tensed up and moved the truck to the right. The vehicle sped by, never slowing down; its draft shook the pickup.

"Asshole!" she screamed as she steadied the steering wheel. *Why would anyone drive like that on a night like this?* After calming herself down, she got back on the road and headed home.

CHAPTER 23

Saturday, August 25, 1984

The following day, the rain stopped. Moisture hung in the air so thick Maddy couldn't see the lake from her kitchen. She sat, feet up on a chair, facing an open window, gazing out into the nothingness, thinking about the Lutheran minister. *Doc is either so scared he's exaggerating what happened, or someone is trying to control the townspeople through intimidation.* She started questioning her judgment. *Am I paranoid?* She needed an outside perspective from someone in law enforcement whom she trusted. She grabbed the phone, dialed a number, and when she heard, "Zepatello here," she thanked God that Zep was in his office.

"Zep, it's Maddy."

No one knew her under stress better than Zep. She wasn't surprised when he said, "Maddy, what's wrong?" She sat on the sofa and unloaded to her old friend and ex-boss. He knew about the Donnellys but did not hear about Silas Glumper. She explained about the Hicks girl, the minister, and the break-in. When Maddy told Zep about finding a bug in her place, he nearly jumped through the phone.

"Jesus, Maddy! What's going on up there? That's not good. My God, you need to stay armed at all times." Maddy could visualize her old boss standing up and pacing around his desk with the phone in his hand. She saw him do it many times. "If those cops are on the take, you won't know what hits you when they come after you. Why don't you come back to Utica and stay with Susan and me?"

"You know how I am about running. I just can't."

"Yeah, I know. The odds are against you, though. You're alone, and you do not know what's going on; you're a sitting duck."

"That's the problem. I need to find out what's going on."

"Have you shared any of this with the state police? Why don't you call Hannah Bates?" Sounding frustrated, he said, "I wish there were something I could do, but you are way out of my jurisdiction."

"It helps just talking to you," Maddy said.

Alone in her house when they hung up, she remained on edge and started moving into a dark place within herself, reliving memories of Cupid when the second victim was found dead. Maddy had gone into a major funk, drinking every night; she felt helpless and questioned her sanity. *That's how I feel now.* She decided to call Hannah Bates.

"Why, hello. How are things going in no-man's-land?" Hannah said with a chuckle.

"Not well. I was wondering if you could answer a few questions for me." Hannah said she'd try.

"Are there any developments in Teddy Donnelly's murder?"

"I can't discuss the case, Maddy, but I'll tell you the Donnellys and Glumper murders are related."

"Hannah, have you heard of The Glades?"

"Who hasn't? It's where the filthy rich go to play."

"Avery Jordan ... how about that name? Do you know anything about him?"

Hannah was silent for a moment. "Why are you asking about him?" She sounded put off. Her sudden defensiveness caught Maddy off guard.

"I'm just curious; he's a bigwig around here."

"He's a bigwig everywhere," Hannah said in a severe tone. "All I can tell you is that my boss's boss's boss would love to meet him someday."

"Got it; he's untouchable."

"Unless he's doing something heinous, I'd stay clear." *So much for getting the state police involved.* Maddy thanked Hannah and ended the conversation.

"Shit, shit, shit!" Frustrated, she walked around the kitchen with her arms folded, talking to herself. She was a dog with a bone and couldn't let it go. "Abigail Hicks! That's who I should talk with."

Maddy showered, got dressed, and set out in the fog for Doc's, hoping he'd give her directions to Abigail Hicks' house. As she approached Blind Bluff, flares glowed, and flashing lights shined in the mist. She moved closer. Three fire trucks and two rescue vehicles idled near the dreaded curve. Maddy slowed to a near stop, and a volunteer firefighter holding a flashlight waved her on.

She stopped. Lester stood, long-faced, with tears in his eyes, and came over. "What happened?" she asked.

Lester struggled to speak but eked out, "Doc drove through the guardrail and into the ravine. He's dead."

It was as though she was sucker-punched. Maddy grew dizzy, gripped the steering wheel, and dropped her head. *Doc, why Doc?* She lifted her head and asked when it happened. She thought about how she'd just met with him up the road less than ten hours earlier.

"Someone said he's been dead about eight to ten hours. A truck driver found the busted guardrail this morning."

Tow trucks pulled Doc's Subaru onto the road; its crushed roof brought the image of what his body must look like. "You're going to have to move on, Maddy," Lester said. She looked in the rearview mirror and saw cars backed up behind.

Lost in disbelief, Maddy edged forward, glancing over at Doc's car as she went by. She felt hollow inside. *He said he was afraid of an accident. Oh my God.* She drove on, unsure of where to go, and found herself on Main Street, heading to Lena's. She pulled into a parking spot. Inside, muffled silence hung in the air, like at the funeral of a beloved person. *This town has lost its patron saint.*

Rose placed a cup of coffee on the counter near Maddy. "Did you hear?" she asked. Maddy nodded. "This is going to be a tough one." Rose left to serve other customers.

Maddy wanted to be alone, to clear her mind enough to gain perspective. She reviewed the night before. *Accidents happen when people ask too many questions. Doc must have been followed to our meeting. The car that almost hit me got him.*

Rose came back, and Maddy asked if anyone had seen Hector. "He's not been around. Hector and Doc were close; he will not do well with this." Maddy pulled out some money for the coffee and asked Rose to write directions to Abigail Hicks's home. Rose scribbled out a map on a slip of paper, and Maddy put it in her pocket.

CHAPTER 24

Sunday, August 26, 1984

After Doc's death, Maddy didn't want to leave Flat Top Rock. She stayed in her pajamas. The darkness of an unstable weather system added to her gloom; every day was cold and rainy. She had little appetite, picked at leftovers, and ate an occasional bowl of cereal. On the fourth day, a gruff voice on the phone perked her up.

"Maddy!" the voice said.

"Is that you, Bob?"

"Yeah, it's me. I've had a hell of a time finding your number. I've wanted to talk to you for weeks."

"Is everything okay?" she asked.

"Everything's fine here, but I've been having those damn dreams again, and they're all about you!"

Bob Bennett was her father's partner in the Chicago P.D. and his best friend. Bob retired after James Reynolds' murder and could never forgive himself for not being with his partner when Cupid killed him. He stood by Maddy the night her father died; they bonded and had been friends ever since. Maddy respected Bob's uncanny sixth sense, and whenever an occasional insight came to him in a dream, she listened.

"These dreams I'm having are weird, really weird. Are you involved in some bizarre shit up there where you're living?" Bob's voice grounded her. It felt like being home on Thanksgiving.

"Bizarre is putting it mildly," she said.

"Hell, I woke up this morning from a dream of a guy chasing me down a mountain trying to cut my head off. I damn near wet the bed!"

Maddy laughed. "Oh, Bob, it's so good talking to you. Yes, things are ugly here, but you're making them better." She explained as best she could what was happening in Berry Lake, and just listening to herself, she realized how surreal her life was becoming.

She finished, and Bob said, "It sounds like with that Doc guy gone, you're in it alone. That kid Hector might be close to going off the deep end; he won't be much help when the shit comes down. What's your plan?"

That's what Maddy loved about cops from Bob Bennett's era; it was always about your plan, your next step. Things fall apart in police work, and you revise your plan and move forward, as in battle. "Bob, you've got to realize I'm not in a position of authority anymore. I'm just a civilian."

"Jesus Christ, Maddy! It doesn't matter if you're a civilian; your life is on the line. Protect yourself. If I were you, I'd act like a detective, civilian or not."

Shit, he's right! Bob threw ice water over her head, waking her out of a stupor. As the events in Berry Lake had unfolded, she grew unsure of her role and hesitated to engage. It was her ass on the line, and she needed to wake up.

"I couldn't agree more, and that's what I'm going to do."

When she hung up, Maddy reprimanded herself for becoming passive. *I've got to do what I do best. I'm going back to Blind Bluff.* Before leaving the house, she searched around and found the directions to Abigail Hicks' home.

When she arrived at the Bluff, she pulled over near the broken guard rail, got out, looked down, and thought of what Doc experienced as he dropped eighty feet. She walked back along the road in the direction he traveled. Within seventy feet, she found what she was looking for: pieces of the red taillight. *Just as I suspected. Doc didn't accidentally drive off the road; he was forced off.*

She gathered the bits of glass and put them in her pocket. *That was one hell of an accident investigation the local police did.* She got back in her truck and started for Abigail Hicks'.

I'm lost, she thought, frazzled from trying to follow the map Rose drew. She turned around and found the gravel driveway that led through a small field a mile back. A dozen birch trees surrounded a cottage. The sun broke through the fog, and streams of light beamed down. *If I were religious, I might think it's a sign.*

Maddy marveled at the charm of the well-kept home; window boxes with red impatiens, a cobblestone walkway lined with deep green creepy jenny, and two large wind chimes with angels on either side the door. *It's like entering a forest fairytale.*

Maddy knocked. As she waited, the sun spread its rays on the magical setting, and she felt at peace. The door opened, she turned, and the woman from the post office stood smiling.

"I'm Maddy Reynolds. Are you Abigail Hicks?" Maddy put out her hand, and the woman took it.

"I am; come inside, dear." It was as though she was expecting the retired detective.

Decorated with simple antiques, the home's ambiance was otherworldly. A sweet fragrance of flowers permeated the room. Wooden and ceramic pieces placed on the fireplace mantel and room corners with interesting, leafless tree branches added a sense of nature's calm. They both sat in soft cushioned chairs across from each other.

"May I call you Abigail?" The woman nodded. "I'm interested in Luellen." Maddy thought that would get a reaction, but it didn't; the woman sat placidly.

"I expected you, Maddy Reynolds." A shiver ran down Maddy's spine. She remembered her old friend Mary Thompson, a very spiritual person, also understood things beyond normal comprehension.

"Surprised?" Abigail asked. "Your courageous soul could never be where evil exists without being drawn in." It was like Abigail looked into her soul. "Don't be afraid. There is no evil in this house."

Maddy didn't know what to say. "You want to know what happened to my daughter," Abigail continued. "I will tell you." Peace seemed to enter the room. Maddy settled back to let her tell her story.

"Like all the young girls around here, Luellen was trying to find herself when she graduated high school. With few opportunities, she was excited when she landed a job at The Glades." A dark cloud seemed to enter Abigail's being. Her face drooped, and her eyes were sad.

"Something happened to her in those months after she started working there; Luellen changed. She resented me, closed herself off, and shared very little. One day, she came home and said she was moving to The Glades. I was in shock. How could someone change so fast?" Abigail looked at Maddy with her head turned as though she expected an answer.

She stopped a moment, pulled out a tissue, wiped her eyes, and continued. "Weeks went by, and Luellen didn't come home. I was worried and drove to The Glades, but they said she didn't want to see me. I went to Chief Smith, he said that Luellen was of age and could do nothing. A few weeks later, they found her. You know the rest, I'm sure." Abigail looked down, gazing at her hands on her lap.

"You must have had some inkling of what was going on."

"I asked the authorities and townspeople a lot of questions. No one knew anything. They said she was depressed, and it was suicide, but my God, the way she killed herself!" Abigail let loose and broke down, weeping.

Maddy waited for the woman to compose herself. She asked if she could look in Luellen's bedroom. *Girls' bedrooms have voices and reveal secrets.* Abigail nodded, got up, and led Maddy to narrow stairs and a bedroom.

"I haven't touched a thing in here since she left. Part of me keeps thinking she might come home someday. Isn't that silly?"

"No, it's not silly at all. My father died nearly thirty years ago. I still think it might be him when the phone rings."

Abigail closed her eyes and smiled. "You go ahead, dear; I'll be downstairs."

The room was small: cedar-planked floors, one window shrouded with yellow, sheer curtains, one dresser, a nightstand, and a maple desk. Maddy went to the closet; shirts, pants, and dresses hung on a crossbar. A few pairs of shoes were scattered on the floor. She opened each of the three desk drawers but saw nothing of significance.

A brass lamp on the nightstand with a hollowed-out base drew Maddy's attention. She picked it up, pulled back the loose green felt bottom, moved her hand around the inside, and pulled out an unsealed envelope that contained hundreds of bits of a ripped-up letter.

She went downstairs with the envelope. "I want to piece this together and maybe learn something about what happened."

Abigail told Maddy to take the letter. She stood, and together, they went outside. With folded arms, she said, "Ms. Reynolds. I made peace with my life as it is. I can never replace the part of me I lost when my daughter died; I know that now. I've learned to live a simple life, surrounded by God's wonders, and I don't want that disturbed. Please don't share what you find out in that letter with me." Moved by Abigail's connection with the other world, Maddy said she understood.

When she got in her truck and headed home, she began thinking of her father. *Dad, I am entering a strange and scary place; please be near me.*

CHAPTER 25

Sunday, August 26, 1984
Avery Jordan

"You were wonderful," Naomi said, with her head resting on Avery's chest and their bodies entwined together after making love. Avery's relationship with the possessive woman was on the mend. He accepted that his attachment to Anna Jean was misguided. Naomi connived, but she could meet his needs better than the innocent girl.

A sound at the door, and Naomi pulled a blanket over their naked bodies.

"Stay here; I'll see who it is," Avery said as he put on a bathrobe and went to the door. He cracked it open, and it was A.J.

"Avery, can we talk?"

"This is not a good time."

"I want you to know how much I love you. I don't know what I did to make you shut me out, but whatever it was, I'm sorry. Please, Avery, I'm dying inside. All I do is think of you." Sobbing, she looked up and asked, "Can't I even come in?"

The smoothness of a silk robe was Naomi behind him. She put her arm around his waist and snidely said, "Good night Anna Jean," as she closed the door. A.J.'s painful, gut-wrenching wail tugged at Avery's insides. He thought of Ronald Aster and what he did to the girl. Avery realized Anna

Jean was not the spring flower she once was. She was more like a pathetic wilted weed.

"Should we call Neri and have him drag her away? That whimpering is so annoying," Naomi said.

"No, she'll go away soon enough." Within a few minutes, the crying stopped.

They returned to bed. As Naomi was sleeping, Avery lay with his mind churning, thinking about the fast-approaching masquerade event. It was the key to paying off his debt, and he ruminated about everything that could go wrong.

Maybe we won't get the turnout we need; perhaps the weather will be bad, and the planes won't be able to land; perhaps Maddy Reynolds is an undercover agent; maybe that Hector kid will go to outside authorities. He gave up on getting sleep, got dressed, and went to his office.

He opened the safe and pulled out the ledger as he'd done at least two dozen times that week. He scrolled down the list of attendees. *If eighty percent shows, I'll be fine. Less than seventy percent, and I'm a dead man.*

He closed it and thought, *I'm going to make myself crazy if I keep doing this.* He turned his chair to the window and waited for the eastern sky to brighten as his mind continued racing from one potential problem to another. *I can't control the weather, but I could take care of Reynolds and the Lemont kid.* He heard his father saying, *Don't fuck this up; it's your last chance.* Avery moved to the table where he kept a bottle of Scotch, poured a glass, and slammed it down, trying to quiet the voice.

A more frightening voice said, *If you don't pay up, you're a dead man.* It was the mob guy who'd been haunting his dreams since the New Orleans bar; he slammed down two more shots and sat at his desk until The Glades came to life at about eight o'clock.

He called Girard and told him to have the Chief, Neri, and Naomi to his office for a meeting right away." While he waited, Avery thought of ways to approach the people he depended on. When they arrived, he began by emphasizing the gravity of their situation.

"We have two critical events coming up: the gala and the masquerade party. The gala is very public and should keep up our stellar image. The masquerade party is clandestine. We must protect our guests' anonymity at all costs. One mistake with either will spell big trouble for all of us."

He leaned forward to emphasize the importance of what he was about to say. "Let me be blunter. We will all end up in jail." He neglected to say that he'd be dead.

"Chief and Mr. Neri, I am assigning Hector Lemont to you both. It's your job to see to it he doesn't interfere. I'm told we have seen him running around in the woods within our perimeter; we cannot afford that runt messing up our operation. Do something about it! The Reynolds woman is another matter. I am convinced she's in Berry Lake on detective business. Chief, what have you found out?"

"We went through her place with a fine-tooth comb. Other than two legal handguns, nothing."

"I plan on meeting with her alone when she comes to the gala," Avery said. "From here on, I'll handle her." He glimpsed at Naomi as she glared at him. "That's it. Keep me informed."

Neri and Smith exited the room; Naomi stayed behind. "Do you have an itch for something on the side, Avery?"

He told her not to be ridiculous, but Avery secretly found Maddy Reynolds intriguing. An intelligent, brave, and beautiful woman, she caused him to believe he was less like a man. *Maybe that's what I find so erotic about Reynolds; conquering her would be like climbing Mount Everest.* He cast the thought from his head. *It makes no difference; she threatens this business and my life.* His fantasy had to take a back seat to his survival.

"I know you better than you think," Naomi said as she sashayed out of the room.

That morning, as Avery reviewed the itinerary for the gala, a call came through from a potential masquerade party guest. A senator was afraid of being exposed, and Avery tried to calm his fears.

"I'm so glad you can make it, Senator.".

"I've never been to one of these affairs before; when should I arrive?"

"The way it works is, all guests must arrive by plane at our airfield by six o'clock PM on the evening of September seventeenth. You can coordinate arrangements for landing with our Mr. Girard."

"Why a weeknight?" the senator asked.

"It's less conspicuous," he said and went on to explain that the theme of the masquerade party was Renaissance Faire. "You will dress in some costume appropriate for the event. Say a knight or a nobleman. To protect your identity, you will wear a mask at all times."

"Ah," the senator said, "that's reassuring. And the financial arrangement?"

"Mr. Girard will help with that. All financial transactions will use bank codes. You will provide him with a code for transferring money based on your purchases, and the transfer will occur within twenty-four hours of the event."

"Brilliant, Mr. Jordan. It appears you've thought of everything."

"We've been doing this for many years. Would you like to go over things again, closer to the event?"

"No. It won't be necessary. You've answered my questions. I look forward to seeing you on the seventeenth."

Avery opened the ledger when they hung up and placed a check mark next to the senator's name.

CHAPTER 26

Monday, August 27, 1984
Maddy Reynolds

The night was warm, and Maddy planned on staying in her house until she pieced Luellen's letter together. She returned from town in the afternoon with three bags of groceries; two twenty-by-twenty-inch glass panes; one roll of three-inch, double-sided adhesive tape; and three bottles of the local liquor store's best zinfandel. *This project is going to put my puzzle skills to the test.*

After clearing the table by sliding the Magical Kingdom into its box, she placed the two glass panes side by side and set the envelope with the letter pieces on top. That was as far as she'd gotten since two-thirty in the afternoon. She'd sat in the kitchen, nursing glasses of wine, staring at the envelope and wondering what the letter might say.

A force emanating from the bulging white envelope tugged at her, and her sixth sense told her it contained answers. She treated the letter with reverent respect. *A torn letter is sacred,* she thought. *It holds a secret the writer wants to hold on to.* The phone rang, and Maddy came out of her thoughts.

"Mom, why haven't you returned my calls? I'm worried sick."

Oh, shit. Maddy had evaded Amber, not wanting to worry her with the bizarre goings-on at Berry Lake. "Hi, honey. How are you?" She tried to think about what to say.

With a sigh, Amber said, "I'm okay. Well, not really."

"Tell me what's going on."

"I thought Cornell would be different. I want to come home, but we don't have our house anymore," Amber said, crying. "I don't think I fit in here. Everyone is so smart. There are tons of kids on a free ride, and it feels like they're all smarter than me."

Other parents warned Maddy about the intense performance pressure at Ivy League schools. Maddy knew she hadn't given Amber much support since she arrived at her new home. "How bad is it?"

"I got a C minus on an analysis of *As I Lay Dying* by William Faulkner, and I just didn't expect that."

"Have you had other disappointing grades?"

"No, but this was an enormous project."

Maddy felt inadequate to help her daughter because she had only attended a two-year community college. She was shooting from the hip, but out of nowhere, the words came. "Some things are worth holding on to," she said. "Others we must let go of. You need to let perfection go. This C minus is an opportunity to learn. Have you discussed it with your professor?"

"No, I'm too embarrassed. I thought I was letting you down."

"Oh, Amber, you're not letting me down. I'm proud of you. Just think about what you've accomplished. You won a scholarship to an elite school in a program you've wanted. I don't want you to put undue stress on yourself. One C minus isn't a catastrophe, and guess what? There will be more. It's all part of learning, honey; the highs and the lows are all part of learning. I think you need to sit down with your professor and discuss the paper."

She heard a deep sigh, and her daughter said, "I'm sure you're right. I'll make an appointment to meet with her." After Amber shared her trepidation over her grade, she chatted about campus life and a few new friends she'd made. Then the conversation got around to Maddy. "How about you, Mom? How are things at Berry Lake?"

Damn! Maddy hesitated. "Well, things are strange. I mean, as far as the surroundings, it far exceeds what I expected. However, a bizarre drama is playing out in the town." Maddy explained everything and held nothing back: The Glades, Avery Jordan, Hector, Doc, the white cross in the woods behind her house, and the torn-up letter. To Maddy's surprise, Amber listened and didn't panic or become overwhelmed with worry. She let her tell the entire story before commenting.

"I know I promised to not worry so much about you," Amber said, "but the situation you're describing sounds extreme." Her daughter hesitated before blurting out, "Can't you stay with me for a week or two? I'll make time to do stuff together. Please!"

"I'm sorry my situation has you so worried, and I know what I'm telling you is extreme. I just can't turn around and walk away. Please try to understand."

Maddy heard Amber whimpering on the other end, and after twenty seconds, Amber said, "I can't think of anyone more capable of handling a difficult situation like that than you, Mom." Maddy wished her daughter was sitting across from her so she could reach over and give her a hug.

It was getting dark, and she was tired. She had too much wine to attack the puzzle, she thought, so she emptied the letter bits onto one of the glass plates and turned them over with the writing side up. After spreading them evenly on the glass, she placed four quarters, one on each corner of the plate, and laid the second plate on top, resting it on the quarters.

Okay, that's where I'll start tomorrow, she said to herself. She finished the last of the wine in her glass and crashed for the night. The following day was cool and overcast. She dressed in comfortable sweat clothes and made her way to the table. After lifting the top plate of glass, Maddy put her knees up and began moving pieces of the letter around with the blunt end of a knitting needle. First, the four corners. *There we go,* she said.

She worked with one piece at a time, examining it with a magnifying glass and using the lines on the paper, the swirls of letters, and the shape of its tear to approximate its location on the glass. When two pieces matched, she used tweezers to lift them in place.

Patience is the name of the game, she'd tell herself when she'd worked a 12,000-piece puzzle. *It's just like piecing together a homicide.*

By one o'clock, she was hungry and needed a break. Tired, she stretched back in her chair. Before getting up to raid the refrigerator, she looked at what she'd accomplished. A few words were readable: I can't, die, and throat. The word throat sent a bolt of adrenalin through her. It was as if she'd drunk a pot of high test coffee, her eyes stuck wide; she forgot about her hunger and kept on working. She stopped, pushed away from the table, and relieved herself about five o'clock. Before returning, she grabbed a dish of leftover pasta, a glass of lemonade and went outside.

It was still overcast but warming up. The quiet of the late afternoon did nothing to silence the questions running through her brain, questions the letter was screaming out to be answered. *Was Luellen murdered? Is The Glades a nefarious operation of some sort? Perhaps it's a front for dark money. Who the hell is Avery Jordan? Why are people dying?* She took a deep breath of mountain air, went back to the dining table, and three sentence fragments were readable: afraid for; people's throats; and; afraid for my.

She sat down, ran her fingers through her hair, and refocused on the monster project. It was nearing seven o'clock, and she readied herself for a long night, determined to finish before morning.

At ten-thirty, she stopped, broke out a bottle of wine, and returned to bull her way to the end. It was after four o'clock in the morning when she finished. Her eyes were blurry, and the note was difficult to read. She placed the glass cover over the letter, walked to the living room, and dropped onto the sofa.

CHAPTER 27

Tuesday, August 28, 1984

Maddy woke up to a ringing phone; it was 11:10. *I've got to cut this shit out,* she thought, thinking about her affinity for wine. She forced herself up and answered.

"Hey, it's me, Jodi."

"Oh, hi," Maddy said, holding her head as though trying to keep it from falling off.

"Did I catch you at a bad time?"

"Oh God, no. It's just that, well, I've got a bit of a hangover."

"Are you sure you're up for talking?"

"I'm fine. I have to get myself moving, anyway." As she shook the cobwebs out, she glimpsed at the letter on the table; it was pulling at her like a magnet.

"I'm calling about the gala. If it's okay with you, I'd like to come up a few days early to visit the ranger school."

The gala! Shit, I forgot. "Sure, that would be great."

"I'm thinking of the fifth; would that work for you?"

"It does," Maddy said.

"You don't sound too sure," Jodi said. Maddy really wasn't sure. Not because she didn't want to see her friend, but because she was putting Jodi in harm's way.

"It's not the date I'm worried about. It's just that things have gotten more strange, and I'm worried about your safety."

Maddy took the phone to a comfortable chair and began explaining all that had happened since they last spoke. "Do you think you're the only one who's ever lived in bizarro land? Jodi said. "How about being eight and alone in Saigon while the North Vietnamese Army was killing people?"

Jodi's admonishment brought a smile to Maddy's face. She remembered who she was talking to. Jodi was the person who'd grown up in Vietnam during the war, survived a work camp, escaped before the fall of Saigon, and saved Maddy's life the night she faced off with Cupid. "Okay, okay, sorry," Maddy said. "The fifth it is." They hung up, and Maddy's mind turned back to the letter.

She prepared the first pot of coffee of the day. *What is it I'm expecting from this letter?* Sitting on the kitchen table, feet on a chair, she stared at the bits of paper in the next room. *Maybe I'm too much in my head. Maybe I'm going off the deep end.*

Working solo was unfamiliar to her. She'd always worked with a team, and whenever she drifted, someone was there to bring her back. She might go off the map in her current situation and not know it. Spending two days piecing together a kid's letter would have gotten her laughed out of the coffee room where she used to work. However, her intuition was strong, and it screamed to her that the letter held critical pieces to The Glades' puzzle.

Maddy hopped off the kitchen table and walked up to the note. "Here we go." She lifted the top pane, laid it to the side, took strips of the three-inch, double-sided adhesive tape, and covered the glass. She finished, and the pane was one large sticky surface. "Now for the hard part." The next step required fine dexterity and extreme patience. She stacked two cushions on a chair and made herself comfortable.

Bringing one paper bit at a time to the adhesive pane, she matched its tear with the last piece and set it in place. "Holy shit. This is going to take forever."

She focused on garnering the concentration required to finish the job and started a heads-down effort. She kept her eyes focused on each bit of paper. Two and a half hours later, Maddy fell back in the chair and dropped her hands to her side. "Done!" Before reading Luellen's letter, she poured a glass of ice water. I hope this was worth the effort, she thought as she approached the mysterious note. It was dated May 23, 1980, and read:

> *Avery,*
>
> *I love you with my whole being. I've given you my all—body, mind, and soul—to do with as you will. You know how much I need you, but ever since the night she saw us, I've lived in fear. She's everywhere I go, watching, creeping around, giving me looks. I've come to Mother's, and I can't return to The Glades. I am too afraid—afraid for my life.*
>
> *Yet, I can't imagine living without you; I don't know what to do. Today, when I saw Naomi in the garden, she sneered and said, "I know what you've been doing at night." She knows, Avery; I know she knows. She said, "You know what Mr. Neri likes to do, right?" Everyone says Neri cuts people's throats. I'm so afraid.*
>
> *I'm sorry, my dear, but I can't go back. My God, I don't know how I'm going to live without you, but I can't go back.*
>
> *Yours Forever,*
>
> *Luellen*

Maddy gazed at the words. Like water gushing over a busted dam, answers and more questions poured into her head. *Neri is the throat cutter; that scumbag! Who is Naomi? Wait a minute! If Luellen was at home when she wrote the letter, how did she fall prey to that Neri guy? Did he come to Abigail's for her? Oh, no, of course not. Luellen must have changed her mind and returned. Why didn't Abigail tell me that? More missing pieces!*

CHAPTER 28

Wednesday, August 29, 1984

Maddy spent the morning deciding what to do about the letter. She walked around her place like a zombie. Hannah was the proper source, but Maddy lost confidence in the investigator. She almost called her again but needed her facts straight before getting Bates involved.

The gap in Abigail's story about Luellen's return home before leaving again for The Glades bothered Maddy. Before doing anything else, she needed to find out what had happened. She got in her truck and started on the thirty-minute drive to the Hicks' house. She tried to imagine what it must have been like for Luellen. She was in love, and Naomi's threat of cutting her throat terrified the girl.

Luellen was Amber's age, and the thought of her daughter in such a situation horrified Maddy. She remembered Avery Jordan's charm and understood how an innocent teenager might fall hard for his sicky-sweet venom. *I'm getting myself too worked up over this; chill out, Maddy.*

She arrived at the cottage and calmed herself. Abigail answered. Maddy said she wasn't clear on something and asked if she could come inside for a moment. The woman hesitated, looked scared, but let Maddy in any way, and they sat in the living room.

"Mrs. Hicks," Maddy started out saying, then realized she sounded like a cop, stopped herself, and said, "Abigail, I respect what you said about finding peace with your daughter's death and not wanting to dig up the pain, but there's a minor detail that I'm hoping you might explain."

Abigail squinted and gave Maddy an untrusting stare. "Go ahead."

"I got the impression from the letter that after Luellen came home, she returned to The Glades. Is that what happened?"

The woman looked down, sighed, and the energy seemed to leave her body. "You have a daughter, right?" Before Maddy could answer, Abigail said, "I read that in a magazine. Do you remember the day she was born and how wonderful you felt? Do you remember all the dreams you had for her, the parties she'd have, her first date, the prom, graduation, and maybe college?" Every word the woman said brought an image of Amber into Maddy's mind.

Abigail looked into her hands folded on her lap. "The last thing you could ever imagine during those precious moments is your daughter, the person whom you love more than yourself, saying, 'I hate you.'" A dagger punctured Maddy's heart when she heard those words. Abigail wept.

Why did you do this, Maddy? Was it necessary? Maddy wished she could undo what she started, turn around, and go home, but it was too late. Abigail continued, "Yes, Luellen came home. She stayed six days—the last six days I'd ever see her. She was quiet and kept to herself. A mother knows her daughter, and I knew she was heartbroken. There was something else I couldn't quite put my finger on, and then I figured it out: she was terrified. She would go to the window and peek out and was always checking the doors to make sure they were locked."

Abigail sighed as though she was getting to the hard part. "I left her alone, gave her space, kept my distance. I got up one morning and saw her packed bag by the door. She was standing next to it, waiting for me. I couldn't believe it. 'Are you going back up there?' I screamed. I was furious but more hurt than angry."

"'I can't stay here!' Luellen screamed at me. I told her she'd changed, grown selfish, and whoever she was going back to at The Glades was evil. That's when she said she hated me. She walked out and slammed the door. I chased after her to say I was sorry. I saw her get in a shiny black limousine, it drove off, and I never had a chance to say I was sorry."

Maddy got up from her chair, walked over, and helped Abigail to her feet. She held her. Abigail buried her face in Maddy's embrace and wept, and Maddy wept too.

On the drive back to Berry Lake, Maddy beat herself up. *You violated the woman's request to be left in peace; why did you do that?* She reached the village and stopped at Lester's Hardware. He was outside arranging a display of lawnmowers and rototillers. He turned, saw Maddy, and stood erect. "Hey," he said.

"Lester. I'm wondering if you know where I can find Hector. He seems to have disappeared."

"Haven't seen him for a week. The last I knew, he was hanging around with Stick Larson. I suspect he'll be coming around for Doc's funeral services on Friday; he and Doc were close."

"Well, can you tell me how to find Stick Larson?"

Lester shook his head as though he couldn't figure out why anyone would want to talk to Stick but gave Maddy directions to Pendergast Farms, where he worked. "If he's not there, he's gabbing it up at Lena's. Yacking is what he does best. There are plenty of people to yack with there." Maddy took the directions and left to find Pendergast Farms.

It didn't take long to find the produce company. Several open trucks of different sizes, filled with fruits and vegetables, were backed up to a building with a dozen open garage doors. She saw a lanky guy fitting Stick's description. Maddy pulled up, got out, introduced herself, and asked if he was Stick Larson. He looked afraid and said he was. She asked if he'd seen Hector and, if so, how the boy took the news about Doc.

Stick started chirping away. "Well, two weeks ago, Hector asked for a ride to The Glades. I deliver up there twice a week, you see. I told him those guys ain't like us, and he better be careful. They patrol the place with dogs and guns. But no, Hector has to go anyway. He wanted to see A.J., that's his sister. Well, when I picked him up the next day to bring him back, it was like he'd seen a ghost; he didn't say a word—just stared out the window. Something awful bad must have happened. I ain't ever seen Hector like that before."

She asked if he'd seen Hector since. "Nope, he's gone to Tupper Lake. Left the next day and ain't been back. He has some cousins there, I guess."

"So he doesn't know about Doc?" Maddy asked.

"No, and I sure don't want to be around when he finds out. Him and Doc were close, you know."

Maddy thanked him and headed back home, thinking it was time to get Bates involved. When she got back to Flat Top Rock, she dialed the state police investigator and got voice mail. She left a message for Hannah to call her back. It was about four o'clock in the afternoon when the phone rang.

"Hi, Maddy, it's Hannah Bates."

"Thanks for returning my call." Maddy got right to the point. "Some evidence has emerged about the death of Luellen Hicks four years ago. They ruled it a suicide, but the new evidence points to murder."

"What kind of evidence?"

"A letter was written by the victim, who supposedly cut her own throat."

"Ouch, that doesn't seem real," Hannah said.

"Exactly. The letter points to someone working at The Glades. He might also be a suspect in other cases you're working."

"I think I'm up for a nice long ride in the mountain," Hannah said. "Are you around tomorrow?"

"If you get here by lunch, I make mean tuna melt sandwiches."

Hannah laughed. "You're on."

It relieved Maddy she finally had the state troopers involved. The next day, when Hannah drove up to the house, it was a little after one, and Maddy walked out to greet her. The tall detective stood outside her car, stretching her back. "I forgot how long it takes to get here; you can't go too fast on those winding mountain roads."

Maddy said she had lunch ready on the deck. "Sounds great, but first, I have to use the facilities. There aren't any rest stops on the way here," she said.

Clouds scattered in a blue sky, and a comfortable breeze blew as the two women talked about their families as they ate. "Much to my dismay, my son, wants to go into law enforcement," Hannah said between bites of her tuna melt sandwich. "He's in eleventh grade, so I still have time to talk him out of it."

"That was my fear as well. I'm a third-generation cop, and I was relieved when my daughter gravitated toward literature. I told her I'd rather have her write about shoot-em-ups than live them." Hannah laughed.

As they talked, Maddy realized Hannah had a gift for putting people at ease. *It's why she rose to senior investigator with the New York State Police at such a young age,* she thought.

"There are quite a few stories out there about you, Maddy," Hannah said, placing another sandwich on her plate and refilling her glass with lemonade. "They can't all be right. Is it true that Cupid killed your father?"

"Yep, on a Halloween night when I was twelve. Almost twenty years later, he tried to kill me too."

"But, you were the one who did the killing that night," Hannah said. Maddy looked off, thinking of the awful ordeal.

"That's why I moved up here. To get away from crazy. Little did I know I was entering something even more bizarre."

"Ahh, yes, the reason I'm here, the letter. Why don't you show it to me."

They went inside. At the dining room table, Hannah looked at hundreds of bits of paper taped on glass. A baffled look came over her. "Okay, so someone ripped this letter up, right?"

"Luellen Hicks wrote it and then tore it up. I found the pieces in an envelope."

"And you taped it all together?"

"I'm a puzzle freak, and it's not that hard for me."

"You should be in forensics," Hannah said as she lowered herself toward the table to read the letter.

"Jesus," Hannah said. "We've got a four-year-old suicide, confirmed by the Chief of Police and medical examiner, and now we want to investigate it as a murder. And, it involves The Glades, a place with strong political ties. It's going to take time, but we'll get it going." Hannah looked at Maddy, smiled, and nodded. "Once a detective, always a detective, right, Maddy?"

"I guess," she said, but thought to herself, *You have no idea.*

When Hannah left, Maddy was confident she did the right thing by getting her involved. *At least I'm not in this alone anymore.*

CHAPTER 29

Friday, August 31, 1984
Hector Lemont

"Another few miles, Hector." Jimmy's twangy voice woke Hector as he rested his head on the passenger-side window; the eighteen-wheeler was old but drove as smooth as ice cream. They were heading into the village of Berry Lake, and it was dark.

"What time is it?" Hector asked.

"Three-thirty-nine in the a.m.," Jimmy said, doing a radio D.J. imitation. Jimmy had picked Hector up outside Tupper Lake and was a chatterbox. Hector believed it was hitchhiker protocol to talk it up when someone offers you a ride, but he was exhausted and opted for a few hours of sleep.

"You can let me off right outside of Berry Lake, Jimmy."

"What are you coming home to?" Jimmy asked. Hector wasn't about to tell him, so he said he was visiting folks. It wasn't a lie because he planned on returning to The Glades to see A.J. again.

"I'm headed right through to Buffalo," Jimmy said. "Got me a nice long haul." The diesel's growl calmed to a purr as he downshifted on the decline into the village; the thrust pushed Hector forward in his seat.

"Up there, past the Berry Lake sign." Hector pointed to an area about a hundred yards ahead, and Jimmy pulled over. He got out. The truck drove off through the sleepy village, and Hector headed for Pendergast Farms.

The eastern sky was pink as he climbed into the back of Stick's truck and covered himself with a tarp. The sound of the truck's steel hatch opening jolted Hector out of a sound sleep, and a burst of sunlight blasted his eyes.

"Is that you in there, Hector?"

"Yea, it's me. Can you make any more noise?"

"I said I'd give you rides; I didn't say you could camp out in the truck," Stick said. "You're gonna get me fired."

Hector jumped out. "Relax, Stick, I ain't movin' in. I needed a place to hide away a few hours, that's all."

"Where you been, Hector? People been asking about you."

"I told you—I went to visit my cousins over in Tupper Lake for a bit."

"Well, the way you acted that day, I thought you might skip town for good. Did you come for the funeral?"

"What funeral?"

Stick went silent, his eyes widened, and he stood, looking like he just got caught stealing at the grocery store. "Who died, Stick?" Hector asked.

"Doc."

Hector's head went blank. He grabbed the side of the truck to keep his balance and lowered himself to the ground. "Are you okay, Hector?" Stick kneeled and put his hand on his friend's shoulder.

From his depths, Hector drawled out, "No." Folding his arms over his knees, he leaned his head on top and moaned, "What happened?"

"He drove through the guard rail up at Blind Bluff. You know how steep those cliffs are. It was a rainy night, and they found him the next morning."

"That doesn't sound like Doc. He's the slowest driver I know." He put out his hand, and Stick pulled him up. Shaking his head, he said, "This doesn't seem real."

"Sorry, Hector. I know you and Doc were close."

Hector nodded and asked when the funeral was. "Today at noon over at the cemetery." He started walking away, and Stick asked if he wanted a ride. He was in a daze and just kept walking.

Unsure of where to go, Hector headed to Doc's house. He walked down the driveway and knocked like always, but his mind didn't register that Doc was no more. He turned the knob and walked in. Still, fresh-looking, the apples in the fruit bowl sat among bananas turned black.

Too numb to cry, Hector stood in his empty aloneness. Doc's kitchen was a place where he went with scraped elbows, bruised knees, and when his mother was dying. The old man gave him love. *Now he's gone.*

Carrying his heaviness out into the sunshine, he started for the cemetery. The cottages he always admired seemed different. *None of this belongs to me anymore; I'm not part of this place; maybe I never was.* An orphan, a loner, an outsider; it was becoming clear who he was.

Hector's house was on the outskirts of town where troubles lived. The town drunk, and the butt of jokes down at Lena's, lived there. He was the kid who was accused of things he didn't do, but the town doctor, the most respected person in Berry Lake, saw something in him. It was something no one else saw. Whenever Hector screwed up, Doc would laugh and say, you wait, boy, someday you're going to be something. You'll show them ... wait and see.

Doc was hope—Hector's hope, his cheerleader, and his mentor. That hope was no more. The hecklers shouting in the crowd would watch him now, waiting for him to fail, he thought.

He went to the cemetery and waited by his mother's grave. Across the way, tall white gravestones stood by a giant stone cross. Cars lined up near a hole in the ground. Hector sat near his mother's small stone and watched men carrying his beloved Doc. Tears streamed down his face when they lowered him into the hole. A few faces turned his way, and Maddy Reynolds' face was one.

She stared at him as though she wanted to come closer but didn't. Marjorie Best, Lester's wife, spoke beautiful words that drifted across the open space like a melody.

"These are the words of Alfred Lord Tennyson," Marjorie said.

Tears, idle tears, I know not what they mean,

Tears from the depth of some divine despair

Rise in the heart, and gather to the eyes,

In looking on the happy autumn-fields,

And thinking of the days that are no more."

Hector's pain blurred out most of the remaining words, but he heard the final stanza:

"Dear as remembered kisses after death,
And sweet as those by hopeless fancy feigned
On lips that are for others; deep as love,
Deep as first love, and wild with all regret;
O Death in Life, the days that are no more!

How can this be! Hector stood up. He turned and began walking away. He reached the edge of the cemetery, turned again, and watched as people laid flowers on Doc's casket—all except Maddy, who stood looking at him.

He headed for his cave. No words could express how he felt, even to himself. It was almost like he had moved out of his body, and someone else moved in. He wanted to save the one person left in his life that mattered: A.J.

The night came, and he lay cuddled in a sleeping bag at his cave, unable to sleep. The sun rose, and he started back to Pendergast Farms and got there in time to catch Stick before his run up the mountain.

"Hey, I'll be going with you today."

"Hector, are you sure? You ain't looking so good," Stick said. "Plus, those people up there have been acting awful jittery. They got some big events coming up, and they're checking every bushel in my truck each time I go."

"I know what I'm doing, Stick. Come on, I'll help you finish loading."

The truck struggled up the steep incline. Stick asked Hector what he planned on doing when he got up there. "I'm going to talk sense into A.J., and if that doesn't work, I'm going to find Avery Jordan. I'm gonna tell him to let my sister go."

"Are you crazy? If you even get near Avery Jordan, they'll kill you."

"Let me worry about that."

Stick told Hector he'd have to jump out soon as they neared the top. "I'll jump out right here," he said." He looked over at his friend. "Wish me luck."

"Good luck, Hector."

CHAPTER 30

Friday, August 31, 1984

Hector made his way through the woods to The Glades. He found the entrance and waited behind the second-floor door. When the hallway cleared, he went to A.J.'s door and stepped in. Lying on her side, knees to her chest, she faced the wall. Hector sat on the bed and put his hand on his sister's arm. "A.J.," he whispered. Her eyes opened, and she turned her head.

"Hector?" she spoke in a soft, barely audible voice.

"Yes, it's me. I'm taking you home."

Shaking her head, A.J. groggily said, "This is my home."

"A.J., no. This ain't your home. Your home is with me. Let me take you out of here." Her head hung limp when he tried to pull her up, and she flopped back on the bed. His eyes rested on a line along her forearm. It was a series of small red punctures. *Drugs!* His sister lay with her eyes closed, and she went unconscious. He shook her. "Come on, A.J., wake up."

Hector tried to lift her again, but she was unmovable. He stared at her, not knowing what to do, and Avery Jordan popped into his mind. *I'm gonna make that bastard let her go.*

Hector left his sister and headed for the enormous hall with the marble floor, and walked into the middle of the vast empty space. He wanted someone to see him, and someone did.

"Hey, you!" Hector didn't run. A guy ran to him, and two others followed. "Who are you. What are you doing here?"

"I'm Hector Lemont, and I want to see Avery Jordan."

The three men turned at the sound of footsteps echoing across the open space. A huge, smooth-skinned man with a mean look on his face approached. "I'll take him," he said. "You three can go."

"Yes, Mr. Neri," one responded.

Neri grabbed Hector's arm, pulled him close, smiled, and said, "You must be Anna Jean's brother."

"I want to see Jordan."

"You'll see him alright, and you're gonna wish you didn't." Neri pushed Hector across the floor to a large oak door and knocked.

"Come in."

Neri said, "You have a visitor," and he shoved Hector into the room. "This is Hector Lemont."

Avery looked up from his desk, took off his reading glasses, and laid them down. "Well, what brings you here, Mr. Lemont?"

"My sister."

"Anna Jean? I want you to know that we are very pleased with the job she's doing for us. I don't know her, of course, but I understand she is a fine employee."

"Don't you try to sweet-talk me, you son of a bitch." Hector snarled, with his lips pulled back and teeth showing. "And tell Frankenstein here to keep his filthy mitts off me."

"So, why are you here, Mr. Lemont?"

"Someone up here has A.J. hooked on drugs, and I aim to make it stop."

"What makes you think shady business goes on at The Glades?"

"My sister was excited to get a job here. I saw her the day before her interview. She bought a new dress with all the money she had. A few weeks later, she's all drugged up and acting like a different person. No, something's happened to her here." Hector's eyes fixed on Avery. "I plan on finding out what's going on, and I'm gonna expose it!" If Neri wasn't holding Hector back, he would have lunged at Jordan.

"I don't know what you are talking about," Avery said. "If shenanigans were going on, I'd know it. I'm sorry, Mr. Lemont." Avery nodded at Neri, and the big man pulled Hector back into the hall.

"You're hurting my arm, you big jerk!" He stomped on Neri's foot, came free from his grip, turned, and kicked his groin. The boy ran across the marble floor to the garden. He heard the large man's footsteps close behind. "You little fuck, I'm going to kill you."

Hector cut through the open area, darted into the brush, and made his way to a ditch alongside the road. Somehow, Neri went a different way, and his towering figure stepped out from behind a tree. "I've got you now," he growled, holding a knife. He charged, and when Hector tried to sidestep, his foot caught Neri's ankle, toppling both down the hill.

Hector stopped by grabbing a sapling as Neri's massive body rolled and tumbled. The boy propelled himself forward by grabbing at tree branches. He looked over his shoulder; Neri got up and started coming.

It was getting dark, and Hector thought his pursuer was out of sight, but Neri's silhouette appeared on a ridge. He ducked behind a tree as the man scanned the area, then turned in Hector's direction and started walking toward him.

Shit, who is this guy? Neri knew every trick Hector had learned. The boy bolted from behind the tree and sprinted toward an area where a stream ran between two steep hills. He could hear heavy feet pounding the earth, crushing leaves, and breaking branches.

Hector raced toward the lake, and, just as he was about to jump down an incline, Neri grunted. He looked over his shoulder, and the big man's outstretched hand was reaching for him. It tugged at his shirt. A jolt of adrenaline pushed Hector forward; he jerked away from the massive hand, ripping the shirt from his back. Neri tumbled as Hector slid down the hill into a stream.

Hector hid behind a bush and listened for at least a half-hour but heard nothing. He stepped out; Neri appeared again and charged. Hector darted to the side, dodging him, then ran up the steepest part of the hill. He thought the guy would never keep up, but Neri stayed with him. He reached the top and slid down the other side on his butt. He didn't look back but heard Neri still charging. *I have to reach the lake,* he thought, realizing it was his only chance against the agile big man.

The land dropped off twenty feet down to the shoreline, and he jumped. A sharp stabbing pain ran up his calf when he hit. He rolled to his side. A broken branch protruded from his leg. He yanked it, and a stinging pain felt like ten bee stings. The monster stood on top of the ledge. He seemed reluctant to jump and looked for a way down the embankment. Hector got to his feet and hobbled toward the lake, as Neri made his way down.

He dove underwater and swam submerged a long way, circled back toward shore, and emerged in a weed bed about fifty yards down the shoreline. Poking his head up, he looked toward where he'd last seen Neri. It was dark and hard to see. Hector waited and heard splashing as the guy searched for him.

"I will get you, and when I do, you'll be dead," a deep voice finally shouted out.

Hector waited several hours before swimming to shore. He started down a path parallel to the water's edge, cold and shivering. He couldn't go back in the cave's direction, so he headed to Maddy's. As he limped through the darkness, his calf was on fire up to his thigh. The numbness inside gave way to sadness. *Mother asked me to watch over A.J.,* he kept thinking.

A bright moon glimmered on the lake and lit the way along the path. Hungry and weak, Hector thought he might pass out. When he reached a grove of beach trees near Flat Top Rock, he got new strength and thought of Maddy, warmth, and food. When he reached Maddy's house, it was dark, and the door was locked. Exhausted, he lay on a reclining chair on the deck.

CHAPTER 31

Friday, August 31, 1984
Maddy Reynolds

Lena's was empty; it was closing time—nine o'clock. Maddy sat at the counter nursing a Coke, talking with Rose. "What a sad day for Berry Lake," Rose said. "I don't know how this town will manage without Doc."

Maddy leaned her arm on the counter, held her head with one hand, stirred the Coke with a straw, and watched the bubbles. Her insides churned thinking about Doc. *He was stolen from these people. It's a good thing the town is in denial. There's no way it could handle the truth.* Maddy kept her suspicion about how he died to herself.

"The person I'm most worried about is Hector," Rose said. "Did you see him at the cemetery?"

"Yeah. I wonder where he went."

Rose wiped down the counter, cleaning up before closing. Maddy put money down for the Coke. She said goodbye and started for home. It was dark, and her mind was on Hector. She wondered where he was and worried about his state of mind. She'd seen young people like him before, who were good inside, but who might turn left or right on their journey. If they met a loving person, they'd be okay. A cruel loss might send them down to destruction. Hector was at the crossroads, and Maddy worried Doc's death was his turning point.

When Maddy arrived home, it was pitch black outside; she walked up the stairs and flipped on the lights. Someone was lying on the recliner; she approached and realized it was Hector. He was sleeping. One pant leg and a sneaker were blood-soaked. Cuts and scrapes covered his arms, and a gash over his eye oozed red.

"Hector!" The boy woke up, his face flush and sweaty.

"Yeah," he said, half awake. Maddy didn't make him explain; she helped him to his feet. He placed his arm around her neck, and they limped inside. She led him to the sofa, handed him an afghan, and told him to cover up. "Take off those pants. I'll get something to clean that wound." She returned from the kitchen with a pan of warm water and a clean cloth. Sponging the blood from his leg, she asked how it had happened. Hector said nothing; he looked scared and exhausted.

"Do you have something to eat?" he asked.

"How about a cheeseburger?"

"Can you make two?"

Maddy wrapped the wounded leg and dabbed ointment on the gash over his eye. "Rest here while I make your food?" She came back and sat across, watching him eat. The boy was famished. He devoured the cheeseburgers, drank an enormous glass of milk, then sighed and leaned back.

"I didn't think I'd make it here alive." Startled by his words, Maddy crossed her arms and listened. "After the cemetery, I went to The Glades to find my sister. Something terrible is happening; someone is changing her, and she's not the same. When I found her, she was all drugged up and wouldn't listen to me." *This sounds like Abigail talking about her daughter,* Maddy thought.

"I had to do something, so I went looking for that Avery Jordan. I got caught. This guy as big as Frankenstein named Neri brought me to Jordan's office, and I told him to let A.J. go. I told him I knew someone was giving her drugs. He acted like it wasn't true, and then I got crazy and threatened to expose him."

Oh my God. Never threaten to expose a guy like that, Maddy thought. *It's the worst thing you can do.*

Hector shivered as he spoke. Maddy kept her gaze, got up, and lit kindling in the fireplace. She closed the screen and sat back down. "Jordan gave Neri a look, and I knew I was in trouble." He described how he broke free from the big guy's grip, and he chased him through the woods with a knife. "I don't know who he is, but for an oversized dummy, he is fast— almost as fast as me—and I'm half his size." Maddy thought Neri might have cut Hector's head off if he got caught.

There was silence. The fire crackled and leaped, and their faces glowed in the darkened room. "Someone turned A.J. into a different person. It wasn't her who told me to go away; it was the person they made her into. I'm gonna find who did it. I'm gonna expose 'em, and I'm gonna bring A.J. home. Can you help me?"

Maddy remained silent as Hector looked back into the fire. "A.J. wanted a job, so we'd have some money for food. That's all. And look what happened." Tears ran down his face. "I'm gonna find out who done it, I swear, I will," he said as he wept uncontrollably.

Fearful of what the boy, desperate to save his sister, might do, Maddy tried to reason with him. "Hector, if they are doing something bad, why not get the law involved?"

"You ain't been around here long enough. There's no law in this town. They're all under the spell of Avery Jordan."

"There are other law enforcement agencies." She was reluctant to reveal she got the state police involved, fearful it might get out and undermine Hannah's investigation.

"I don't trust anybody like that," he said.

"How about me? Do you trust me?" Hector didn't respond. She kept trying to reason with him. "What about A.J.? If you get in trouble, she won't have anyone."

He said nothing. He wiped the tears from his face and kept staring at the fire. "If it weren't for A.J., I'd have run away when Ma died. She's the one good thing worth staying for. My ma wouldn't be too happy with me if I ran."

When she asked if he was close with his mother, he nodded. An occasional flicker from the fire landed on his face, and she saw his sad eyes.

"Just before she died, we talked," he said. "She told me Pa was going bad with the booze, and I'd have to watch over A.J. I promised I would."

That struck a chord with Maddy. She remembered the promise she'd made to her father at his grave to follow in his footsteps and become a detective. *End-of-life promises,* she thought. *They have a way of hanging around.*

"You know, I lost my parents when I was about your age," she said. Hector turned and looked at her. "I was lost and alone."

"Did someone help you?" he asked.

"I moved in with my grandma. She helped me get through the worst of it."

He looked back into the fire. "Doc helped me, and now he's gone." Maddy had nothing to add. The hard-shelled boy, who seemed to carry a heavy burden with him, looked like a tender child yearning for a mother's love.

He asked her if she was close with her mother, and Maddy said she died when she was ten. "I remember her being loving, but recently, I realized I forgot what she looked like. It scared me. I started digging through boxes of old photos until I found one that reminded me of how much she loved me. She was smiling as I stood next to her. I was leaning my head on her shoulder, and we both seemed full of love for one another."

"I'll never forget my ma," Hector said as the fire dimmed to embers. There was silence before he added, "And yes, I do trust you."

Maddy saw warmth in the boy's eyes when he looked at her, and it melted her heart. He lived in a cruel world, where he was being forced to grow up before his time. Circumstances beyond his control hardened him. *The world does that,* Maddy thought.

She kneeled, put a few logs on the fire, and when she turned, Hector was sleeping. She brought a blanket and covered him, then dug through old clothes. She laid a pair of sweatpants, a shirt, and socks on a chair, and the following morning, he was gone. Staring at where he had slept, she thought, *He asked me for help, and I said nothing.*

CHAPTER 32

Wednesday, September 5, 1984

Time dragged on as the gala approached, and Maddy's thoughts were with Hector. She wondered where he went. It had been a week since he'd stayed at her place, and the image of his tear-filled face asking for help would not leave her.

Riddled with guilt, she hoped the troopers would make a move soon. She worried the investigation might not proceed fast enough to save Hector's sister. The few times she called Hannah, she was told the investigation was underway—nothing more.

The sound of a car driving up her road pulled her out of herself; it was Jodi. "Hey, you.," Maddy called from the deck as her friend got out of her old Volvo.

"That's a lot longer drive than I remember," Jodi said.

Maddy walked down to help bring Jodi's things inside, and each carried arms fulls to the house. After Jodi rested, they ate fish tacos and went to the deck. Late-day clouds streaked across the sky, and Maddy opened a bottle of Riesling.

"To a great visit." Maddy held up her glass, and they drank. She asked Jodi if she was feeling better about George.

"George, who?" Jodi responded, and they both laughed. "I've finally stopped thinking about him. How about you? How are things in la-la land?"

"Well, la-la land is now the land of the macabre." Jodi twisted her head and asked what she meant. "A lot has happened, none of it good, and I am anxious. I don't know where to start."

"The last I remember, Doc died in a car accident, and you were suspicious it wasn't an accident," Jodi said.

"What if I told you a girl killed herself by cutting her throat right behind this house?"

"What? Is that even possible?"

"It's possible but highly improbable. The girl's name was Luellen Hicks. I visited her mother and found a torn-up letter that I put back together. I have a copy. Hang on, I'll let you read it."

When Maddy returned and gave Jodi the letter, Jodi squinted as though it was painful reading. "Oh, my God. The poor girl. Is that the Avery guy you had lunch with?" Maddy said it was, and then Jodi asked about Neri. "Have you met him? He sounds like a monster."

"No, I haven't. Nor have I met Naomi, but we'll see these characters at the gala. Now you know why I'm so concerned about getting you involved. Maybe we should skip the entire event."

"I don't think that's a good idea," Jodi said. "If they think you're running scared, you'll be even more vulnerable."

Sounds like a girl after my heart, Maddy thought to herself. Maddy asked Jodi if she remembered her mentioning Hector, and his sister, A.J., and Jodi said she did. "Well, A.J. is in the same predicament at The Glades as Luellen Hicks, and I fear Hector has been putting himself in danger trying to save her. I think he's headed for real trouble."

"Have you gone to the police?"

Maddy explained the local cops were on The Glades's payroll, but the state police were now involved. "I fear by the time the troopers intervene, it'll be too late for A.J."

A cool breeze kicked up, and Maddy grabbed the wine bottle. "Let's take it inside."

Jodi got comfortable as Maddy built a fire. She broke out another bottle, filled the glasses, and sat. "I'm so glad you're here," Maddy said.

"Me too. It's been a rough few months. I've realized some things about myself through it all." Maddy remained silent. "I have a hard time fitting in with American kids. I got along with people in Vietnam well; they seemed more genuine."

Maddy gave Jodi an understanding nod. The fire crackled, the light outside grew dim, and they shared their troubles without judgment.

Jodi continued, "Maybe it's just me, but it seems these kids are all hung up on the competition and outdoing each other. After midterms, a boy jumped off a cliff near campus and killed himself. How can that happen? What is so important about school that you kill yourself?"

Maddy's mind drifted to Amber, who worried about getting a C minus on a project. "I worry about that with my daughter. She's been under a lot of pressure as well."

"I came into this world with nothing," Jodi said. "I'll leave the same way; the rest is just a free ride."

Neither spoke for a while. The fire glowed, snapped, and sparkled as each became lost in thought.

"How do you see tomorrow going?" Jodi asked. "You know, the gala."

"We observe, and after, we compare notes. Maybe we'll figure something out. That's about the best we can do." Tired and about to pack it in for the night, Maddy noticed Jodi hesitating as though she wanted to say something. She asked if she was okay.

"I said I am over George, and I think I am, but something isn't right." Maddy sat back down. "Deep inside, I don't believe I was good enough for him."

Maddy sensed the depth of her friend's vulnerability as the girl looked down and continued. "I dream about my mother a lot lately. She left me at the work camp and said she'd return. I'd watch the road for her to appear each evening after we returned from the rice paddies. She never did. I'm sitting by the phone in the dreams, waiting for my mother to call. I wait and wait and wait. It's an awful feeling."

Maddy wasn't a psychologist, but she knew enough about abandonment to understand Jodi's dreams and was careful with her words.

"It sounds like when George cut you out of his life, it brought back feelings of your mother. Any child would feel unworthy if their mother left and didn't return."

Maddy saw tears dripping down Jodi's face in the dim light of the fire. She sobbed softly as though she carried a lifetime of sorrow. Maddy sat next to her and held Jodi in her arms. An aching, painful moan came from her friend's depths. The girl wailed into the embrace as Maddy comforted the abandoned child Jodi carried inside. When the flood of emotions ceased, Maddy handed her tissues she'd pulled from her pocket.

"Well, I didn't think I was coming here for a therapy session," Jodi quipped as she wiped off her face. Blowing her nose, she added, "You can send me a bill."

"You are a beautiful person, Jodi, inside and out. Anyone would be lucky to have you love them. I'm glad you're my friend."

Jodi gave her a grateful glance and finished cleaning off her face.

As Maddy lay in bed that night, she thought about what might happen at the gala. She wondered if Hector might make an unannounced appearance, spoil the party, and get his revenge on Avery Jordan. *I'm walking into a den of horrors, but I'm damn grateful I'll be with Jodi.*

CHAPTER 33

Friday, September 7, 1984

Jodi finished her shower while Maddy laid out her gown on the bed. Blue sapphire, strapless, sleek, and with an open back, it was perfect for what might be a warm evening at The Glades, but she planned on bringing along a matching lace shawl to carry over her arm just in case.

When Jodi came out in an emerald gown, two women looked at each other and roared. "Our dresses are identical except for the colors," Maddy said. "I almost picked that green; wouldn't that have been a hoot?"

The laughter helped relieve the tension building in Maddy's gut all day. Luellen's letter had been running through her mind, yet she'd tried to remain upbeat for her friend. They brought their giddy moods to the pickup.

Each woman struggled to climb into the front seat of the truck. Their long, snug dresses required them to lift their butts and slide onto the seat. "I wonder how many guests at the Single but Not Alone Gala will arrive in a Chevy pickup truck," Maddy said, snickering. Jodi held her stomach and whooped; Maddy joined her. Their laughter provided added release. Yet, for Maddy, deep inside, a sense of foreboding lingered.

As they approached the turnoff to The Glades, the traffic backed up. Behind Maddy's Chevy truck was a Lincoln Continental, several Mercedes Benz, and a few Cadillacs. Uniformed men directed traffic, and one approached them.

"Hello, can I have your names, please?"

"Maddy Reynolds, and Jodi Novak." Maddy noticed he was wearing a holstered revolver. That's odd, considering he's only directing traffic.

He flipped up several pages on a clipboard and said, "You may think this is a strange question to ask you ladies, but are there any weapons in your vehicle?"

Maddy looked at Jodi, turned to the guy, and said, "I have a Glock 17G5, 9-millimeter, semiautomatic in my door panel."

The man tilted his head, smiled, and said, "Cute," as though Maddy was joshing.

"If I reach down and show you, you won't shoot me, will you?"

He seemed to realize she wasn't kidding. "Just open the door, please." He looked at the holster with the gun inside, squeezed into the door panel. "Is it loaded?"

"It only works if it's loaded."

"You're going to have to check it with me and can pick it up when you leave." He tagged the weapon, ripped off half the ticket, handed it back, and told her to move ahead.

The truck climbed upward through the tall, white pine forest, and when it reached the top, Maddy pulled under the overhang. Men walked around, opened the doors, took Maddy and Jodi's hands, and helped them out.

Maddy stepped down. A warm breeze from the woods, carrying a scent of pine, brushed up against her face. One guy drove off with the vehicle, and the other escorted them inside, where the temperature cooled, and everything was different. Delightful aromas of food cooking permeated the air. Maddy and Jodi stood in a massive open area filled with people, elegantly dressed, milling about, holding glasses of wine, laughing, and chatting it up.

"This is amazing," Jodi said, looking up at the opulent chandeliers.

"Let's walk around," Maddy said. Scattered throughout the open area were serving stations, each with meat or fish, where people stood waiting to eat. She saw at least four bars where crowds talked and laughed.

"I see where I'm headed. Come on, let's get a glass of wine." They meandered through the crowd. Thousand-dollar gowns and diamond necklaces adorned prominent society women. They spoke to one another like old friends, laughing and moving around as if accustomed to luxurious surroundings.

A lone piano player played contemporary music in jazz-like arrangements, the likes of which Maddy never heard. As they walked through the mass of bodies, several men, all wearing black tuxedos, turned their heads toward Maddy and Jodi as they walked by.

Surrounding one bar, a group of men blocked the way, laughing and smoking cigars. They parted when an older man gazed at the two women. "Gentlemen, there are two beautiful women who are trying to get through." He smiled as the throng parted, opening a path to the bar.

With glasses of wine in hand, Maddy and Jodi moved to a wall made of glass where three tall French doors opened to a tiered stone terrace surrounded by magnificent gardens. Water fountains, scattered about, and groomed foliage with flowering trees, enhanced the beautiful setting. Maddy saw it before when she visited Avery for lunch, but somehow it looked even more spectacular with celebrities meandering about. The two found a place to stand.

"This is not your typical Sunday social," Jodi joked.

"It's hard to say what this is," Maddy said.

"Senator Johnston, how wonderful to see you," a woman said loudly to the powerful man. *She wants everyone to hear,* Maddy thought.

"Where should we go?" Jodi asked.

"How about some food?"

"You don't have to ask me twice," Jodi said. They found serving stations in the garden, and as they filled their plates with savory shrimp, scallops, beef, and pork hors d'oeuvres, Maddy heard someone call her name. She turned, and a guy in his late twenties, with long hair, walked over. Unsure of who he was, she shook his hand out of politeness and said she couldn't remember where they met.

"We haven't. I'm Randy Gardner. I do a radio talk show—Late Night With Randy; maybe you've heard of it. I recognized you from your magazine photo."

"I have listened to your show," Maddy said, then introduced Jodi. "You can pick your jaw up off the floor now." Maddy laughed as the young man gawked at her stunning friend.

"Oh, I'm sorry. I didn't mean to stare; it's just, well...."

"No apology needed," Maddy interrupted. "Everyone stares at Jodi."

Jodi blushed, stuck out her hand, and said hello. Randy took it, nodded, and seemed to be mesmerized by the girl's beauty.

"What do you think of this shindig?" he asked.

"It looks like every politician in the state is here. I'm surprised I don't see the governor," Maddy said.

"I heard he's supposed to be here later," Randy quipped.

Maddy noticed a huge, dark-complexioned man standing alone with a beer in his hand, attempting to be one of the crowd, looking her way. The slight bulge on the side of his tuxedo jacket told her he was carrying. She turned her attention back to Randy and said she listened to his show on sex trafficking. "Pasha's story was moving and most disturbing."

Randy's demeanor changed. "That stuff is real. After that show, I couldn't sleep for a week."

The man with the gun kept staring. Maddy said, "Let's check out that room." She walked ahead as Randy and Jodi walked behind. She heard them talking and Jodi giggling. *How cool would it be if she met a nice guy tonight?*

They entered a library adorned with black walnut woodwork and shelves filled with interesting-looking books. "This is bigger than the library in my hometown," Jodi said. Leather-bound ancient texts looked like something one might see at the Vatican.

Jodi walked over to gaze at the library, and Randy stayed with her. Maddy slid through people. She noticed a plaque with an emblem resembling the symbol on the invitation to the event propped up on a desk. Latin words encircled a lion's head were similar to the invitation, but the words were different. The invitation read simul os sunt, which means "together we are one." The words on the plaque read ad victorem spolias, "to the victor go the spoils." *Those are cruel words*, Maddy thought and sensed a hidden mockery of the more favorable version.

"Please don't touch the items on Mr. Jordan's desk," a voice said. Startled, she looked up, and the huge, dark-complexioned man was standing next to her. He took the plaque and set it back in its original position.

"Oh, I'm sorry. I didn't know Mr. Jordan was so particular."

"That's an understatement," he said with a touch of sarcasm.

"I take it you work security here?" Maddy inquired.

"Why do you say that?"

"They took my weapon at the first checkpoint, and you're still carrying yours."

"Very observant, Ms. Reynolds."

"You know my name; not fair. What's yours?"

"Sedgwick Neri, Director of Security."

A chill ran through her, and she almost asked where he kept his knife but didn't. She calmed herself. "This is quite a library Mr. Jordan has. I see books a few hundred years old and several in foreign languages. He seems like quite a guy."

"Would you like to meet him?"

"We've already met, but if he wants to see me, I'd be glad to accommodate."

"He'd very much like to see you," Neri said.

"I'm here with some friends. Can they come along?"

"Just you, Ms. Reynolds!"

"Lead the way," she said, and Neri started for a door. Maddy followed and noticed the distinctive scent of the big man's cologne. "Mr. Neri, what is that cologne you're wearing? It's very different."

"Clive Christian Number One," he said.

She wasn't familiar with the scent but heard of the brand and remembered it cost $1,500 an ounce. *Cutting throats must pay well.*

Neri's gait was agile and graceful, which she thought was unusual for a man of his size. Then, when he pushed off his right foot to turn down a hallway, a bulge in his right pant leg revealed the outline of a knife. *There's where he keeps it.* When Neri grabbed and opened a door, his hand covered the entire knob. *I bet he can hold a person's head with one hand and cut their throat with the other.*

"This way," he said. Avery Jordan sat alone, looking at the party through a window. He turned and swung around in his chair, and his eyes lit up when he saw her.

"Maddy, how are you? This party was bringing me down until now. Come, have a seat near me," he said, gesturing to a nearby chair.

His welcoming smile and warm voice made it difficult to reconcile the two Avery Jordans—the slime bag in Luellen's letter and the pleasant, father-like man before her. Maddy had the advantage of knowing Rusty. He acted like her friend but turned out to be Cupid, the child killer. She since developed a filter to screen incoming social cues, analyzing and taking time to determine who people were.

"So, talk to me; how do you like the gala?" he asked.

"I'm afraid it's not my cup of tea."

Jordan laughed. "That's what I like about you; you're so honest."

"Aren't you?"

"Only when I have to be." He walked to a bottle on a table. "Join me in a glass of Penfolds Grange Shiraz, 1977; it's a wonderful wine."

"I'd love to."

"Mr. Neri, would you pour Ms. Reynolds and me a glass? Neri brought the wine, and Avery asked him to leave. "I'd like to speak with Miss. Reynolds alone." Maddy noticed a contemptuous look on Neri's face. *Avery Jordan should never let this guy stand behind him.*

She took a sip and thought, *Oh, my God, this is outrageous.* Avery asked her if she liked it, and she said it was quite nice.

"Do you mind?" he asked, holding up a cigar. She gave a nod, then complimented him on his book collection.

"You must speak quite a few languages; I noticed books from around the world."

"A necessity of the trade." *What trade?* she wondered. "Let's talk about you," Avery said. "How are you enjoying your time in Berry Lake?"

"Most interesting," she said.

"How so?"

Where's he going with this? "You know," she said, "the people and the scenery."

Avery laughed and exclaimed, "The people! Oh, come on."

What an asshole.

"I would have thought you'd have gone back among equals by now."

"Are you saying you're not my equal?"

Avery put the cigar down. He looked at Maddy and said, "Level with me; why are you in Berry Lake?"

Ahh, he thinks I'm here undercover. He's paranoid; I wonder what he's hiding. I'm not inclined to ease his mind. "Well, I'm multifaceted, if that's what you're wondering. That's what makes a diamond glitter, isn't it?" she said with a coy smile.

She detected a hint of anger in the way the corners of his mouth turned downward and knew she'd hit a nerve. "Multifaceted," he repeated with a muffled, cynical tone. As though he realized he was losing control, he said, "Well, as much as I'd rather stay here and chat with you, Maddy, I must mingle with guests."

She noticed a wolf's head mounted on a wall. "Did you shoot that wolf?"

"I did indeed. Right here at The Glades. I would have killed her mate too, but he moved."

"Lucky for him," Maddy said. "He must be lonely since wolves mate for life."

"It's too bad I didn't put him out of his misery then, isn't it? We have seen him, and I'll get him."

Seething at the man's arrogance, she tried to calm herself, and she returned to the library, looking for Jodi, but it was empty. The sounds of people in the garden led her back to the glass doors. She walked out, and a crowd gathered, waiting for fireworks to begin. A hand reached out and grabbed her arm. It was Jodi. "I thought you were lost," she said.

"I was visiting with Avery Jordan." Several loud booms above and scatterings of sparkles floating down from the sky marked the display's beginning and stifled their conversation. People looked up and watched as the flashing colored lights shone on their idolizing faces, adding to the evening's surrealism. Maddy signaled for Jodi to walk inside.

They stopped in Castile Room, and Maddy asked where Randy was.

"He said his boss is here. He went to speak with him and said he'd be back."

"He seems nice," Maddy said. Jodi nodded.

Maddy noticed Avery standing with Neri and an exotic albino woman, all looking at them. *Shit, they're coming over.* "Hang tight, Jodi. Avery Jordan, that Neri guy and a woman are coming to visit us."

"How fortuitous. We get to see one another again," Avery said when he approached. "I couldn't help but notice your dazzling friend. I also want you to meet Naomi. I believe you've already met Mr. Neri."

"This is Jodi," Maddy said before saying hello to Naomi and nodding to Neri. Jodi gave a slight nod as well.

"One hears a lot about Maddy Reynolds these days," Naomi said with a plastic smile.

"Oh, and what have you heard?"

As if unable to think of anything polite, Naomi hesitated. "All good, I assure you."

I bet, Maddy thought.

Avery's eyes kept bouncing over to Jodi. Maddy noticed Naomi's face stiffen as she watched. "Jodi, you appear to be of Asian heritage, but your blue eyes tell me something different," Avery said. "There must be a story behind that."

"My mother is Vietnamese, and my father was Irish-American."

"You use the past tense for your father; is he long deceased?" *That's a very personal question to ask, you asshole.*

"He was a marine and killed in the war."

Avery looked as though he wanted to continue his dialogue with Jodi, but a venomous look set him back when he glanced at Naomi, and he stopped himself.

"Avery tells me you have a daughter who's a freshman at Cornell," Naomi said to Maddy.

Red flags and alarm bells went off in Maddy's brain; her face flushed with anger. She glared at the albino, then moved her head to Avery. "You do your homework well, Mr. Jordan."

He turned his head, embarrassed, glared at Naomi, and his look said, *What the fuck are you doing?* Naomi smirked and moved closer to Neri than Avery, as though she were sending him a warning that he'd better stay in line.

"Oh, I see the senator. Excuse me, it was very nice meeting you," Naomi said. She took Neri's arm, and they walked away, leaving Avery standing with Maddy and Jodi.

Avery seemed to strain to maintain his composure and said, "Yes, I should go as well. Have a pleasant evening."

"Holy shit," Jodi said when she and Maddy were alone. "What was that all about?"

Dozens of loud booms from outside rang through the great hall, one after another. "It's the grand finale," Maddy said. "They will mob this room soon. Let's get out of here."

The women headed for the front door, but before they walked outside, a voice rang out Jodi's name, and it was Randy. He walked over, and Maddy said she'd wait outside, leaving them alone.

When Jodi came out, Maddy was waiting inside the truck. "So?" Maddy said.

"So, what?" Jodi said, smiling.

"You know."

"Yes, we're going to stay in touch; maybe get together in a few weeks."

"Alright!" Maddy roared. The joy of the moment soon passed, heaviness set in, and the truck was quiet on the ride home. Maddy couldn't stop thinking about how Naomi mentioned Amber. *What was that all about? A shot across the bow; that's what it was. It was a warning!*

She didn't want to discuss it with Jodi, worried she had already exposed her to the dangerous situation. The evening was too much to digest, and the women settled in before a fire when they got back. Jodi sat in her pajamas. "I don't know," she said. "The Glades seems very strange."

"Something awful is happening there," Maddy said. "Their behavior verified everything in Luellen's letter in spades tonight. There's more— much more; I feel it. Something bad is coming down, and I'm worried about Hector."

Numbed by the weirdness of the evening, they retired early.

CHAPTER 34

Saturday, September 8, 1984

The morning after the gala, Jodi packed her car and was ready to leave for home. She and Maddy sat out on the deck, talking with their morning beverages; Jodi with tea and Maddy with a cup of coffee. "That Randy seems like a decent guy," Maddy said.

Jodi smiled and nodded. "I like him. But I'm going to take it slow."

Maddy was about to say that was a good idea when a siren screamed not far away. Her mind flashed back to the streets of Utica.

"Maybe it's a fire," Jodi said.

The phone rang. Maddy went inside to pick it up, and it was Rose. "Maddy, something awful has happened." Maddy's stomach tightened, and thoughts turned to Hector. "A.J. Lemont jumped off Wheeler's Point." Like she'd been kicked in the gut, she was breathless. She eeked out, "Where's Wheeler's Point?"

Rose gave her directions. Maddy and Jodi ran to the truck and took off. As they went, the morning grew dark, and rain clouds gathered. When they arrived, cars lined the road, lights on rescue vehicles flashed, and men dressed in mountain climbing gear assembled in a group. Lester wore a volunteer fireman's rubber coat. *This is déjà vu. That's how he dressed when Doc went off the cliff.* She pulled her vehicle forward, rolled down the window, and asked Lester if it was true. "Did A.J. jump?"

Unable to speak, Lester nodded. He seemed to be fighting tears, cleared his throat, and said, "They're getting ready to go into the ravine and retrieve the body."

Maddy pulled over and got out. She walked over to the edge of the road, and Jodi followed. "Oh, my God," she said, clasping her hand over her mouth. The cliff was a steep, unimaginable fall that no one could have possibly survived. Jodi stood next to her, put a hand on her shoulder, and pulled her away. Maddy fell into her arms, weeping.

"I can't believe this." She remembered Hector asking for help to save his sister, and she didn't. She had held back, hoping the state police investigation would intervene at The Glades and save A.J. *I was wrong for doing that.*

Large cold drops of rain peppered the ground, and pedestrians ran to their cars. "Let's get out of the rain," Jodi said, then led Maddy to the truck.

"Hector asked me to help him," Maddy bellowed, "and I did nothing." Overwhelmed with guilt, Jodi's efforts to console her friend were useless. "I have to find Hector," Maddy said. When the rain let up, she got out, went up to Lester, and asked if he knew where Hector was.

"I ain't seen him, but he knows what happened, I can assure you. He always keeps an eye out for his sister; he knows alright." Before the two women turned back to the truck, the sound of ropes on squeaky pulleys froze Maddy's gaze. Men reached out to haul in a rescue basket. Someone ran over with a tarp, but not before Maddy saw A.J.'s caved-in head, contorted leg, and a missing arm. Her knees gave way, and Jodi kept her from falling.

Jodi pulled Maddy to the truck and told her it wasn't her fault. "There was nothing you could have done to prevent it." Maddy put her head down on the steering wheel. "Let me drive home," Jodi said. Maddy said she'd be okay, and they started back to Flat Top Rock.

The sun came out in the afternoon, and Jodi said she would skip classes to stay with Maddy until she was doing better. "No, I want you to go." Maddy's guilt turned to agitation. "I'm more concerned with your safety now than ever. I never should have let you come here." She looked across the lake to the Glades. "This is a hellish place. I need you to go, please. I couldn't bear it if something happens to you."

Jodi resisted, but Maddy wouldn't relent. "Look, I know you're my friend; I know you saved my life with Cupid, but this time, give me your support from afar. Please, do this for me."

Jodi agreed. The friends looked at one another, and there were no words, only hugs, and tears.

CHAPTER 35

Saturday, September 8, 1984
Hector Lemont

Hector sat on the hill across from Wheeler's Point, watching rescue vehicles extricate his sister from the vast hole in the earth. A crowd of onlookers gathered near its edge, trying to glimpse the body. It started to rain, and he leaned back against a tree as the wind picked up. A hollowness grew inside of him, and numbness filled the void.

The rain let loose, driving onlookers back to their cars, while ropes pulled the basket with A.J. inside onto the road. Somebody covered her with a blue tarp and slid her into an ambulance.

There'll be plenty for everyone to talk about over dinner tonight, Hector thought cynically to himself. He tried to lift himself off the ground but could not move. It was as if his body weighed 600 pounds; all strength had left him. He sat in rain-soaked clothes, chilled from the outside of his body through to the inside.

He dragged himself up and started for his cave. Walking to the crest of the hill, he stopped, and before descending the other side, he turned. "Goodbye, Anna Jean," he said, looking once more to the place where his sister died.

As if he was a robot, he started down the other side of the hill, putting one foot in front of the other. His mind wandered, and Avery Jordan entered his thoughts. *He watched that young woman, naked, with her hands and feet shackled apart, and the albino woman probed her with the feathered wand. That would have sent my sister running for the cliffs.* The thoughts flashed to his sister crashing into the rocks. *I bet she called out to Jesus for help. That's what she always does when she's scared. But Jesus didn't come.*

Hector's feet sloshed in the muddy earth. With each step, he moved further away from the person he was. He never felt so strange. There was no pain—just an odd emptiness. *Mother's gone, so are Anna Jean and Doc. Pa's gone too; there's just me now.*

The clouds cleared by the time he reached the hole in the hill he called home. The stars burned, and it was a clear night. The moon seemed from another world, and something moved inside of him—a spirit, he thought. It was always there, but he had paid it no mind. Now it was giving him strength and purpose. He didn't need to think of what to do next, and he didn't have to worry about hurting his loved ones anymore. He could do as he pleased.

Hector took the wood he'd stored beneath a tarpaulin and placed it in the pit. He lit the kindling and watched the flames rise. Surrounded by the smoke-scented air, he looked out to the mountains; they seemed alive in the moonlight, and somehow he was at one with them. *This is who I am now; this is my home.* He realized the village of Berry Lake held nothing for him anymore. *There are no more dreams,* he said to himself. He always hoped he'd have a family someday, a job, and live like other people he knew. But, now all that seemed like a cruel fantasy.

He breathed, exhaled, and sank into his new reality. In the distance, a wolf howled. Hector climbed on a rock, stood, and listened as the wolf bellowed into the night. Feeling like he was being summoned by the fierce beast, his heart overflowed with excitement. The past melted away along with his illusions of the future. Everyone he loved was gone, and Hector could finally get what he wanted. And what he wanted was revenge. Like Moses with his staff, he grabbed a stick, left his cave, and ascended the mountain to The Glades.

CHAPTER 36

Saturday, September 8, 1984
Avery Jordan

Avery sat, facing an open window, staring out into the darkness, trying to grasp the loss of Anna Jean. *She's gone. Sweet Anna Jean is dead.* He tried to remember the first time he'd seen the girl. *Ah, yes, that awkward gait and her nervous smile. She wore scuffed-up shoes and a new dime-store dress.* He laughed to himself, yet mused, how her innocence made him want her.

She was like a ripe peach hanging low on a tree. Perhaps it was her virginity. I always enjoy being the first. Luellen Hicks came to his mind and thought about how virgins fall hard. He felt a similar sadness when Luellen killed herself.

The door opened, and Naomi walked in. He turned back to the window and asked what she wanted.

"Are you going to kill that wolf? It's been howling every night and is putting everyone on edge."

"I have more important things on my mind than a damn wolf."

"Oh, you mean like poor, sweet Anna Jean, who turned her perfect little body into hamburger meat this morning?"

"You are cruel," Avery said.

"You do not know what cruel is, I assure you," she said.

"Anyway, I'm not thinking about Anna Jean. My mind is on raising enough money at the masquerade party to pay off our debt."

"You mean your debt and to save yourself from becoming fish bait."

"Did you come here to irritate me?"

"I came to tell you The Guy is on the phone."

Avery flung around in his chair. "And you're keeping him waiting? Send the call through."

The phone buzzed, and Avery's heart thumped. "Avery Jordan, are you ready for your deliverance or for your judgment?"

The air left his lungs, and he struggled to speak. "I'll be ready with the money when the time comes." A clunk, a dial tone, and the ominous howling continued to reverberate in his head. *I'm going to kill that damn thing.*

He returned to his quarters, and the howling stopped. Avery lay in bed, and his mind raced as he worried about everything that might go wrong. He reran the same old script in his head. *What if the weather's terrible? Maybe not enough people will show? What if that Lemont kid makes good on his threat to expose us?* Tossing in bed, his mind spun like a merry-go-round. He was most worried, however, about Maddy Reynolds.

She's too damn smart for her own good. The beautiful woman gnawed at him. Naomi's manipulations were bad enough, but being outsmarted by Reynolds made him feel less than a man. Deep down, he doubted she'd find him appealing.

Avery fell into a restless dream. He was naked in a room with mirrored walls. Unable to escape the image of his nakedness, he covered himself. *What am I doing here?*

A woman's voice whispered his name mockingly; it grew louder and became a giggle. It was coming from beyond the glass. He pounded on the mirrored walls, trying to get at it. The giggling turned into roaring laughter, and the image on the other side was Maddy Reynolds.

Avery squatted, trying to cover himself with his hands. His face was feverish as his humiliation grew. His throat tightened, and he tried to hide from his reflection, but it was everywhere around him. His body appeared deformed. Dumbo ears and a bent, witch-like nose made him look ridiculous.

Running from Reynolds's image, he began to trip as his feet became enormous, and they flopped as he walked. His fingers were long and stringy, his head was bald, and three front teeth were missing. In his reflection, he saw his penis. It had shrunk to the size of an acorn and was barely visible. The laughter turned into a high-pitched cackle; he covered himself, screamed, and fell to his knees.

Avery awoke, soaked with sweat, and his pajamas stuck to his body. The veins on his neck were bulging, and the room spun. "Are you alright, sir?" Girard asked from outside the door.

Avery forced out the words, "I—I—I'm okay. I'll be fine; I'll be fine." He tried to convince himself he'd be okay, but he wasn't sure. He got up, and he went to the phone. "Mr. Girard, I want another meeting with Naomi, Neri, Chief Smith, and yourself in my office as soon as possible." Avery went to the table where he kept the scotch and poured a glass. *That Reynolds woman is getting to me. I'm sure she's working behind the scenes to bring me down.* Keeping her from interfering with paying off The Guy was his highest priority.

Ragged from lack of sleep, Avery waited for the others to arrive. He poured through the ledger to drive out the shame-filled dream, counting and recounting the number of guests. The phone buzzed, and Girard said everyone was present. The door opened, and The Glades's inner core took seats. A noose was tightening around Avery's neck, and it was imperative to make the others understand the seriousness of the situation.

"September seventeenth is a critical day for our futures," he started out saying. "Our fates will be determined. Your necks are on the line with mine." Avery looked at each person to emphasize everything must go as planned. "One misstep might spell disaster, and merciless people will take over."

He crossed his arms and leaned back in his chair. "That's why I've asked you here. I am imploring you to leave no stone unturned and to stop all preventable problems." He stood, walked to the window, looked out, clasping his hands behind him.

"I see four possible disasters. Weather and turnout we can't control, but Hector Lemont and Maddy Reynolds, we can." Avery flashed back to his dream. He saw Maddy Reynolds pointing at his penis, laughing, and a bolt of shame ran through him.

He looked at Smith. "Chief, I've asked you to take care of Lemont. What do you have to report?"

Smith shifted in his chair. Loosening his collar, he said, "Hector has skipped town, and no one's seen him. We found his cave, and there was no sign of him. The word is he's gone to stay with relatives."

"Good," Avery said. "Now let's talk about the problem that's causing my insides to twist into a knot; that damn detective. I am sure she's in Berry Lake undercover. I spoke with her at the gala. I asked why she had moved here, and she said she was multifaceted, like a diamond. Who would believe such nonsense?" He felt his disdain for the intelligent woman erupt. "She's enjoying the scenery at our expense. What are we going to do about her?"

"She has a daughter, remember?" Naomi said.

"Go on," Avery prodded as he sat back down.

Naomi got up. She moved with her hand up to her chin. "The famous detective is not the type to scare. We know she won't run from a fight based on what she did with Donnelly, right?" Avery nodded. "In fact, she sounds like the type to react against anyone who might try to intimidate her."

Naomi sat back down. She seemed in complete command of the men in the room. "If Maddy Reynolds were to show up dead—throat cut, shot in the head, killed in a fire, or even dying of a heart attack—all of her fellow detectives would swarm to Berry Lake looking for answers. We can't kill her. Are you all following me?" Everyone returned an affirmative look.

"Where is this going?" Avery barked.

"Hear me out," Naomi snapped back. "She has a daughter. Even if Reynolds will risk her own life for what she believes is a good cause, which she's already proven that she will do, the question is, will she risk her daughter's? I suspect not." Avery's eyes glued on Naomi.

"How do we make this happen?" he asked.

"We put her daughter in jeopardy, make the good detective aware that we're in control, and threaten harm to the kid if her mother doesn't fall in line."

Avery looked at Naomi. "It's risky, and there are big issues to be addressed, but I think it could work. The most dangerous thing we can do is nothing, so I think we should try this plan."

For the next few hours, they discussed the issues. Neri said he knew a young guy, Jimmy Bond, who could go to Ithaca and befriend Amber. "He's handsome, not much older than the Reynolds kid, but he's a killer and shrewd. I'm sure he can finagle his way into her situation. We'll have photos taken of them together and make Reynolds aware her daughter's life is in jeopardy and that we are in control."

They seemed to agree it was a good plan. When they finished and everyone was leaving the room, Avery asked Naomi to stay. He walked up, stroked her hair, and said thank you.

"As of late, I've questioned if you were with me or against me." He kissed her forehead, and she put her arms around his waist. It was their first embrace in weeks, and at that moment, he thought he might love the woman. "Come to my room tonight," he whispered.

"Maybe," she said, smiling as she walked out.

CHAPTER 37

Sunday, September 16, 1984
Maddy Reynolds

Maddy spent the days after A.J.'s suicide at home. She tried to unravel the layers of craziness that had taken place in her world. She believed The Glades somehow influenced A.J.'s death, and Hector would try to get revenge. Frustrated that the state police were moving slowly, she called Hannah to push for more information but got her voice mail.

"Hey, Hannah, it's Maddy. There was another suicide here. It might relate to The Glades; please call me. Thanks."

Maddy felt alone and called her daughter. "Hi, honey. I thought I'd call you to see how things are going."

"Oh, I was going to call you today. Things are great here. Any more weird stuff going on in Berry Lake?"

Maddy said things were about the same and asked what was going so well with her.

Amber said she took her mother's advice; she met with her literature professor and now understands why she got a C minus on her project. "I know what she's looking for, and I've brought my grade up to an A. And Mom, I met a great guy. His name is Jimmy, and I can't wait for you to meet him."

Amber started describing the guy. Maddy's mind wandered, thinking Hannah might call her back, and her daughter noticed. "Mom, you seem distracted. Are you sure everything's okay?"

"I didn't want to worry you, but Anna Jean Lemont killed herself yesterday. I think it's related to The Glades." She tried to assuage Amber's fears. "The state police are handling it now. I'm sure they will get things under control."

"Are you safe?"

"I have my weapon with me at all times."

"Just one? What happened to the other two?"

Shit! Maddy didn't want to explain the break-in but ended up telling Amber everything. "I will not try to talk you into leaving Berry Lake," Amber said. "I know what you'll tell me. All I'll say is, please be careful."

They hung up, and Maddy thought, *It must be awful to have a mother like me. I'm stubborn and constantly in danger.* Within a minute, the phone rang, and it was Hannah Bates on the other end. A wave of calm came over Maddy. She hoped Hannah would say the police were closing in on The Glades.

"I'm so glad it's you. There's been another suicide, and I'm sure it resulted from activity at The Glades. Can you tell me if you're making a move?"

"They might tap this phone," Hannah said. "We shouldn't be talking about this."

Of course, Maddy thought. *How careless of me.* "I'm sorry."

"Goodbye, Maddy," Hannah said before hanging up.

Fuck, I'm in the dark; that's where I am, isolated in darkness. Doubts and thoughts of self-recrimination began tormenting her. *Am I falling apart? I've always handled stress, no matter how intense, but now I'm not doing well.* She sat on her sofa, placed her hands over her drawn-up knees, and leaned her forehead down. "Oh, God, what will I do?"

The sound of crunching stones startled her. She ran to the kitchen. *What the hell!* A black limousine waited with the door open. She ran to her bedroom, grabbed her Glock, and slipped it into the back of her jeans. She walked to the limo, and Sedgwick Neri got out. Avery Jordan followed.

"Hello, Ms. Reynolds," Avery said with a smile. Maddy said nothing. "Please get in."

"No, thank you."

"Get in," Neri said. "Wait!" he added as he grabbed her arm, reached behind her, and pulled out the gun. "Now you can get in."

"What's this all about?" she asked. The two men smirked. Thoughts came to her, one after another. *They must be desperate to kidnap me like this; they are not dumb. They know they've already committed a crime; what's their end game? They must know I'm talking to the state police and want to silence me. They can't kill me; how would they explain it?* She sat between the two men as the driver proceeded through the village.

Maddy saw Rose standing outside Lena's having a smoke and wanted to cry out for help, but it was an impossibility. They passed Doc's place; overgrown grass and no cars parked out front made it look as abandoned as she felt. *It appears they got me too, Doc.*

Maddy grasped her father's badge and prayed. *Please help me, Dad.* She then thought of Amber. *Oh, honey, I'm so sorry.*

"You realize what you're doing is kidnapping, don't you?" she said.

Neri gave her a sideways smile. "Spare me, Reynolds; you don't scare me."

"That's because you're not smart enough to be scared, but Avery is."

"We have a proposition to discuss with you," Avery said, but Maddy noticed a slight quiver in his lower lip.

I bet, she thought.

When they arrived at The Glades, two men waited at Castile Room to escort them inside. Avery and Neri went off in one direction, and the men brought Maddy to a room without windows in the basement. "You have everything you need in here," one said. She heard the door lock, and she was left alone, looking around the wood-paneled room. The emptiness inside of her was as palpable as the emptiness around her. She sat in one of the two leather chairs and began contemplating her situation.

They've got to be hiding something huge for Avery to take this risk. She opened the door to a furnished bedroom with a king-size bed. Garments lay on the bed—sweat pants, shirts, socks, sneakers, and underwear—all the correct sizes. *How the hell did they find out my sizes?*

She walked to another door. It opened to an enormous bathroom with a ceramic floor, marble counters, a walk-in shower, and a jacuzzi bathtub. Soft lighting and the scent of burning jasmine candles made what might otherwise be inviting seem bizarre. Maddy walked to the bed and sat. *I'm a prisoner!* She held her father's badge to her chest, lay back, and closed her eyes, whispering, "This can't be happening."

Staring into the stillness of the room, she lay for hours. She was living her worst nightmare. It was like being twelve again after her father's murder, falling into a downward spiral; her life was out of control. She endured several life or death crises since that Halloween night when Cupid killed her dad. She knew to survive this one, she'd have to find new weapons. Her shooting skills would not help; instead, it was all about her intellect.

There was a knock at the door. "Can I come in?"

"Yes," Maddy said, without thinking. The door unlocked. A woman rolled in a cart, and a man with a gun waited at the door. "I'm Lucia. I brought you breakfast."

Maddy sat up and realized it was morning. "What time is it?"

"Seven thirty-seven," Lucia said as she parked the cart. She began unloading food trays onto a table near the bed. Lucia spread the food out neatly: a coffee pot and cups, baskets covered with cloth napkins containing rolls and bread, silverware, and covered silver plates. The man with the weapon stood in the doorway, observing Lucia's every move. Maddy watched him observing.

Lucia finished and turned to push the cart past the guy holding the door. He said, "You're to meet with Mr. Jordan at ten; I'll be back at nine forty-five to escort you."

She asked him his name, and he froze as if unsure whether to answer. "Come on," Maddy said. "Nobody's going to shoot you if you tell me your first name." He said his name was Steve.

"Thank you, Steve," Maddy said as she walked to the table with the food. The door closed, and she sat looking at the spread of pancakes, bacon, sausage, muffins, cornbread, eggs, yogurt, bananas, blueberries, toast, and coffee. She craved a cup of coffee but dared not drink, thinking it would be the easiest of all the items to poison. Scrutinizing a slice of toast, she bit off a tiny piece, waited, and then ate the entire slice. She peeled and ate a banana but didn't touch the pancakes.

After she dressed in the clothes they provided, she waited, and at 9:45, Steve appeared in the doorway.

"Are you ready, Ms. Reynolds?"

"As ready as I can be. What is this about, Steve?" He said nothing. "I'm concerned about my daughter. She's nineteen and worries about me. I bet Amber has already called my house several times and is in a near panic." She tried to work the fringes with Steve and Lucia. *They can't be part of The Glades' core sickness,* she thought. *They just work here.*

"I'm sorry I have to do this," Steve said as he held out a pair of handcuffs. He closed them around her wrists behind her back.

"Don't lose the key," she quipped. "I did that once, and my captain was mad at me for a week." She dropped reminders that she represented the world where criminals got handcuffed and not cops, hoping Steve would realize The Glades was a false reality.

He led her by the arm to a room. It was below ground level and much different from her suite. It was illuminated by dimmed-down recessed lights and had burgundy curtains covering three outer walls. Maddy recognized the mirror at the front of the room was see-through, and people were probably watching from the other side.

She was forced into a chair and told to sit. Steve waited by the door. Footsteps in the hall grew louder, and when close, Steve stepped away. Neri and Avery walked in.

"Hello, Maddy." Avery sat at a table between the mirror and Maddy. "Are you wondering why we brought you to The Glades?"

"The thought crossed my mind," she snapped.

"You didn't think we'd be so gullible as to believe your charade of coming to Berry Lake to be near nature, did you?"

He thinks I'm here undercover. "I hoped you might," she said.

"Do you admit you're here on assignment?"

"It's moot why I'm here. Kidnapping is kidnapping, and jail time is jail time. How much damage to yourself are you planning to do?"

Avery winced at her words. Neri shrugged his shoulders and said, "Enough of this." He walked around the table holding a manilla envelope, pulled out a glossy photo, and handed it to Maddy.

Neri stood with a handsome young man next to him in the photo. He then gave her a second with the same young man's arm around Amber. "His name is Jimmy, and he is enjoying your daughter," Neri said.

"We want you to work with us," Avery said. "We can make it worth your while."

Her body tensed up, and she struggled to breathe. She tried not to appear intimidated but could not control her trepidation. She forced air into her lungs, waited, and exhaled. The men's eyes were on her. *The worst thing I can do is make them think they have me scared.*

"You guys keep adding years to your jail time. I dare say, Avery, you'll be well into your eighties by the time you'll be eligible for parole." Neri took out three other photos and handed them over—one of Amber walking to class alone, another of her returning to her dorm alone at night. The last was Amber entering a shower.

Maddy's heart pounded; her child was vulnerable. Her face grew hot with rage, and she looked at the mirror, wondering who was running the show. She didn't think it was Avery. He was too frightened and Neri too stupid.

"If Cupid couldn't intimidate me, you will not."

"Mr. Neri, I don't believe Ms. Reynolds believes we're serious," Avery said. "Let's let her think awhile." Avery went to the door, and Neri followed. Steve returned and escorted Maddy back to her suite. She sat on her bed, ears ringing, head-spinning, and the walls closing in.

CHAPTER 38

Monday, September 17, 1984

Time passed slowly, in the room with no windows. A minute felt like an hour, an hour, like an eternity. Maddy sat in a chair, moved to the bed, paced around, then went back to the chair. The afternoon dragged on. She heard the sound of the door unlocking. "It's me," Lucia said as she wheeled in lunch. Steve watched from behind.

Maddy asked if they always eat at the same time.

"Seven-thirty, noon, and five o'clock," Lucia said. "We are always on schedule." Maddy made a mental note.

When Lucia left the room, Maddy asked Steve to wait a minute. "You seem like a nice guy, Steve. Do you realize who you're working for? They are threatening to kill my daughter. Help me get out of here."

Expressionless, Steve reached for the knob, walked out, and closed the door. "Shit." Maddy kicked the steel cart and stubbed her toe. She threw herself on the bed, wept into a pillow until she was spent, and drifted off.

She woke up dizzy and weak, with her stomach growling. *I've got to eat something.* If she was to survive, she needed to accept the situation as it was and stop bemoaning its unfairness. That meant taking care of herself, physically and mentally.

She took a few bites from a bagel and drank half a carafe of orange juice. She was reluctant to take a shower, afraid they rigged the room with cameras. She slipped behind the shower curtain wrapped in a towel, turned on the water, and tossed it on the floor. The showerhead's stream revived her, reactivating her brain, and thoughts started pouring in.

I need a plan. I could charge Steve when dinner comes, grab his gun, tie Lucia with cords from the hairdryer, then take Steve at gunpoint to a car. She disregarded the idea because too much might go wrong.

She had already tried unlocking the door with a butter knife, but it was the type that prevented tampering. She finished her shower, got dressed, and fell back into helplessness. Back on the bed, she lay on her side with her knees up. She kept running into brick walls; every good idea was a dead end. Time lost meaning; she wanted to roll into a ball and disappear. Rumbling from above sounded like furniture moving around. She lifted her head, listening. *That's Castile Room. Are they setting up for an event?*

"Lunch, Maddy," Lucia said at the door. Maddy didn't look at her and Steve when they came in. She lay looking into space. The door closed, and she waited for the clunking of the lock, but it didn't come. She listened and waited, but no clunking. They're gone! She jumped up and went to the door. The knob turned, the door opened, and hope rushed into her veins. *Was that a mistake? Did Steve do that on purpose?*

Stay calm, Maddy. She looked into the hallway; it was empty. She stepped outside the room as the sound of furniture moving continued, then ran beneath the stairway and hid.

Listening for footsteps above, she heard none and started climbing the stairs. With each step, she looked for signs of someone walking down. When she reached the top, Castile Room was unrecognizable. They converted it into a theater, and it looked a third of its normal size; curtains created a pleasant setting. Dozens of workers assembled a stage, and she hid in the darkness behind the curtains.

Maddy observed the room through an opening in the drapes. Thirty leather chairs made a semicircle around the stage, and the ramp extending into the seating area was a runway. She made herself comfortable and waited for an opportunity to escape.

Her curiosity grew as time passed, and leaving her perch of cushioned blankets to peek out, she saw Avery Jordan inspecting the carpenters. Her rage grew as he paced about with his arms folded. She needed to know more and decided to stay put.

Several hours passed, and Maddy grew groggy. With little sleep and not much food in her, she started nodding off. She snapped out of it at the sound of people talking, and when she looked out, dozens of men in costumes milled around. They drank from snifter glasses, smoked cigars, and laughed. Strange music played in the background. *What the hell is this all about?*

The music stopped when Naomi walked out on stage. There was silence, and everyone took their seats. Naomi wore a long black gown, and her white hair was tied high on her head. The albino's face was partially covered by a dark blue glittering mask, but her haughty eyes remained uncovered.

She moved with odd smoothness, like a serpent. When she held up a blank card, the men held cards in response, each with a number. "We shall begin," she said.

The men talked among themselves, and the intensity of the moment grew. One said, "Alright, let's see what they've got." Their eyes were lustfully glued to the stage. The air of refinement exacerbated the hypocrisy, Maddy thought.

A girl about eighteen walked out from behind the curtains. Two men escorted her along on the runway, each holding an arm as though she might stumble. *She's all drugged up*, Maddy said to herself.

The girl's long black hair shined beneath the bright lights. She wore a silky red robe and was barefooted. Naomi came to her, and the men stepped aside. She loosened the girl's robe tie; it fell to the floor, and her naked body was exposed.

A moan went up from the crowd. The albino spoke, "Language, Russian." The girl stood rigid, elevated high on the platform of the smoke-filled room. Naomi took a baton with feathers, and she ran the feathers up and down on the girl's stomach. She groaned, and the men let out a roar, clapping loudly.

Maddy recoiled in disgust. *I can't believe this.* She realized The Glades was a sex slave marketplace for very wealthy men. Everything Pasha Lermontov said on Randy Gardner's radio show returned to her.

I know about evil people, Maddy thought. *I even understand the reasons behind their despicable deeds. Cupid had an abusive mother and a criminal father. His mind became twisted by finding pleasure in raping and strangling children. But this is different. These are rich people who, collectively, have assumed the right to ravage the innocence of young girls.*

Maddy had entered hell on earth. The room reeked of wickedness; it hung in the air with the cigar smoke, filling the souls of like-minded men who believed they were above reproach.

"Shall we start at one hundred and fifty?" the albino said. Several cards were raised. "One hundred and fifty thousand. Do I hear one hundred and seventy-five?" Five cards remained. The girl sold for three hundred and fifty thousand dollars. The bidding ended, and she was escorted off the stage.

The following specimen was Asian. "Vietnamese," Naomi said. She untied the gown and used the feathers. The child tumbled. Men ran to grab her, and the bidding continued.

The sale price was four hundred thousand dollars. *My God, this is like a cattle auction,* Maddy thought, fighting back her tears. *They're just children!*

Maddy snuck backstage to see the girls put into rooms. They returned in wheelchairs, dressed in street clothes. Limousines drove them to the airfield, where airplanes waited. She had stumbled into something more sinister than she could ever have imagined.

The criminality on the streets involved poor people who fought with police over broken laws. *Some people in this room make the laws. This must be what Sidney Myers meant when he said the devil transforms himself into evil of a different kind. This isn't about just a few individuals stealing or committing murder; this is an industry exploiting the essence of a child's innocence. It's diabolical.*

Maddy returned to the auction. A tall man with a swagger and a mask walked among the audience. She knew it was Avery Jordan. *There's that bastard.* Jordan waltzed around, chatting with guests, acting in complete control. Maddy fought an urge to run up and knock him down.

Naomi started the bidding of another girl. Someone asked, "Please tell us what that mark is on her neck." She looked closely at the girl.

"It's a tattoo."

"What is the tattoo's image?" another man asked.

"A crucifix."

The crowd recoiled with a rolling grumble, and men escorted the girl offstage. *It's their conscience,* Maddy thought; *they know what they're doing is evil.*

The event seemed to be ending, and Maddy realized the bidders followed a certain etiquette. No one left the proceedings until the bidding was finished. The last auction was completed after midnight, and everyone remained seated. After the final sale, Avery Jordan stepped onto the stage.

"As is our custom, all transactions will be honored," he said. "You will hear from us soon about the next gathering. This concludes tonight's event. Thank you for coming."

The men stood and clapped as Avery walked off stage. They shook hands the way old friends do when they know they won't see each other for some time. Masks covered their faces as they drifted to the doors. Maddy maneuvered to an empty room, looked outside, and saw limousines waiting out front.

One by one, the guests filled the vehicles before they were driven to the airfield. Their purchases waited in the airplanes, ready to take off. She marveled at the operation's precision.

Twisted minds conceived The Glades, and they had the gall to place it amongst one of God's greatest wonders, she thought.

Her mind shifted to herself. *I have to find a way out; the world must know about this.* A stabbing light assaulted her eyes; she squinted and turned. Two men stood, pointing guns at her heart.

CHAPTER 39

Tuesday, September 18, 1984
Avery Jordan

Elated the masquerade event was a grand success, Avery waited until the early hours of the morning for the figures. The accountant, a large man with glasses, a suit, and a bowtie, came in and sat. He pulled out a notebook. "Friday night was a very profitable evening, sir."

"How much?" Avery asked.

"Ten million, two hundred, and eighty thousand."

"Do we have all the bank codes?"

"Yes, sir."

"Where are they?" Avery said insistently.

"I have them right here," the man said, holding up his briefcase.

"Give them to me," he said, grabbing the envelope. "You can go."

Avery held the envelope as though his life depended on it. The codes were his passport to freedom. "Over ten million dollars," he marveled, almost giddy. Naomi walked in. He placed the envelope inside the ledger and closed the cover where it lay on his desk.

"It looks like we're going to be okay," he said, smiling. It was his first moment of relief in months, and when Naomi walked near, he held out his arms and pulled her close.

"See, all that worry for nothing," she said, putting her arms around his neck and kissing his forehead.

Another knock at the door, and Naomi moaned, "Oh, don't answer."

"I have to, dear," he said.

Neri and Girard walked in.

"Sir," Girard said. "We had a mishap."

"What happened," Avery said with concern.

Girard looked at the floor and said, "Maddy Reynolds escaped." Avery rocketed from the chair.

"Please, let me finish," Girard said. "We apprehended her, and she's secured."

"But—" Neri added.

"But what?" Avery snapped.

"Reynolds saw the entire auction."

"What!" Avery threw himself down into the chair. "Oh, my God. What are we going to do now?"

Naomi walked around the desk with her arms crossed. "She did not take your threats to kill her daughter seriously. It's imperative to make her know you mean business."

"And just how do we do that?"

"I'll tell you how," Neri said. Avery braced himself for Neri's idea. He explained his plan. Avery looked at him as though he had just heard a believable horror story.

"I can't witness that," he said. "You'll have to handle it on your own."

"No problem," Neri said, seeming to relish executing his idea.

When everyone left the room, Avery walked to the window and took a breath of air. He tried not to think of Neri's macabre preoccupations.

The eastern sky was red, and the grounds around the great lawn were at rest. As relieved as he was about raising the money, Avery would not relax until the money was transferred.

The Reynolds problem opened a new set of worries. Maddy knew enough to put himself and many famous people in jail. As repulsive as Neri's idea was, it was his only hope.

CHAPTER 40

Tuesday, September 18, 1984
Hector Lemont

After Hector witnessed the auction, he knew why his sister killed herself. *I bet they did those things to A.J.*, he thought. Disturbed, he hid in the woods while electricity buzzed through his veins, and he couldn't sleep. Morning came, he watched a lawnmower edge its way across the open space near the airfield and a guy refuel an airplane.

He had familiarized himself with The Glades since his sister's death, each night after everyone was asleep. He had watched Avery Jordan come and go. The albino woman entered his quarters at night, and Neri roamed the halls. *He ain't as sneaky as I am,* Hector thought to himself, recalling the morning he'd broken into the big man's quarters and stole a handgun from his desk.

He had snuck around The Glades for days, living off the food he snatched from kitchens. He had explored basements, storage rooms, and attics. He had become preoccupied with a room in the basement where a woman wept inside. The door was always locked.

Hector stayed hidden in the trees, and although the sun was up, he was overwhelmed with exhaustion and fell asleep. A high-pitched squeaky sound woke him, and he crawled to the lawn. When he saw a guy winding a hose to a fuel tank, an idea flashed into his head. *I'm going to burn it down.* He raised his arms with a thunderous silent roar and danced around;

his life finally made sense. When his revelry subsided, he sat, ate a banana, and began contemplating a plan. *I don't want innocent people to die, and I have to save the locked-up woman I heard crying.*

He waited for the right time to move, then left his spot in the woods to check the building where the girls were staying. The first floor was empty. *Them sons-a-bitches took those girls away in airplanes.* There was no one on the second floor either, but he found a girl sleeping in a room on the third. She didn't move. "Hey," he whispered. She snapped her head around. *She's the one no one wanted to buy because of her tattoo.*

She seemed horrified and pushed herself against the wall. "I won't hurt you," Hector said. "I want to help you get out."

Her eyes were wide, and she seemed not to trust him. "How do I know you'll help me?" she asked.

"I am leaving. You can come with me, but you can't stay here because I'm gonna burn it down." Hector reached out his hand and kept it there, and finally, she took it. "I'm Hector. What's your name?"

"Rosa," she said as she put on her shoes. "Are you really going to set it on fire?"

"Yes. It's evil."

A door clanked, and Hector looked into the hallway. Footsteps clunked on the stairwell. "I'll hide across the hall and come back when it's clear." He went to the utility closet, and two men walked into Rosa's room.

"I hope the bitch doesn't give us a hard time," one of them said. They entered Rosa's room, and Hector heard screaming. *The bastards!* They dragged Rosa into the hall; each held an arm, bound her, and forced her to the stairwell.

Sitting among brooms and mops, Hector was like a deflated balloon. He almost saved the girl, yet the Glades snatched Rosa from his grasp, just like it had A.J. He checked the remainder of the floor and found it empty. There was one more thing he had to do before he headed to Castile Room.

Keeping low, he crawled between the building's shrubbery and C-wing to the fuel tank. It was about five o'clock in the afternoon. A small airplane was parked near the tank without a guard, and The Glades seemed dead.

He noticed an open window on the first floor where Jordan watched the tied-up girl.

The fuel tank nozzle was thirty yards away, and Hector made a dash for it. He hid when he got there and his heartbeat was hard against the inside of his chest. He calmed himself, waiting to work up the courage to make his next move. Finally, he launched at the nozzle, grabbed it, and bulled his way back to the shrubs, pulling the hose behind. Hector peeked out and sighed; he'd gone unnoticed. Staying down, he moved forward, dragging the hose over his shoulder toward a basement window near Jordan's office.

It was hot, and the hose got heavier the further he went. Halfway, he stopped to rest. The thick black rubber tube felt like he was dragging ten cords of wood. When he started again, he focused on the basement window. With all his power, he pushed, grunted, and sweated. Despite raw knees and an ache in his back, he kept moving. One thought gave him the will to drive forward: Anna Jean.

Finally, he stopped at the basement window. He looked in and saw a storage room with concrete floors; it was dark and lined with metal shelves piled high with boxes. Ten feet further, the curtains in Avery Jordan's window blew in and out. Hector left the nozzle behind and crept forward to look in. No one was inside, and he returned to the nozzle.

He scanned the area to see if anyone was within earshot, then using his elbow, he nudged out a glass pane. It shattered on the concrete floor. He kept still, hoping no one heard, waited, then lowered the hose onto the basement floor.

Tempted to turn The Glades into a Fourth of July celebration right then, Hector's conscience would not let him. He needed to find Rosa and the woman held prisoner in the basement. He left the hose and headed to Castile Room's basement, where he heard the woman. The door was unlocked, and the room was empty.

CHAPTER 41

Tuesday, September 18, 1984
Maddy Reynolds

Maddy was blindfolded, with her hands tied behind her back, as Neri shoved her down a hallway. "So, you think we're not capable of taking your daughter out?" He kept pushing her along. "You don't know me very well." He yanked her hair, jerking her head back, sending a jolt of pain from her scalp down her spine. She heard keys jingling and a door open. This way." He shoved her into a room and forced her into a chair.

Maddy knew Neri had a plan. She was at his mercy and knew her chances of escape were slipping away. *Maybe Jordan decided that it's time for me to go; perhaps I'm too much of a threat, and he's willing to risk killing an ex-cop.*

"Tie her to the chair," Neri barked. A rope wound around her feet before tightening, then her torso and her wrists. Maddy was bound as tight as the inside of a baseball.

"Unmask her and leave." She felt a yank on the blindfold and saw Darius Girard leaving the room, followed by Neri. She was in the room alone.

A single empty chair faced her. Behind it, several objects wrapped inside a tan cloth were on a tabletop. A rubber matt covered a large area beneath the table and chair. Maddy looked at the mirror, wondering who was looking at her from the other side. A single light shined down on the empty chair, it was bright, but the rest of the room was dark. *What the hell are they going to do?*

Loud shuffling sounds in the hallway and a woman screaming, "Stop!" turned Maddy's attention to the door. Neri pushed a blindfolded girl into the room; she tripped and fell to her knees, crying in pain. He yanked her off the floor by the arm and plopped her in the empty chair. The two women faced each other as Neri tied the girl to the chair and removed her blindfold.

The light shined down and seemed blinding to the girl; she squinted. Maddy recognized her from the auction. *It's the girl with a crucifix tattoo.* "What are you going to do to me?" she screamed. Crying between pleas, she whirled her head around several times, trying to free herself until she choked and vomited. She coughed, trying to clear her throat, and her eyes were swollen shut.

Neri looked at Maddy and smiled. She glared back, wondering what he was going to do. She looked at the two-way mirror. *Is Jordan watching this?*

Maddy tugged at the ropes, and they dug deeper into her flesh. Her stomach twisted as the tormented girl's head hung low, drooling as she wept, as snot dripped onto her lap.

The monster's gleeful expression enraged Maddy. He was like a kid running to a swing on a playground. His maniacal expression reminded her of Cupid's, who, before he killed a child, raped them. *It's a look of pure evil,* she thought.

Neri turned, facing the table. Like a priest at the altar during high mass, he pulled back the tan cloth and arranged several large steel knives of different sizes. They gleamed in the light. *Jesus, he's going to cut her head off!*

Maddy gagged. She breathed hard, fighting to catch her breath as she watched the crazy man select his tools. The girl seemed passed out, her head still hanging low. Neri reached down, picked up a poncho-style raincoat, pulled it over his body, then slipped on rubber gloves. *He's going to do it.*

With his back turned to Maddy, Neri held a knife high over his head and examined it to ensure it was what he wanted. He turned to Maddy and smiled.

"So, you don't think we mean what we say about your daughter." The girl turned her head and looked at him. She began shrieking high-pitched screeches, and her face filled with horror.

Maddy twisted in her chair, trying to free herself. Something was tugging on the ropes behind her, and she heard Hector whisper, "It's me; I'm trying to cut this damn rope. I have a gun I'll give you when I free your hands."

"Pretend this girl is Amber," Neri said. He grabbed the girl's hair, pulled her head back, and her mouth stretched wide open. He looked at Maddy. "Just imagine."

Hurry, Hector.

Neri brought the knife to the side of the girl's neck. Maddy's hands came free. The gun handle slipped into her hand, and as Neri stiffened his gaze, tightening his lips to send his power to the hand with the knife, Maddy blasted a hole in his right shoulder. The blade dropped, and Neri reared backward, glaring at her in disbelief. He crashed into the mirror, and it shattered. She shot again, tearing a hole in his chest, and he fell back out of sight into the next room.

The albino was behind the mirror. She looked at Maddy as if caught stepping out of a shower naked. Maddy pointed the weapon at her but did not shoot, and Naomi ran out a back door.

A cloud of smoke filled the room.

"This is my gun," she said in amazement. "Where did you get it?"

"I stole it from that guy's desk."

"Help me get the girl to her feet."

"That's Rosa," Hector said as he cut the ropes from Maddy and Rosa. They revived the girl, helped her up, and Maddy asked if she could walk. Rosa tried to stand but seemed too traumatized; her knees kept giving out.

They each grabbed an arm, lifting the girl to her feet, and Hector said to Maddy, "So you're the one they kept prisoner in that room. I came by and heard you. I've been roaming these buildings at night for over a week and saw them bring you in here. When that big oof left the room, I snuck in and hid behind the curtains."

They got Rosa up, and the three walked to the doorway. "We need to steal a car," Maddy said.

"No!" Hector said. "I'm not going with you. You take Rosa. There's something I have to do."

Annoyed, Maddy snapped, "What?"

"It's for A.J." His tears told Maddy the boy was on a mission, and nothing she did or said would stop him.

"Okay, Hector. I think I understand."

Hector's look softened, and he looked down as if saying goodbye. Maddy grabbed his arm. "Thank you for saving our lives." She pulled him close; he rested his head on her shoulder a moment, turned without looking at her, and ran off.

CHAPTER 42

Tuesday, September 18, 1984
Hector Lemont

It was nearing seven o'clock when Hector left Maddy and Rosa. The sun was low in the sky as he made his way back to the fuel tank. He smelled the fumes as he kneeled next to the spicket, and when he turned the handle on the release valve, the limp hose stiffened. *Now we're going to see something.*

He crawled to the basement window, and petroleum fumes filled the air. The sound of liquid rushing through the rubber conduit excited him. He waited, listening, and when the splashing sound in the basement ceased, he lit a match. Holding it in his fingers, he stared at the yellow flame. "This is for you, A.J.," he said, then let go of the tiny flame.

A loud woof, a burst of heat, and his face scorched like under a hot sun. Flames spread along the basement floor, and Hector reveled in what he'd done.

For reasons he did not understand, he moved toward Avery Jordan's open window and looked inside; it was still empty. He saw a familiar object on a shelf of collectibles near Avery's desk; it belonged to A.J. It was the brass ballerina his mother gave her. It stood with several other items, and it was like A.J. was one of Avery's souvenirs. *That's what my sister meant to him, something to show off.*

Determined to save the memento, Hector lifted the screen and climbed inside. He noticed smoke coming through the air vents and knew he had to hurry. Grabbing a crumpled-up paper bag from a wastebasket, he placed the ballerina inside. He noticed an important-looking object sitting on Jordan's desk as he was about to leave. It was a ledger covered with green leather, with a shiny crest of swirling letters that said The Glades. *It's beautiful*, he thought. He ran his finger along the metal's smooth surface. *It's like gold.* The ledger gave the appearance of importance, and Hector thought taking it might harm Jordan, so he shoved it in the bag with the ballerina.

Smoke filled the room, and he rushed to the window ledge. About to jump, he heard, "Stop, or I'll shoot!" He turned. The albino was holding a gun with two hands, pointing it at him. Hector jumped. Before he cleared the opening, a shot rang out. A hot poker penetrated into his upper back, and he cried out in pain. When he fell forward and hit the ground, he jumped up. Panicked, he ran for the woods. When he reached the trees, he dragged himself back to where he'd hid before. Weak and light-headed, he rolled over on his side as the burning in his back grew hotter. Sweat beaded on his forehead; he was warm all over, then cold and very thirsty.

He heard people running out of C-wing. He crawled up to the tree line and watched them gather in the large open area. Thick, black smoke billowed from ground-floor windows near Avery's office. Screaming women held their heads as they ran from doorways to the green space. People huddled together; some held on to one another, others looked on with horrified faces pointing at the growing flames. A few seemed to be amused.

He lay for a long while; he wasn't sure how long. A loud blast shook the earth and brought him to his senses. Flames shot skyward like a roman candle, towering a hundred feet or more in the air. In an instant, all C-wing windows were aglow. The sun was dropping behind the hills, and the inferno's light merged with the remaining daylight, creating a haunting amber hue that clung to everything.

As the heat reached Hector, his clothes warmed, but his insides were cold. He realized he had to move, struggled to his feet, looked at his creation one last time, and saw the albino and a bald man run to a lone airplane. In minutes, the engine popped, and the plane rolled down the runway. It was soon out of sight. *They got away,* he thought.

As he turned to begin down the mountain, Hector noticed the flames near C-wing jump to the forest. Holding the paper bag with one hand, he used the other to grab tree trunks to keep from falling and edged his way down the mountain.

He began the long decline, thirsty and with his legs weak. There was a strange metallic taste in his mouth, and he spat out a large amount of blood. "Oh, Mama," he cried, stopping to rest on a large rock, fearful he was going to die. He thought of his mother, A.J., and Doc as he entered a trance-like state and began speaking to them as though they were there.

"I don't want to die. Doc, help me." Coughing and spitting up blood, Hector imagined his mother and sister were waiting for him at the foot of the hill. He forced himself up and continued downward.

His consciousness was distorted, sometimes in the present, then back in the spirit world. His back felt like molten lava, and it moved around when he walked. When he came to a brook, he stopped to rest. After struggling to bring water to his lips, he dunked his head in the stream, and its cool wetness revived him.

Sitting and looking up the mountain, The Glades became an out-of-control inferno. Flames leaped into the forest like a monster with many heads. Trees exploded, and burning embers rained down, starting smaller fires around him. A downdraft blew smoke his way, and he began choking. The fiery monster was chasing him; he forced himself up and continued.

He moved by rote memory while in and out of a dreamy state. Hector's experience living in the mountains guided the way. He heard A.J.'s laughter as she pushed him down and ran that day, and he heard himself laughing behind her, letting her think she'd won. "Don't worry, Hector; Jesus will take care of us," A.J. was saying.

Hector found himself at the bottom of the mountain near Route 3. He collapsed, and his mother began speaking lovingly to him. "I love you, son. You're a good boy." His mind was in a far-off place, and he surrendered.

"I'm with you, Hector," he heard A.J. say. "You're not alone."

Barely conscious, he lay facedown holding the bag. His mind was in the next world, but his body was not. There was no more pain. He wandered through memories, pleasant and painful, his life made sense to him, and it was good.

CHAPTER 43

Earlier on the Evening of Tuesday, September 18, 1984
Avery Jordan

Avery looked out his window as The Glades's lights glowed. It was early evening. He reflected on ten long years of living with a noose around his neck. He gloated. *Now, my future is secure! I bet my father thought I'd never do it.* He remembered almost blowing his brains out in the dingy New Orleans hotel and the first time he saw Naomi in her brothel. *We drove up the mountain in winter to see The Glades. We made love in the limo on the way home. It was special. I believe all of this is my fate. My life is like fiction, an exciting story with a happy ending.* The phone rang, and he went to his desk. "Hello."

"It's The Guy, sir."

Of course, it is, Avery thought. "Put him through."

The deep voice asked, "How much?"

"A little over ten point two million," Avery said.

"Good. The money is to be transferred on the appointed date," he said before giving Avery a bank transaction code. "Goodbye, until we meet again," he said and hung up.

Never! Avery said to himself, relieved that he'd soon be free. He buzzed in Darius Girard and asked him if he'd like a glass of brandy. Girard seemed uneasy and surprised by the sudden shift in his boss's mood. Avery went to the credenza, poured two glasses, and handed one to Darius. "Here's to The Glades." The glasses clinked, each drank, and Avery added, "I don't believe I know where you are from, Darius."

"Excuse me, sir?"

"You know, where did you grow up?"

"I grew up in Charlotte, North Carolina, Mr. Jordan."

"Ah, North Carolina. That explains your exemplary manners," Avery said as he lit a cigar. "I grew up everywhere. I don't think there's a state in the union where I haven't lived."

"Yes, sir," Girard said. "Will that be all, sir?"

"Yes, you may go." As Girard was walking out, Avery added, "Oh, before I forget, tomorrow I'd like to take an airplane ride. I want to enjoy these wonders. Have a pilot ready a plane by nine."

"I'll have your plane readied tonight," Girard said before he left the room.

Avery strolled about, reminiscing. He looked at rare paintings and other artwork accumulated over the decade. *This is all mine now.*

His eye rested on a photo of Naomi, and a desire for his beautiful lover grew. He looked at his watch. *That's strange. I wonder where she could be; she should be here by now.*

He changed into a bathrobe and was about to get comfortable when a loud banging startled him. Before he could answer, the door burst open. Two security men ran inside, yelling that he needed to evacuate. Irritated, he screamed, "What's going on here?"

"Fuel vapors are rising throughout C-wing, and it looks like an explosion is imminent. Please come, sir." They escorted him to the hall; he felt confused and disturbed; his mind rambled. He wasn't in control.

They led him outside to the lawn where The Glades' staff were gathered. People chattered about what might happen; many wondered if they were safe. "The place might blow any minute," someone said.

Avery asked about Naomi, but no one knew where she was. He milled around, looking for her, but she wasn't there, and he panicked.

A flash of light and a loud bang pushed the crowd back. Heat, like a hot towel, pressed against Avery's face. His nostrils and lips burned, eyes watered, and his clothes felt hot. He grappled his way through the panic-filled throng, trying to get closer to the building. A second eruption engulfed the structure; fiery plumes reached high into the black sky.

Oh, my God, the bank codes! His heart raced as he thought of The Guy. *Without the codes, I'm dead.* He ran for the building, and men tried to hold him back. He swung, hit one in the face, and broke free. Runny into the conflagration, covering his face with his robe, he rammed through Castile Room's front doors. Smoke, thick and black, rushed into his eyes, nose, and mouth. He gagged. Terror-struck, he panicked. Extending his arms like a blind man, he felt around for his office door, and using the wall to guide him, he found the handle.

His desk was in flames. "Oh, my God!" he screamed. He choked on black billowing soot as he thrust his hands into the fire, feeling around the desktop for the ledger where he put the bank codes. He cried out in pain; his hands and arms burned. The ledger was gone. "Where the fuck is it? Maybe I put it in the safe." Avery struggled toward the safe. His hair burned. He tried to put it out with his hands, but his hair was gone. He felt only stubbles and screamed.

When he reached the safe, he screamed, "The dial is melting." The soft plastic was out of shape and hard to read; numbers blurred. He repeated the combination—thirty-four, twenty-two, ten, six—over and over. "Is that a ten or a twelve?" The safe door finally popped open. The ledger wasn't in the safe, but his father's gift was.

He fell to his knees as the security men outside the window called to him. Avery didn't respond; his life was over. He didn't want to be saved. "This is what it's come to," he said, weeping. "I had it all. Why did this happen?"

He stood and took the gun from the safe. His mind went back to the dank New Orleans hotel when he almost pulled the trigger. *I wish I had done it then.*

Avery looked into the tiny hole at the end of the barrel. "We meet once again," he said. When he lifted the gun, he glimpsed the wolf's head on the wall, and its eyes glowed red from the flames. It seemed to be looking at him. He recalled Neri's words when he shot the beast. He told him the Cherokee believed a slain wolf's spirit would avenge its death. "It looks like you win," he said, weeping. He placed the barrel in his mouth, and this time, he pulled the trigger.

CHAPTER 44

Tuesday, September 18, 1984
After Hector departed from Maddy and Rosa
Maddy Reynolds

After Hector went on his way, Maddy hobbled to a stairway with Rosa's arm around her neck. They heard voices on the stairs above and stayed hidden. "Are you sure you're okay?" Maddy asked.

"I'm diabetic. I've been without insulin for two days; I'm dizzy. I need to get my medication in my room."

The men on the stairway kept talking. "Is there another way to your building?"

"That way," Rosa said. She pointed in the opposite direction of the stairs. They moved out of the darkness into an open space and entered a hallway. The girl's weight slowed Maddy down; she kept looking around, afraid someone might walk through and see them. They cleared the open space. A sign showed they were heading to C-wing. *We're moving too slowly*, Maddy thought. "I'm not sure I can make it up these stairs," Rosa said, panting. "My room is four flights up on the second floor."

"Just rest a minute. We can make it, honey," Maddy said. "I'll help you."

"You should leave me; I can't go on."

A powerful smell of petroleum filled the hallway. "We can't stay here. Come on, Rosa, push hard." Maddy lifted the girl. They started up the stairs, and after the first flight, Maddy felt nauseous from the fumes. Rosa collapsed. Her eyes closed, and her mouth opened.

Oh my God, she's fainted. I can't move her if she's unconscious. "Rosa! Come on, wake up!" Her eyes fluttered. "That's good, dear; you can do it."

As Rosa stood up, a loud woof shook the building. Rosa and Maddy fell into each other. *What the hell was that?* The heat from below rose up, making it hard to breathe. Maddy realized there had been an explosion. "We have to hurry." She lifted Rosa's arm and forced her to move. At the third flight, Maddy looked down and saw smoke billowing into the hallway below.

"You're doing fine," Maddy said, trying to keep Rosa motivated. Deep inside, she didn't think they would make it. Rosa lifted one foot and then another. They reached the second floor.

"We're here; which is your room?"

Rosa pushed her head forward to the right. "Three doors." They reached her room, and when Maddy looked outside, the flames rose to window level. The girl went to her bed, grabbed a plastic box, and prepared the insulin shot. Sitting on the bed, with the drug in her system, Rosa sighed. *The flames block the view outside the window.* "We have to go; the building is on fire."

"Hector," Rosa said.

"What about Hector?"

"Hector did this. He said he was going to burn it down."

Son of a bitch. Hector is burning it down. Of course, he is; this place took everything he loved. She shook her head, wondering where the boy was, then turned to Rosa. "Let's move!"

Rosa grabbed her insulin kit, and they rushed to the stairwell. When they reached the ground level, the smoke was so thick, Maddy felt hot granules burning her throat when she inhaled. She coughed, her eyes burned; she rubbed them and saw the blur of a red exit sign. The fire raged, heat pressed against them, and the sound was near deafening. Maddy shouted, "We've got to get outside!" as they bolted for the door.

They burst it opened, and a plume of smoke followed them outside. Maddy and Rosa ran to the smokeless air, collapsed on the grass, and filled their lungs. Maddy rolled over and lay on her back. She looked up at the glowing sky, wondering how they'd made it out alive. *Thank you, Dad.*

"Don't move, or I'll shoot!" a voice shouted. Maddy turned her head. Two men walked over with guns drawn. She felt for her Glock; it wasn't there. *Shit! It must have fallen out.*

"Get up." Danny Mosher, the Chief's deputy, and Steve, who came each day with Lucia, waited. Maddy helped Rosa up.

"Wait until the Chief sees what I caught," Mosher said. "You ain't such a hotshot now, are ya, Reynolds?" "I could shoot you right now, and no one would care. You're on private property. I'd say you burned the place down, even though Hector did it."

"What about Hector?" Maddy asked.

Danny laughed. "Oh, Hector? You won't be seeing him anymore— alive, that is. He took off through those woods. He wasn't moving so good with that bullet in his back." Maddy cringed, and her face tightened. "Ooh, look it, Steve," Danny said. "She's getting mad. She ain't so tough with no gun, are ya, Miss Big Shot Detective?"

"Why don't you two turn around and start walking toward that crowd," Danny said. Maddy turned. She put an arm around Rosa. *I know what comes next: a bullet in the back.* The girl must have known it, too. Maddy felt her body shake.

Click! A revolver cocked. A shot rang out. Maddy stood frozen; she turned. Steve stood over Mosher's body. Smoke flowed from the barrel of the gun in his hand. Danny lay, blood leaking from a hole in the side of his head.

"I'm Inspector Adam Forsyth, with the New York State Police. I've been undercover here for ten days." He holstered his weapon. "Steve was my cover name. Hannah Bates will be here soon with a fleet of helicopters.

We have to evacuate these people. If you join that group, you can fly out with them."

"What about my daughter? She's in danger down at Cornell."

"We apprehended Jimmy Bond this morning," Adam said. "He's a real bad guy, a friend of Sedgwick Neri's. We've been watching him for a while. Your daughter is safe."

"Thank God!" Maddy said. She looked at Rosa, then back at Adam. "I can't leave Hector to die alone in the woods." Smoke drifted to where they stood as the wind picked up and her eyes watered. She spoke over the roar of the fire. "You take Rosa to safety. I'm going after Hector." Maddy noticed three men running toward them and stiffened.

"Don't worry," Adam said. "They're ours. If you're going after Hector, I'm going with you." Adam pointed at Danny's body and told the men he had no choice. "He was about to shoot these women. I think he's dead, but we better get a medical team here quick." He gave them orders to take Rosa to the helicopters and said he was going with Ms. Reynolds to find Hector Lemont.

Maddy turned to the girl, who was nearly a child. "You're a brave one."

"Thank you for saving my life," Rosa said. The men led her to where helicopters were landing. Maddy and Adam headed for the woods.

CHAPTER 45

Tuesday, September 18, 1984

Maddy and Adam entered the wall of flames. It felt like walking into hell. Heat descended, and smoke swirled in the surrounding wind. Adam shouted, "Over there. Look!" He pointed to an opening in the firestorm; they ran to the spot, and the gap closed behind them.

Trees snapped and crashed to the ground, exploding thousands of tiny embers into the air. The rumbling, like thunder, was deafening. Adam yelled, "They told me the best way down is a dried-up creek bed!"

"I'll follow you!" Maddy shouted back. She felt the heat singeing her hair and wanted to move.

Adam shined his flashlight, looking for the creek bed. A cracking sound like a thunderous whip and a large branch snapped, floating embers onto Maddy's shirt. She brushed them off. A high-pitched squeal signaled a colossal tree was about to fall; Maddy grabbed Adam's shirt, pulling him out of its path. The forest was alive with death.

The fire screamed and roared as Maddy and Adam coughed. "I think I see a brook," he yelled. They moved toward a rock pile; a stream reflected white and yellow flames. "Water," he said, "let's rest a moment." As he was about to sit, Adam froze. Maddy looked; the flashlight's beam rested on several blood-splashed rocks. A sick, sad weakness formed in her gut.

"He's bleeding bad," Adam said. "We need to get to him before he bleeds to death."

Nearby, another crashing tree vibrated the ground, exploding flames and shooting sparks in all directions. Covering their faces, they moved back. "We have to find another way," Adam said as he started around the fallen tree to an open area.

Maddy's throat was raw, and her eyes burned. She took the lead, skirting ground fires and avoiding falling branches. Adam screamed, "Goddamn!" He scampered around, grabbing his shin. His pant leg was on fire.

"Stay still!" Maddy shouted, then tackled him. She smothered the flames with her jacket. Adam lay back with his hand over his face; the wound appeared severe. His skin was exposed, and he moaned in agony. Maddy dug beneath the leaves and twigs, scooped up moist soil, and applied it to the raw flesh. "This will help with the pain." The flames moved down the mountain toward them, and she asked if he could walk.

"I think so." Adam put an arm over her shoulder, and they struggled to keep moving.

They reached a steep ridge with no trees to hold on to. "We'll have to walk along the top," Maddy said, hoping they'd find a place to cross over." Adam was unsteady and winced as he hobbled. She worried Adam might pass out if they had to jump.

They approached an area where the ridge was not too steep. "Can you make it down?" she asked. Adam seemed determined and said he could.

Holding tight to one another, they took a step down, but Maddy's foot slipped, sending both sliding. Adam cried out when he hit bottom, and Maddy went to him. He lay on his back, gazing up, and eeked out in a painful voice, "That was fun."

Maddy gazed at him. *He entered a firewall to find a boy he didn't know.* She suddenly felt a deep affection for him. She wiped the mud from her pants and said, "I think these jeans are ruined."

"Stop, you're making me laugh," Adam said in pain. She helped him up. He looked at his burned-off pant leg. "I might cut these into shorts." Maddy smiled, and he smiled back. Surrounded by danger and barely knowing the guy, she let Adam into her heart.

"Shit, I lost my weapon!" he shouted.

"We can't look for it; we've got to keep moving," Maddy said. Her footing remained uncertain, slipping on wet spots and tripping on rocks. The heat, smoke, and Adam's weight drained her, and she felt light-headed. "Let's rest," she said after several hundred yards. They sat against a tree and gazed at the holocaust raging at The Glades.

"What a sight," Adam said.

The sound of a wolf howling rose above the chaos. Maddy leaned forward, looking for its silhouette against the glow. She was sure it was the magnificent animal she and Jodi had seen months earlier. A shiver ran through her body. In a trance-like state and exhausted, she leaned her head on Adam's shoulder, staring at the calamity above. "I've seen nothing like it."

Maddy thought that the wolf's repeated painful howls were announcing to all at The Glades that his mate was avenged. "Avery Jordan must be dead," she said, engrossed in the moment's mystery. *I hope Hector can hear this.*

They continued moving, and the burden of Adam's weight seemed less. There was a comfort in the wolf's bellowing. Adam said his leg hurt, but the sound of the wolf was taking his mind off the pain. They slogged their way with care, knowing a sprained ankle might prove catastrophic if the fire caught up. When they came to a slight rise, Adam said he was concerned the strain on Maddy's body was wearing her down. "Let's rest," he said. The two dropped onto a soft bed of moss, sweating and exhausted.

Huffing, trying to catch her breath, Maddy lay back, looking up, and glimpsed the moon through the smoke. "A gibbous moon," she said.

"What was that?"

"I've seen bad things happen under that moon." Adam said nothing. "Was Mosher the first person you killed?" she asked him.

"Yes. I wish it didn't have to happen. I had no choice. He was about to put a bullet in your head. He would have killed the girl, too." Maddy didn't say it, but she had taken six souls, which bothered her every day.

"Look," Adam said. He held the light beam on another blood-covered patch of ground ten yards away. They got up and gazed at the matted-down red spot. "He can't be in good shape," Adam said. "We better get moving."

She heard the splashing sound of rubber on the pavement. "That's the sound of a tractor-trailer. We're near Route 3." A few hundred feet further, they climbed up onto the road. "The village is just up there," she said.

The howling stopped, but the trail of blood continued; red smatterings appeared every six or eight feet. "I know where this is going." She realized Hector was headed for Doc's.

It was still dark, but dawn was approaching. They were close to the center of town and saw people gathered watching the fire, spellbound in the streets. A shower of white ash fell like snowflakes. Not knowing any better, little kids chased them as though it was snow in winter.

Sirens filled the air, and Maddy realized they called units to the tragedy from miles around. Emergency vehicles moved through the crowd. One chubby lady, whom Maddy knew was Rose, stood before Lena's, wiping tears from her face.

Maddy turned to Adam and pointed to Doc's house. "There's where we'll find Hector." The place was dark; Maddy remembered the day she brought the bee-stung boy there unconscious. Doc had carried him into his office and brought him back to life.

Adam flashed the light on the doorknob. "Look, blood," he said.

Maddy's heart raced as she pushed the door open and hurried inside. The kitchen remained dark when she switched on the lights. "They shut off the electricity. "Hector," she shouted, and there was no answer.

They walked to the living room, and Adam moved the beam of the flashlight around. A white arm dangled from a sofa. *Oh, my God, it's in the same position as the day the bee stung him,* Maddy thought. "Hector!" she shouted again, expecting him to pop his head up in surprise. She stopped cold.

Hector lay on his side. His eyes were frozen open, and he had a blank stare on his lifeless face. The boy was dead.

"Oh, Hector," Maddy said as she fell to her knees, sobbing. Adam placed his hand on her shoulder, leaned over, and slid Hector's eyelids closed.

She had come to Berry Lake to escape senseless violence. On the streets, wicked people took life as though it were meaningless. *It's the same here,* she thought as she wept. *All life is vanity.*

She pushed the boy's bloodied locks from his face, moved close, and kissed his forehead, giving him the mother's love he so needed. Her tears dripped onto his face as she wailed, "I'm so sorry I didn't help you save A.J. when you asked."

Adam consoled her, rubbing her shoulder. He handed her a blanket when she looked up. She stood and covered the body. Clive Christian Number One filled the air. *Oh, my God, he's not dead!* She turned. A giant silhouette stood before her. The arm was raised, and an object came crashing down, smashing Adam's head. He fell, unconscious.

Maddy thrust her palm upward into Neri's chin; his teeth clattered, and he fell backward into a bookcase. The iron man struggled to regain his balance as Maddy steadied herself. He stammered from bullet wounds and Maddy from exhaustion.

"I'm going to disembowel you, you bitch." He lunged at her with a knife, slashing the blade. She pushed a dining room chair before him, and he tossed it aside. Thinking of the medicine cabinet, she ran into Doc's office. *I hope he left the keys.*

Neri was close behind her, and Maddy stopped, fell to one knee. Like a mule, she thrust her heel up and out, slamming Neri's groin. He let out an agonizing growl. She looked over her shoulder and saw him leaning against the wall, holding himself. She bolted to the medicine cabinet and hoped the keys were in the lock.

Maddy heard Neri struggling to stand up, and she moved fast. She felt around the inside of the cabinet where the Demerol bottle was the day Doc treated Hector. She grabbed a glass jar. *I hope this is it.* She opened the drawer, grabbed an object, and ripped open the seal. It was a needle.

Neri crashed through the office door, and when she heard a grunt, she moved to the right. The blade clanked on the counter, and he fell, huffing. She tried running past him to the next room, but Neri swung the knife around and sliced her calf; she cried out and struggled forward.

Ducking behind the couch where Hector lay, she stuck the syringe needle into the bottle's rubber top, pulled back the plunger, and filled it. *Dad, let this be the right drug.* She peeked around the sofa. Neri's Frankenstein-like image was silhouetted in the dim light. He stood with the knife in his left hand, hobbling toward her. As he passed by, Maddy jumped on his back. She drove the needle deep into his neck, emptying the syringe.

Together, they smashed into Doc's dining room table, Maddy on top. She tried to break away, but when Neri spun around, slashing the blade, she felt the flesh of her lower back rip open. "You fuck!" she cried out.

She tried to limp to the kitchen, but he grabbed her ankle, and she fell. In an instant, the big man crawled on top. She rolled over and saw the knife plunging down toward her face. Jolting her head to the side, the blade missed and penetrated the wood-plank floor.

As he loosened the knife, Maddy embedded the syringe into his right eye. The monster screamed, fell to the side, and brought his hands to his face. It lessened the weight on Maddy, allowing her to wiggle out from beneath him. She crawled toward the backdoor and tumbled to the pavement.

As she pushed herself to her feet, her calf gave way. She used the side of the house as support and gimped toward the street. Screaming as he crashed through the kitchen door to the outside, Neri looked and started limping toward her, blood dripping down his face. *The drug is working!*

She made it to the street, turned, and taunted him to come after her. She hoped his effort would speed his heart rate and hasten the Demerol. His steps slowed to a trudge until he stopped, leaned against the house, and looked to the sky. After a long minute, the throat-cutter collapsed with a thud.

Maddy let herself go limp and folded down in the middle of Main Street. A voice from the crowd in the center of town called her name. The first face to hover over her was Lester's.

"Are you all right?" She looked up and felt like laughing.

A crowd gathered around; Rose kneeled next to her and asked what she could do. "Hector's inside. He's dead." Rose covered her face, whimpering.

"There's a state trooper in there, and he's badly injured. His name is Adam Forsyth. Someone needs to get him help. Contact Inspector Hannah Bates from the state police."

"I'm right here, Maddy." Maddy looked up, and Hannah kneeled next to her. "I think you're running out of your nine lives," Hannah said. Maddy gave her a half-smile, a shrug of the shoulder, and a slight nod. "We have ambulances coming," Hannah said. "Neri's not dead, but he's near to it."

"I want to see Adam," Maddy said. Hannah asked if she could stand; she said she could.

"Let's move these people away from here," Hannah shouted to the troopers. They brought bandages and dressed Maddy's wounds." Rose came over with a wool blanket and wrapped it over her shoulders. Hannah helped her up, and together they walked to the house.

"Is he conscious, Hannah?" Maddy asked.

"They said he was."

The house was lit up with lanterns and full of investigators. She saw the rubble from her battle with Neri. They walked into the living room, where Hector lay on a sofa, now covered with a blue tarp. On a second sofa, Adam sat, holding an ice pack on his head. Maddy sat next to him and put her arm around his shoulder. "Are you okay?"

"I think so, but I'm worried about my daughter; I don't want her to hear about me on the news. She's thirteen and worries."

"How about your wife? Can't someone get a message to her?"

"I'm a widower. I'll have Hannah tell Gabriella. How about you? Are you going to be okay?"

"Yes," she said. "I'm just a little cut up." She leaned her head on his arm.

"That feels nice," Adam said. "I wish there weren't so many people here."

Maddy looked up into his eyes. "Maybe another time."

As they slid her into the back of an ambulance, she heard the wolf howling again. She smiled and thought of Hector, and the words *kindred spirits* came into her mind.

Two Days Later

Maddy sat in a day room watching boats move across Lake Colby outside her window. She was in the hospital at Saranac Lake. Her mind tried to piece together the previous few days' events and fit them into the puzzle of her life. *Why me?*

A nurse came to tell her she had a phone call, and she'd put it through to the day room phone. It was Hannah Bates. "How are you doing, Maddy?"

"They stitched me together pretty well; I'll survive."

"I thought you might want to know that Neri didn't make it. You gave him enough Demerol to kill a large animal; he was dead before he got to the hospital."

"Thanks for letting me know. Do you know what they're doing with Hector's body?"

"The villagers are taking up a collection; they'll bury him next to his mother and sister."

"And Adam?" Maddy asked. "How's he doing?"

"They brought him to the burn unit down at Albany Medical. He'll be there a while, but he's okay. I saw him this morning, and he asked about you. He's a good man, Maddy; I hope things work out."

"I sensed that about him," Maddy said.

When she hung up, Jodi stood nearby with an arm full of orange lilies. "Hey, you," Maddy said, remembering the orange lilies Hector left on the woodpile a few weeks earlier. It seemed like a century ago.

Jodi sat next to her. "I've been torturing myself for leaving you alone the day A.J. killed herself. I'm so sorry."

"Don't be sorry, Jodi. If you'd stayed, we both would have been hostages." Maddy took the flowers and held them up near her face. "The lilies are beautiful."

"They reminded me of the ones in your kitchen when I visited you before the gala," Jodi said.

"The gala!" Maddy responded. "I wish I knew then what I know now. Anyway, how did you hear about what happened?"

"Amber called me. She'll be here this afternoon."

She put out her hand, Jodi took it, and Maddy began to weep. With no words spoken, Jodi sat next to her friend in silence. Maddy reached over, picked up a box of tissues, and laid them on her lap, wiping tears from her face.

"What made me think living surrounded by nature would be different from a city?" Jodi remained silent. "I can't seem to get away from the craziness." She lamented that trouble followed her everywhere. "It just never stops. Is it something I'm doing?"

Jodi piped in, seeming uncomfortable with her friend's anguish. "I think you're looking at it all wrong." Taken aback, Maddy asked what she meant. "From where I'm sitting, it's obvious you're being called to do what you're doing. You've saved a lot of lives over the years, Maddy."

In an instant, Sidney Myers's book flashed into Maddy's mind. "You just reminded me of something I read. *In The Changing Faces of* Evil, Sidney Myers said people who are often drawn into conflict with evil perceive themselves as victims, but in reality, they are beckoned by forces of good. He believes it's always without the person's knowledge or consent because if they knew the powerful role they play, they might wane under the weight of their calling."

Jodi sat smiling and said, "Exactly!"

After Jodi left and Maddy waited for her daughter, she thought about something else Myers said. *Understanding why you have the life you are given is like emptying the ocean into a bucket. It's just too big. It's better to accept your fate, not fight it, and live with dignity.*

Maddy smiled to herself, and an overwhelming sense of peace came over her. "I think you have that right, Sidney."

THE END

ACKNOWLEDGMENTS

A special thanks to Megan, my writing coach, and Anne-Marie, who shared meaningful insights. Julia, your proofreading was enormously helpful. To the beta readers, Gary, Susan, Pat, Nichole, Marcia, Jean-Marie, John, Holy, Denise, Maria, Donna, and Mike, your feedback helped to improve the story. Thank you to my wife Jean, children, David and Laura, and grandchildren, Alexis and Tyler. You are always there for me. I want to thank you, God, for the newfound gift of writing.

ABOUT THE AUTHOR

John spent the early years of his career as a rehabilitation counselor offering a hand to people in need. Some took it, and with them, John was privileged to share their journeys. He learned of real human suffering, the tragedies, and the victories of life. But most of all, he realized we share a never-ending quest to be known. He is dedicated to making his characters known to his readers, even if just a little while. John now writes full time, has published *Cupid and The Glades*, and has plans for several other novels.

DON'T MISS THE SEQUEL!

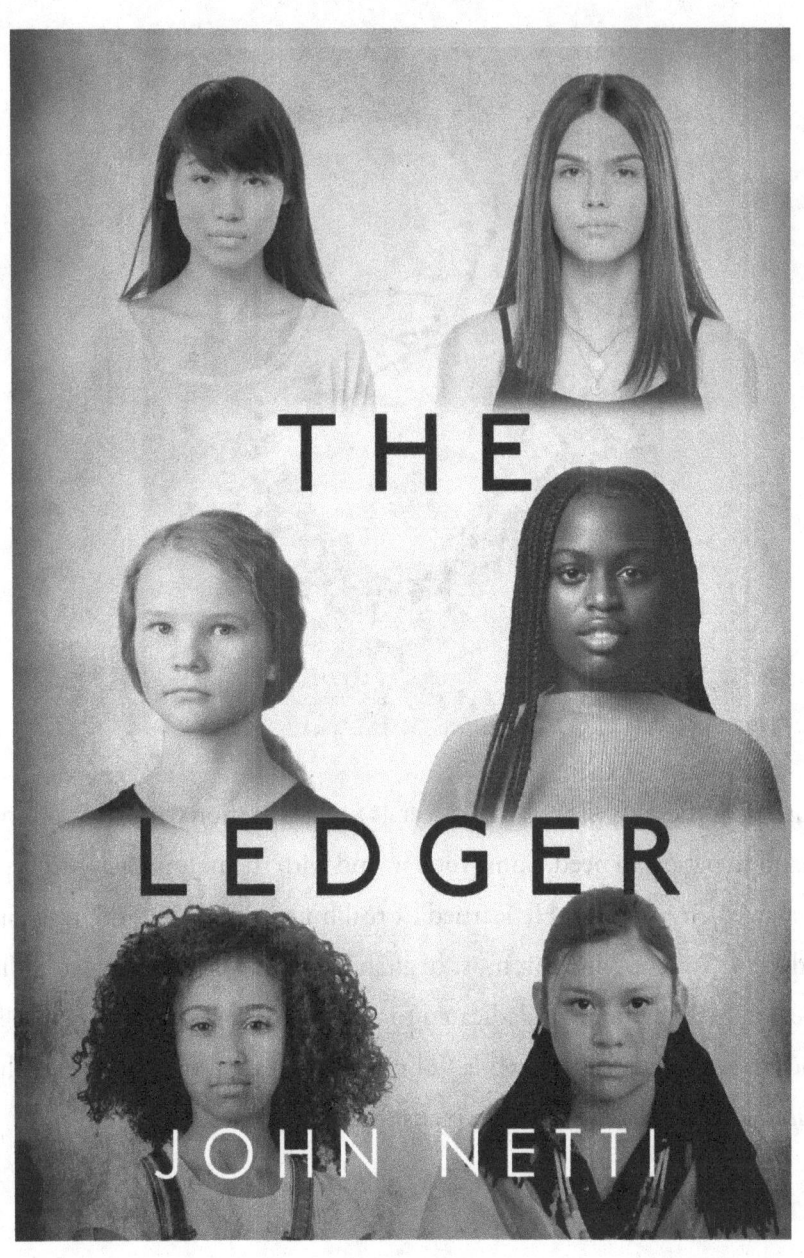

THE

LEDGER

JOHN NETTI

NOTE FROM THE AUTHOR

Word-of-mouth is crucial for any author to succeed. If you enjoyed *The Glades*, please leave a review online—anywhere you are able. Even if it's just a sentence or two. It would make all the difference and would be very much appreciated.

Thanks!
John Netti

We hope you enjoyed reading this title from:

Subscribe to our mailing list – *The Rosevine* – and receive **FREE** books, daily deals, and stay current with news about upcoming releases and our hottest authors.
Scan the QR code below to sign up.

Already a subscriber? Please accept a sincere thank you for being a fan of Black Rose Writing authors.

View other Black Rose Writing titles at
www.blackrosewriting.com/books and use promo code
PRINT to receive a **20% discount** when purchasing.